A Dance with Fire

D.B. Forest

Book Cover by D.B. Forest

1st edition 2026

CONTENTS

Dedication V
1. Chapter 1 1
2. Chapter 2 23
3. Chapter 3 40
4. Chapter 4 48
5. Chapter 5 56
6. Chapter 6 65
7. Chapter 7 73
8. Chapter 8 79
9. Chapter 9 91
10. Chapter 10 110
11. Chapter 11 124
12. Chapter 12 141
13. Chapter 13 154
14. Chapter 14 160
15. Chapter 15 181
16. Chapter 16 195
17. Chapter 17 204

18. Chapter 18 221

Sneak Peek! 233

Many Thanks! 248

About the author 249

Also by D.B. Forest 251

Dive into the World 253

Please leave a review 255

To all of those who want to write a book and then realize how hard it is. You've got this! It just takes some grinding sometimes. Keep at it.

Chapter 1

"Ha! Get ready to weep," Alessi says as she prepares to throw down her tiles in triumph, but with a bigger bump and the rattle of horse hooves on cobblestone, the wagon tosses us. Settling, we stare at each other for a moment.

We've switched from dirt road to stone.

Gribble whoops, and Surrilo says, "Finally."

Abandoning our tiles, we scramble to the front, poking our heads to see past our driver, Haweth. We've been to this city before, but rolling into any place we can perform never fails to thrill. Alessi and Gribble point out landmarks over Haweth's right shoulder, while Surrilo and I peer over his left. Surrilo mentions the changes he can see from here. "Oh, they repaired that broken post," or "that sign wasn't here last time."

I only vaguely mark the changes. Excitement prickles my insides too much to note the mundane. It's the people I'm here for.

Haweth clucks at the big horses, urging them a little faster as he steers them onto the bridge and toward the city gate. The horses' heads bob a little faster with the quickened rise and fall of their shoulders and rumps. Their ears swiveling backward for a moment before flicking at the flies and perking up toward the city with the new sounds, sights, and smells.

We're almost there! And I know our family in the other wagons is just as excited.

I wish Haweth would make the horses go faster. But he's stuck behind the lead wagon. *They* decide the pace. And knowing Della Gianna, she'd prefer a smoother ride into town than a fast one. There's a lot to complain about in old age. Bumpy wagon rides are one of them.

As the front wagon passes through the wooden gates and into the city, we hear the shouts of the townsfolk, hailing our arrival. Jitters in my chest make me want to leap from the wagon and run into town faster to soak in all the anticipation of the people. We'll get the chance. It'll come soon enough.

But that's not the point.

The point is that we're missing the first notes of the people's welcoming song...Figuratively speaking. They can't sing like we do. Or they'd not be so delighted to have us here.

Our wagon is next.

Through the gate, we go and into the midst of a gathering crowd, where children run alongside us while dogs bark and chase, not exactly sure why the humans are fussing, but wanting in on the fun. And women with babies or baskets on their hips shade their eyes and point, while men stop their work to come gander as well. One drops his wheelbarrow; another leans his tools against a wooden post while another chucks his arm load of timber and jogs to the front of the forming line of adulators.

We wave. Surrilo leans around me, already performing. Charming the masses with his friendly, open manner. Alessi is on the other side, blowing kisses and laughing her tinkling laugh, fiddling with her blonde curls. Gribble waves as well, of course, but he doesn't stand out next to Alessi. He serves more as a backdrop for her. The same way I serve as a backdrop for Surrilo. Although technically I'm in front of him right now because...manners.

Though we need no guide through the town, a man takes it upon himself to direct the wagons to the square where we'll set up the stage. Invited to entertain at their fair, we intend to stay the entirety of the week. Not with the best accommodations, it may be noted. Welcomed, we are, but we're not 'of' them. We're not fully accepted. Traveling entertainers have reputations. Sometimes for good reason. Pickpockets, tricksters, and crooks often roll into towns like us, offering special tinctures to heal anything, elixirs to make women beautiful, or claiming they can tell fortunes. Unfortunately, because we're 'unsettled people,' that stigma clings to us as well and drives a wedge between us and those we perform for. Like we're not decent folk because we don't have a house. Or because we're cast-offs. Which isn't incorrect. A lot of us have run away or been driven away. Or are orphans.

So, they sequester us in the square, which is better than being asked to camp outside the town where the wild animals are. There's at least some safety within the walls. But we won't be allowed to take rooms even for money (which we're not inclined to spend our money on anyway). We're quite fine living out of our wagons.

Haweth pulls up the horses on the other side of the elder's wagon, and the four of us inside scamper to the back. Gribble lets down the gate while Surrilo stands backwards at the very edge, holding onto the wagon posts that hold up the canvas. With a smooth motion, he thrusts himself away from the wagon, flipping backwards and around at the same time, his body twisting so that he lands on the ground facing the crowd with the flourish of his hands. Just a little taste of what they expect to see later tonight. Several of the townsfolk 'oh' and clap for him while he grins and bows. He reaches back into the wagon to help me down while Gribble helps Alessi.

She descends gracefully and then bends in a dainty curtsey, blowing kisses and waving while she poses and preens. Her delicate hands become instruments of faux modesty, fluttering like a butterfly around her rosy cheeks and on her neck. While she plays coy, Gribble simply moves around the wagon, unloading what needs to be unloaded.

Surrilo works the crowd, shaking hands with the menfolk, seeking out those he recognizes from our last visit and asking after their families. He laughs and shares some jokes with a few, moving through the crowd as if he's a nobleman and not a lowly entertainer.

Big Henri, our giant, helps the matriarch from their wagon. The aching, white and gray-haired woman straightens, and her hand lands on her lower back while the other clutches her cane. Della Gianna works her way to where Haweth has placed a log for her to rest on while we set up. Della Gianna isn't her real name. 'Della' is a title she's given herself to create her character as an entertainer. Some of our names are that way. Mine, for instance. Though I didn't choose the name 'Whistle.' It was given to me.

I stand still, eyes moving between my fellows and the crowds. Never really sure what to do in these moments.

Not good with the relations like Surrilo.

Not good at simpering and acting shy about the attention, especially from young men who come to speak with Alessi. She tilts her chin into her chest, with her large blue eyes pinning the young stags in place, her cheeks pinked with blushes. As some of them speak to her, she laughs lightly and gestures that they're too funny. Her yellow-blonde hair is up with flowers pinned in, but the ends of her loose curls are left wild and fluttering around her face as she shakes her head.

Her clothes are also a tool she uses to attract attention. *Too* bright, they are, blue like the deeper blue of the sky over warm pink trimmings (an older style with high collars and wider skirts with a bright pink petticoat). 'Normal' women consider the style and color as clashing. Oranges, reds, and golds are what's 'in' right now. And 'normal' women wouldn't wear their hair like hers, wild and free as it appears to be. But the most condemned of all is her stockings. Stockings should *never* be seen; however, Alessi shortened her dresses and devised ways to hold the skirt up, as if she were grasping it in her hands. It falls about mid-calf at the highest, but still enough that her wildly dyed or embroidered stockings can be seen over the tops of her boots.

The negative attention from 'decent' women only fuels her fire, serving to embolden rather than shame her. In spite of our diminished state, she's made do. She utilizes old styles because they're what we can afford or are given. And she alters the clothes herself, spending nights by campfire or candlelight taking apart, reattaching, and in essence, redesigning her own looks until she's satisfied. And she takes tender care of her bright, treasured stockings (visible as they are), which she buys new when she can and stockpiles in her special cedar chest.

And she may catch attention with her bold style, but she masters it with her charm.

I can't help but notice that not a single one of the young stags looks my way once she's got their attention. Not one. I'm not afraid to admit I'm bitter about it. I'm not too proud to say it bothers me that this happens every time we roll into town. But there's nothing to do about it, so I move around the wagon to avoid the scene.

I hear one of the men ask Surrilo to grab a drink at the tavern. He declines, pointing out the work he has to do here to set up for tonight.

"Later then," one of them says.

"You know a minstrel's schedule," Surrilo says, but he's grinning and waving, telling them to greet someone or another for him. Then he bats his hat in his hand and pops it on his head, a giant smile on his face as he comes to help us unpack.

He moves to untie some of the boards we transport on the bottom of the wagon. I grumble to myself as I smack the wagon's back gate with the flat of my palm. Surrilo pushes the boards out from under the wagon and then measures them, too buried in his calculations to notice my frustration.

"Why does Alessi get all the praise. Every time we roll into town? After every performance?" I ask, leaning against the wagon now, arms crossed.

"Probably because she doesn't scowl at everyone," he answers without looking up. He crouches near the beams, holding his arms out to measure and compare.

"I don't scowl."

"Yeah, you do."

"Do not."

"Do me a favor?"

"Yeah," I answer, rolling my eyes. I'm certain what he's about to ask has something to do with the thing he's working on. He wants me to hold or grab something, probably. I intended to grumble, not get roped into his project.

"Think of your face right now. Freeze. Hold your face still. Then step outside your body and imagine what that looks like to someone else." He's not even looking at me. I guess by now, he doesn't have to.

And I heave a sigh, kicking my leg out, but I do imagine what my face looks like. My brows are turned down and crunched inward. My mouth is tight, and my dark eyes bore holes in things.

"It's just my face," I reason. "That's just how I look."

"Exactly," he says with a gesture like 'now you've got it,' "You have two expressions: hungry and angry. They're not that different. You could be contemplating daisies and still look like you're planning murder."

He pauses his calculation to stand and adjust his pants at the knees. He sends a half-cocked smile my way as he crouches around the other side of the beams now to tick something with his knife.

"Besides, what would you want with a townie anyway? You know we're not here for long. We're only here for a week or two, and then we move on. Hardly enough time for a relationship. Not enough time to get to know someone. And townies stay put. They don't travel. They don't perform. They don't get to do the things we do."

"It's not about the *men*," I say, rolling my eyes. "Or a relationship."

I don't have the time or the inclination. And he's right about townies.

"Oh, so it's about the *attention*?" he says, marking another spot on the wood so it matches the other board.

Admitting that I want it stings. Like I should be above that. I try another direction.

"Every time we roll into a town, the young stags see Alessi and go wild for her. Inviting her to the pubs or to meet their mothers. They don't even *know* her," I reply as if the moral high ground is something to argue in this context. As if I *have* it.

He moves to the other side of the boards and crouches down to make more of the marks. I push off the wagon and square up with him, because I don't feel like I'm getting the sympathy I'm after. I want to snap at him to look at me. To notice my frustration and be kind with it. Or at least validate it.

"This isn't about her," he says. "It's about you."

"What about me?" I challenge, waiting to see if he'll say something that's remotely what I want to hear.

"You're upset because you're a closed door to men. And most people in general, but it's mostly the men hanging around Alessi that you get frustrated by. Because you don't know how to open that door to initiate an introduction or conversation without being awkward or too much, while she draws them in like flies. You don't know how to flirt like she does. She makes it look easy while you look like the awkward sister that was kept in the attic all her life."

My jaw hangs open, and my eyes pop. How could he say that?

"I am *not* awkward," I shoot back.

He sends me a sardonic look, smiles, not at all chagrined, nor is he trying to hide that fact. He goes back to his work, saying, "Not at all. Clearly, you're a natural at flirting with men. That's why you're growling at me right now, isn't it?"

Reeling back, my arms drop to my sides, and my mind blanks from the sheer shock of it.

"I'm not trying to flirt with *you*," I point out, barely containing the tone of my voice.

"You couldn't if you tried."

"I *wouldn't* try."

"That's probably for the best. Keep your awkwardness to yourself."

I screw my mouth shut to keep my anger from pouring out. My fists clench as my mind churns over what insult seems appropriate.

Or a retort. Or something that he does that's dumb or lacking. But I can't think of anything at the moment. So, I make a frustrated noise between a growl and an 'ugh' and stalk away.

I don't dare look back. He'll only be smiling, delighted to have set me off. Self-satisfied toad. The *audacity*. The pure, unrestrained, infuriating gall of him.

No sympathy. No understanding...Not at all how I wanted that to go.

The stage is set, the players dressed up, the sun sets, and we wait with as much anticipation as the audience. Some of the company clasp hands, hoping that things will go well. Their eyes closed in silent prayers as their faces turn towards the sky with stars beginning to peek between the soft, translucent clouds.

Torches dot the square, casting orange light across the faces of the townsfolk, some standing, some sitting. Most of the kids have found their way to the front of the crowd to be nearer the wooden platform. The curtain is closed, but the posts have been dressed with pretty, shimmery draping of bright orange, white, and yellow.

And then the musicians break into a song. Ollio, our magician, steps out onto the stage, waving his hands as Surrilo dives into a flurry of flips and twists, going across the entire stage while the children erupt into a chorus of 'yay!' They clap and cheer at the tops of their voices as Surrilo, finished with his warmup phase, moves to the center of the stage. Ollio begins his starter act, pulling scarves out of Surrilo's ears while Surrilo greets our fans here tonight.

"Welcome!" he begins to another round of squeals from the children and whoops from some of the adults.

This is it. The beginning. When anything can happen. This is the best part because there's so much ahead, and the possibilities are endless. The mind can't yet conceive of what it will see, but it can imagine. And imagination is powerful.

We intend to enliven that tonight.

"Are you ready to see some daring and incredible feats that will bend the mind and entertain beyond anything you've seen before?" Surrilo's voice rises as he stares intently at the children, hyping them with his tone, raised eyebrows, and the way he waits.

They all shout, "Yeah."

"What about your parents? Are they ready?" he asks the adults now. And they, too, shout 'yes' and whistle.

"Then let the entertainment begin," Surrilo says, and he flourishes a bow to them and then to Ollio, who's already started his act to make the transition as seamless as possible. Surrilo moves off the stage to allow our colleague to work.

Ollio doesn't announce his tricks. He bends with his magic as if sharing a secret between himself and them, pulling the audience in with how he moves. Inviting them to lean in and then revealing the trick's end for all to see. And sometimes a single trick blends into another.

An older man with a long, gray beard, he seems mysterious because he doesn't speak much to the audience (even when not on the stage) and wears spectacles and a pointed hat. The accoutrements are part of his character. Like Della Gianna's name.

As he pulls a live bunny from his hat, the audience cheers, and he gestures for one of the children to come hold the rabbit for him, showing them to hold tightly so it doesn't escape. Then he waves his hands over the animal, which wiggles its nose with discomfort and sneezes, and a little cape unfurls over the little creature's back while the child squeals with delight, barely containing the impulse to jump and shake. Then Ollio reclaims the animal, putting it back into his hat, and then flipping the hat to show the crowd that it's now empty and the bunny has disappeared.

Their mouths hang open in awe, and they look at each other like, "Did you see that? Where did it go?" Sometimes astonishment likes an ally.

Then Ollio bows and steps back to allow the tumblers their space, as they've already entered the stage with flips and tricks.

Ollio moves off the stage, while Letta puts her hand on the old man's shoulder and congratulates him on a great performance. He says nothing, but his cheeks rise in a smile hidden under his beard. And he moves to his tent to reset the mechanisms for the next performance.

It ought to be noted here and now that Ollio is not a real magician or wizard, and everyone knows it. If he were a sorcerer, he'd have been arrested long ago. Real acts of magic are dangerous. Long ago, those who had magic were captured by the nobles of this land and hunted for sport because it was a sign of strength and cunning to be able to defeat one. Even if that sorcerer was tied up or crippled in some way that prevented them from using their magic. Extinct now, they are. Even still, even a whiff of real magic drives them mad.

But Ollio doesn't work in acts like real magic anyway. He doesn't blow wind through the trees or summon rain or disappear through the sunlight. And thus, with everyone knowing he can't *really* do magic, he's safe. There's relief in knowing it's only trickery of the mind.

I wait off to the side of the stage where I can see both the players and the crowd. Where I can be ready with my bit as soon as I'm needed. Surrilo comes up beside me, throwing his arm over my shoulder and half leaning on me while I stand, arms crossed, and not acknowledging him after our earlier spat.

He wears a loose, light tunic of fiery orange with red laces on the ends of his sleeves and down the front. A teal sash rests around his waist and loose brown pants that cinch around his ankles and disappear into his black leather shoes.

"You ready?" he asks.

"Always," I answer curtly. He makes no apology or gives any sign that he's even surprised that I'm still angry. Because when it comes to it, we're professionals on stage regardless of what happens behind the scenes.

"Good, because I've got something special I want to try tonight."

I groan inwardly.

"What did you do?" I ask. I hate it when he changes the routine. Especially late notice like this. We're literally about to go on. He knows I'm no good at improvisation. *He's* the showman. The actor. Not me. I need practice and time and space to get it right, and even then, I-

"Before you go freaking out about it," he begins, with his fingers splayed as if telling me to stop, "I promise it'll be good. You're up for it. And if you screw up, remember that I'm always right there to make it look fine. That's what I do."

"You *say* it'll be fine," I answer, shooting him a sideways glare. "But what if it turns out like that time in Olocillo? I almost broke my ankle."

"It was just a sprain, and you were fine in a week."

"You know I'm not a tumbler."

"It's not tumbling. Not this time."

"I don't like surprises," I remind him.

"You'll like this one," he assures, and when I pin him with my gaze, he says, "Trust me."

I'm not sure I do. Just because things usually turn out fine doesn't mean I like it. And quite frankly, I'd rather have a set routine, but he insists that fresh is the way to go since there are only so many towns. Only so many crowds. Plus, with an ever-changing act, we can generate curiosity. If the act changes from town to town, word spreads, and people travel to see what we're going to do next.

This is why he has his own act. Because he's good at pretty much everything, and I just happen to be incorporated into his act because I can't tumble, I don't sing like Alessi, I can't play as well as the musicians, and I don't have stories to tell. Not to mention Ollio's talents. Basically, I'm Surrilo's project. He's not wrong. He makes me look good on stage.

When I was a child, I could get away with merely playing my whistle well. Not so much anymore. Gotta earn my keep somehow.

The crowd cheers the tumbler-aerialists as Theliane and Riccard climb back up the silks and into the rafters of our stage. As they make their bows from atop and exit, Surrilo nudges me and then dances back out onto the stage, arms outstretched.

"Aren't they amazing?" he asks while the crowd cheers. "Don't forget to show your appreciation for our talents with the coin dance, please." And as he says it, several bits of gold and silver rain upon the stage from the crowd. Little Benji takes his cue, running across the stage with his sack, collecting the coins, bowing, and smiling to the crowd in his little outfit.

He's a little Surrilo in the making. And they've been dressed to match. Little Benji's costume is just a smaller version of Surrilo's, and the crowd loves it. The two carry out a very short routine of the child balancing on the young man's shoulders and then stepping out onto Surrilo's hands. After a moment, Little Benji is launched into the air, caught by his partner, and carefully let down. Then Little Benji bows and hops off the stage, carrying his treasure back to Big Henri. Several of the other performers clap for the little guy and ruffle his hair as he runs past with a huge grin on his face.

"And now...you know her, you adore her. The musician, the dancer, the other half to my act, the daring, death-defying artisan of dreaded deeds. Let's have a round of applause for Whistle."

That's my cue.

So, with a flourish, I stand straighter, setting my shoulders back, letting my arms fly high, and then cartwheeling behind Surrilo and landing in a split. He then grabs my arms, and I flip around so he can twirl me, spinning in circles as he does.

After a full two circles, he gives the cue with his hand, and I twist and bring my legs to my chest as he slows our momentum, and with a hard flick of his hands, he pulls me up, catching me with one arm under my legs and the other around my back. I wrap an arm around his neck as I wave at the crowd.

He keeps hold of me for a moment as the crowd cheers. Mostly for him. He's the true artist. I'm merely here to be acted upon. Like Ollio's bunny.

Then he puts me down, and our hands stay clasped as we both give a bow. Then he motions to Haweth off-stage. Two unlit torches are tossed to him, and he catches them easily.

"Now, I did promise death-defying, did I not?"

Oh, curse...where is this going? What am I going to have to do? Why didn't he prepare me for this?

But despite the flutter in my chest, I keep smiling for the audience.

The crowd cheers in assent, curious now as to what he'll do with them. And he holds out his hand to me.

"Your whistle, please," he asks, and I whip the whistle, my most precious possession, from the leather holder on my waist. I hand it to him carefully, but also with play since we're in front of people. He takes it and then hands me the torches in exchange.

"Never before has our Whistle danced like this. You're the first to see it, so be kind and give her a round of applause for courage."

He puts the instrument to his lips and toots a few playful notes of a popular festival song for harvest. Satisfied, he turns to me.

"Dance with the torches," he whispers with a wink, and then puts the whistle up to his mouth again. He starts with a lively tune that farmers sometimes sing to synchronize work with one another.

I'm honestly at a loss as to how I should be dancing with sticks...Was this really his plan? His ill-conceived plan?

But I settle myself in, finding the beat of the song, and I begin to move to it. The tune sort of rolls in a way, predictable for a while, but then with a flourish or two to keep things interesting. So, it's easy to follow and easy to fall into while still adding some personal touches and switching it up once I fall into a comfortable pattern. The unlit torches become something of a tool for those little extra things. They're small enough that I can twirl them around my arms and around myself, catching one against the other and flipping them both. My wrists flicker around and back and forth, letting the torches twirl, and as the song ends, the crowd cheers.

But Surrilo's not done. He gestures to Haweth again, and the older man moves forward with a *lit* torch.

Curses...

"Shall we have some more instruments?" Surrilo invites the musicians, and I see them moving into position near the stage as Haweth lights both ends of my twin torches. The heat reaches towards my face, neck, and arms. I feel it, watching a bit of burning...whatever's on the end of the torches to keep them lit...drop from the end and fall to the stage. It blinks out instantly but leaves a little black mark on the wood. I'm tempted to rub the burn with my toe.

Turning back to the flames at hand, I blink slowly, holding the torches far away from my body. The light bounces and bobs so quickly, I can't mark where it was from one moment to the next. It's so fast...It's so warm. The base of it glows right against the wood like waves of something devouring, but it reminds me of water, and I'd love to quench them both in a trough right about now. I'm not sure my heart is beating anymore. I can't see or hear the crowd anymore, fixated on the fact that now Surrilo thinks I ought to dance with fire.

"Ready?" his voice breaks into my thoughts, tearing me from that safe place I could stay locked inside.

There's a crowd to please. There's an act to finish.

So, I take a breath and then nod, contending with the dryness in the back of my throat suddenly and reminding myself not to let them touch me or my clothes. No flipping these ones around my body now.

I'm going to murder him after this. He'd better enjoy this while it lasts. Once this show is over, he's a dead man. And he must know what I'm thinking because he's grinning from ear to ear with an eyebrow cocked as if saying, 'You can't get me right now.'

The crowd is the power over our lives. And we must bend to it. Or at least learn to lean with it until we can shape it whichever direction we want. Which Surrilo can do. I cannot. Nor do I think I could wiggle out of this if I *were* charismatic.

So, I accept my fate. He strikes up the band with a note from the whistle. A new song (never the same twice in one performance), and I pay attention, bobbing my head along with the music until I can get the beat down.

Just dance. Just dance and let it flow. And keep the fire away from my body.

Just start slow. Don't be afraid to let it build. Don't be afraid to play. So, I swish the flames swirling my wrists, twisting this way and then the other. The fire whooshes and flutters with the movement, but the more I move, the more I watch, the more I hear, and the more it seems to want to dance too. As if it's *already* dancing in its own way. I just need to understand *it*. The strange thought makes me smile a little, but I close my eyes, feeling the movement rather than seeing it. Feeling the heat bouncing near my skin with each twirl, and then the coolness of the night air rushes in to replace the heat when the fire is away.

I dip and move with the music, dancing around Surrilo on the tips of my feet, twirling my body with the flames and hearing them sputtering to keep up. High above my head, turning and fluttering and down around my body once again.

But there needs to be a climax. And I've only been making this up as I go along. What's daring enough? Something that the crowd will love? But also, safe?

Tumbling is out. Throwing it up is out. It could catch the stage on fire or me if I can't catch it.

Not having practiced, this isn't the best place to do anything incredibly stupid, so I merely combine the sticks into one, do one more twirl, and then separate the sticks. Nothing too crazy. Different though. And that may be all it needs to be at the moment.

And as the music dies, the crowd cheers and tosses coins at us. I breathe, taking it all in, the fact that we survived. No burns. No accidents. And they loved it.

Someone shouts for an encore, but Alessi is on next, so I'm sure they won't be too disappointed that I don't repeat the performance. As I grin and bow, I catch sight of a man in a black cloak with the hood up near the back of the crowd. Torchlight around him bounces off his eyes, lighting them with a strange orange glow. The orange glow outlines his chin covered in dark stubble. His arms are crossed, and he stands still as stone. But the steadiness of his gaze makes me shudder.

Recalling myself, I move off the stage, handing the torches off to Haweth so he can quench them. Without a word, he takes them and dips them in the bucket of water he has on hand. At least there was a backup plan of sorts.

Letta claps and hugs me quickly, which isn't unusual for her, but is a little uncomfortable for me. I let it happen anyway. And it's kinda nice to have that comfort after the ordeal. Which I'll admit, isn't an ordeal now that it's over. My skin still buzzes, but it's not entirely a bad buzz now. Like a bee without the sting. And relief of a job well done settles in my chest like a calming cloud. I did it. I did something good. Something the crowd loved.

Alessi takes her place on the stage now. The young stags cheer especially loudly for her as she giggles and waves coyly. Her arms are extended with her fingertips up delicately as if she's a marionette, held up by invisible strings. And on her head is a crown of fabric flowers she sewed herself.

Tonight, for the performance, she's wearing a bright purple dress that took her especially long to get the way she wanted it. It has a large rear end meant to spread the purple fabric out behind her to show off all her hard work of pleats and bows. She asked Surrilo to build a light, wooden frame that attaches around her waist. It looks uncomfortable, but...I'd never try it, so I don't know. The purple fabric plays intermittently with bright pink and white trimmings, and in the front, the skirt is lifted to show off her bright stockings with the embroidered birds.

Hoot bobbits are a particular kind of bird with beautiful songs and opalescent feathers with purple wing tips. Often, Alessi is compared to hoot bobbits, and it's an apt comparison. She leans into it, warming up with a sound resembling the call of the little birds. She laughs appreciatively at the crowd's delight and then settles in for her song as the players begin.

Her repertoire is extensive. She sings one that she's particularly fond of and then lets the audience decide what she'll sing next. She also dances, but not usually on the first night we roll into town. That will come later.

Our styles of dance are different. Hers are delicate and light. Surrilo directs mine to juxtapose with hers.

And as the night winds on, my gaze is drawn to the crowd. In a snap, I recall the man in the black cloak, but I can't see him now. He'll be hidden behind the wooden wall if he's still there. He might be gone. But he might *not* be. We've had troublemakers attend in the past. Things can turn ugly. It happens. But usually, the heckles start first. If we're not being heckled, we must be fine...

So far, so good. The crowd has loved everything we've done. Without giving it another thought, I hurry to the wagon to change into my costume for the play.

The first night's act is just the warm-up for the rest of the performances. We don't go all out. Just a taste. The next few nights will have more from each of us. Not just a couple of songs or a few minutes on stage. Keep it moving, keep the people happy. Keep the coins raining onto the stage and dancing on the wood.

And then when it's over, we'll pack up and be gone before the sun rises. Where our wagons and stage were, it'll be like we were never here.

Changed out of my costume and back side-stage, I catch sight of Surrilo talking to Haweth and pointing to the stage.

"Hey," I say, not loud enough to interrupt the performance or break the crowd's concentration, but enough to get Surrilo's attention. He turns, and when he finds me, a wide grin breaks across his face.

"Great performance-"

I smack his arm. "What was that? I might have burned down the stage. Someone could have gotten hurt."

"It was a risk," he admits. "But it-"

"'Went well?' Let's not do that. Consider what might have happened."

"Or..." he holds up a hand, "We could consider what *did* happen."

"That was reckless and irresponsible. I shouldn't have done it. You put me on the spot in front of everyone."

"Okay, I'm sorry about that. But sometimes you overthink things. I thought that if you were in front of a crowd, you'd perform without that barrier. And let's not forget, it was a huge success. They wanted more." He holds up his hand to the crowd as if that helps his argument.

"Is that all you care about?" I ask, accusing more than asking.

"Of course not. I knew you'd be okay," he says as if pricked now. As if a blow to his 'having everything figured out' is a blow to his person.

"How?" I challenge, crossing my arms and cocking a hip now.

Go on. I dare you to make it right somehow.

He gets a peculiar look on his face now as if wondering how I could possibly ask that. Almost like it's a stupid question.

That is *not* a stupid question.

"Because I knew you'd be careful…?" he answers, but he's still staring as if confused. "And I wouldn't have let anything happen to you. We're partners."

I stab a finger at him as if attempting to deflate his confidence. "Don't do that to me again. No more surprises on stage. We rehearse everything first."

He rolls his eyes but then attempts to placate me. "We'll practice for tomorrow night. A routine would really help. The ending needs to be bigger anyway."

"Fine," I answer, crossing my arms and turning to the stage. Because I've won a small victory here. No longer will I have to be subject to surprise on stage and be forced to improvise, and that feels nice. I'm no marionette. I don't like having to dance like one.

This feels like an assertion of my own designs on the world, and I like that. Freedom tastes…like air. But still…like *good* air. Fresh air.

As Alessi finishes her song and coins rain down, she blows kisses to the crowd, giving curtseys to their requests for an encore and promising more tomorrow night. Then Surrilo moves onto the stage again, taking her hand and planting a kiss on the knuckle before ushering her off stage and announcing the play while Haweth and Big Henri move a backdrop into place.

He sets the stage while the players get into position behind the curtain.

"Once long ago, this land was ruled by dragons," Surrilo says, leaning toward the audience to arrest their attention. "We know dragons to be greedy for hordes of gold, with impenetrable armor of scales, and great wings that cause the trees to bend and the seas to retreat. Our ancestors lived in fear of these terrible beasts, but one day they'd had enough…"

He sweeps his hand toward the curtain as he removes himself smoothly from the stage while the large drapery lifts away dramatically to reveal our backdrop.

A red dragon sits atop a worn-down, partially destroyed castle with a claw curled around one spire and its belly hanging over the portcullis. It's clawed foot rests over the crumbling roof, and its head stretches up into the sky as its eyes glare down with its wings spread wide as if the creature might take flight at any moment. Of course, it's just a painting, but it still looks intimidating.

The children 'ooh' at the painting, some hiding their faces.

And as Big Henri voices the dragon, we move into place, acting out the first part of the story where the dragon has taken over, but there are brave people to stand up to him.

The next part will come tomorrow. And as night wears on, we bask in the cheers and watch the coins raining down with delight and satisfaction.

Then the curtain falls.

CHAPTER 2

I wake to the smell of smoke and pottage wafting through the wagon. Morning already? I groan and roll over, pulling the blanket over my face to block out the light, sounds, and smells. Morning hang itself. I'll sleep more.

But then Surrilo's voice calls out from outside the wagon, "Whistle, we gotta practice the fire act."

"Half an hour," I negotiate.

"No. Breakfast will be cleaned up by then. Get some food and come practice."

I rip the blanket from my face and slap it back down where it was before, heaving a sigh and dragging myself up. I rub my face and run my hand through my hair. He taps on the wagon cover now.

"Let's go," he says.

I mutter a string of curses back at him in the "low" language, and he just laughs. I hear him move away, though, as if he's not worried about it. As if he's certain I'll come. And so, I curse at him in my head.

I give the thin blanket one more smack before I pull my overdress on and smooth it out. Wrestling my long, dark hair into a loose side braid with only a few twists, I use some of Alessi's scrap fabric to tie it. Then I pull on a black leather vest, not lacing it very tightly, and move to the back of the wagon.

I'm lucky to get to sleep in a wagon. Few do, and we trade sometimes. Alessi and I share this one while Gribble and Surrilo sleep on the ground underneath for protection. It's a different story if the weather is disagreeable or if we're in the wilderness where the critters are.

Lalina, Letta, and Della sit around the cook pot talking about last night's performances while Letta stirs the pottage. She hands me a bowl of the stuff and then points out the wooden spoons.

"And the fire was a nice touch," Della says. Her old voice is layered with dust over decaying leaves. Her face is lined with craggy branches like trees have in winter. And fitting it is since a layer of snow-colored hair hangs over her shoulders, hiding her one incredibly long earring strung with various beads. She sits on a log, with her bent back pushing her towards her cane. Her middle is a barrel while her limbs are like sticks. Her bony hands show the rivers of blue veins underneath, juxtaposed with knobby knuckles like an awkwardly pruned bush.

So much of her looks earthen, I'm surprised she hasn't joined the dirt yet.

She waves her cane at me as if hearing my thoughts. "It's a good thing Surrilo keeps you busy. Don't dawdle here at the cookpot and leave him waiting. That act needs work."

I say nothing to the old woman, but I flick my eyebrows, while I move off a way to be out of their circle of gossip, shoving a spoonful of pottage into my mouth.

Ugh! It's cold still, but I swallow it down anyway, feeling it slide down into my stomach like a weight. Bracing myself for the next bite,

I force it down for the sake of having energy later. Rehearsals with Surrilo can be intense.

It's a battle to get the last of the pottage down, but I do it with sheer willpower and then toss the bowl into the washpot as Della shakes her cane at me to get going. I throw up my hands and move away.

Surrilo is by the stage, leaning against one of the poles, speaking to a townie as Haweth and Big Henry work on the set behind the curtain. As Surrilo catches sight of me, he pats the man on the arm and shakes his hand, telling him that we've got to get to work. The man turns to me, touches his hat to us both, and moves away. It's not uncommon for townies to want to talk to us. But they usually keep their distance for obvious reasons. Surrilo likes the challenge, though.

"That's the third townie who's mentioned your daring fire dance from last night," Surrilo says with his arms crossed and a cocky smile on his face that says, 'I told you so.' He's wearing his plain white tunic with brown trousers. Plain and relaxed for practicing whatever stunts he has in mind for us tonight.

I glance at the man again, noting how he ducks into an alleyway, head bent as if on a mission. Something about the bend of his body, how intent it is, makes me uneasy. Like he's hiding something. Not wanting to be seen with us? Not wanting to be known?

I'd ask who he is, but it doesn't matter. My suspicion is just the shivers of a time past that tell me danger's lurking. That sense isn't always accurate, but it's a habit I haven't relaxed out of. Our debased societal standing keeps it with me.

It's probably nothing.

"We'll start with the torches unlit and get that down before we light them," Surrilo says, bending to pick up the sticks with burny ends. "We'll pick a few songs to work to first, then add from there. Take your usual moves from the previous dances we've worked on and apply them here if you get into a bind. And that's a great place to start from."

I take the one he hands to me, breathing and lifting my chin to stretch out my neck and drop my shoulders back.

"Are you going to dance with fire, too?" I ask, motioning to the torch he still holds. He laughs and shakes his head.

"No, I'll be playing your whistle. It's easier to keep an eye on you that way. If something does go wrong, I won't be distracted."

"How noble of you," I answer sarcastically, knowing he'll understand the meaning behind it. He does. I see it in the roll of his eyes.

"I'm just that kind of guy," he says with the playful raise of his brows. I roll my eyes now.

"Mm hmm," I answer, twisting the torch between my fingers. Twirling it like I might do a thinner stick. It's slow going in my unpracticed hands, but I could probably get faster with time.

Surrilo shows me a few moves one might make with a sword or a spear that we can put to one of the songs, and the twirling that jugglers sometimes do. We practice a few throws and catches, too, including behind the back. And a spin around the back of my neck. Those particular feats will *not* be done with a lit torch. I can't risk the damage. But it still can be done with the unlit torches.

We will begin again with torches *un*lit. Gotta have somewhere to start, and then we'll build up. That's how it's done. Start small, but with plenty of possibilities. Give a little hint here and there so the audience can anticipate where we're going and then follow through. The payoff must be equal to or greater than their expectations. That's how we keep our audiences entertained and engaged. And Surrilo is an undeniable master at it. So, while I practice the moves and we pull together a routine out of what he thinks will work best, he asks for my whistle and puts the moves to a tune, tapping a beat with his foot.

It's midafternoon when he decides we have enough of a routine down to work tonight. We'll keep shaping the act as we go.

But for now, I'm released to find a bit of supper to keep me going until after the show.

"Looking better," Della says as I approach the fire, tucking my whistle safely into its leather holder on my arm for now. "He works you hard, but you need that."

I roll my eyes at the old woman, and she snorts.

"Yes, that's exactly why," she says, vindicated by my 'acting out.'

I answer nothing.

She's one of those who's old enough to know everything and doesn't let anyone forget it. It's really not worth the energy burned to debate her on it. I know because I have. And it's fruitless.

She loves Surrilo for his talent and easy nature with people. She doesn't like me.

Her love for him might also have to do with the fact that he's her grandson.

The rest of us are strays who've globbed together like mud.

For instance, there's Letta and her husband, Braun. Letta has pin-straight, dark hair that falls to her shoulders. And she always wears a cap that had once been fancy but frays now with strings hanging haphazardly from the ends, and little holes wearing through. Braun keeps saying he'll get her a new pretty one, and she keeps protesting, holding onto this one because it's the first one he gave her. They ended up here separately: Letta was kicked out of her childhood home for falling in love with someone who told her he loved her and then left her; Braun fell in with Della as a child when he ran away from home. He's been with the company ever since. Never considered leaving or making a different kind of life for himself. Even after he married Letta.

Lalina sits by the fire now. She mends someone's trousers with a needle sticking out of her mouth and a thimble on her finger. She's a wide woman with red hair and a plain, ruddy face. When she was young, an accident left her leg pointing in the wrong direction. It was a miracle that she lived, but she was deemed a freak. She was run out of her village. In the depths of winter, holding a worn, wooden cup to strangers on the iced-muddy roads, she finally found mercy in the wagon train of people, not much better off than herself. She makes costumes, does hair, paints faces and sets with Letta. The two are as close as sisters now.

Haweth is a suspected defector of the mariners (though his name suggests he may not be from the islands but from the mainland). He has some stories that he's careful with. Doesn't say much and always has a piece of straw, wheat, or something sticking out of his mouth. He helps Surrilo build whatever Surrilo desires. Drives the wagons, takes care of the horses, and keeps to himself. He was the one who found me hiding in one of the trunks in the back of the wagon when I was a child. Didn't say a word to me. Just pulled me out of the trunk and plopped me on the wagon seat next to him. Then he clucked to the animals, and we kept going. His hair is much grayer now than when we first met. And his face has more lines like Della's.

Little Henri and Little Benji came together. Twins, but Little Henri died of a fever last winter, leaving Little Benji broken in a way we don't quite understand. It was like the child lost a piece of himself. Sometimes we still catch him looking around as if Little Henri might just appear. When he gets excited about something, he still tries to show his brother.

Despite the loss of Little Henri, Big Henri remains Big Henri. We don't have the heart to just call him Henri now. It's like denying that

Little Henri existed. And Little Benji remains Little Benji for the same reason.

Big Henri was rejected as a baby because of his odd size and because his mother died giving birth to him. Luckily, Della and the company were in town, heard of the misfortune, and Della bought the child from the father, who, despite not wanting the child, insisted that he be compensated to let the child go. Della tells us how she chastised the man for being a terrible father while counting out the coins. She wrapped the baby in her red scarf and took him away. He still wears that scarf around his neck. Worn as it is, it's still a badge of honor and belonging to him.

Surrilo's father never wanted the traveling life. Della's son got out as soon as he could, settling into a 'respectable' life, marrying, and farming. But he and his wife fell on hard times when an unusual spring frost ruined their fruit crop for the third year in a row. Then they both became very ill and passed their only child to Della to keep him safe, healthy, and fed. They passed away not long after. Della is protective of Surrilo, and he is her bright, shining star despite the other children she's adopted over the years. She sees in him a natural successor and proof that her way of life was the right thing for her and for her family.

The sounds of laughter and talking break me from my reveries.

"Eat," Letta says cheerily to us as she brings out a tray of hunks of bread and cheese. "Eat for strength and energy." Gribble, Big Henri, and Haweth dig in. I do too, choosing to take mine to the wagon to enjoy by myself before preparing for tonight.

There are some of the stories. Definitely not all of them but gives a range of the ways we've arrived here.

The darkness of the trunk presses on my mind as it did at the time, but it's no longer frightening. It's hope now. It's being taken away from a time and place seared into memory. So, wherever the company goes is home. Wherever the wagons park for the night, the animals feed. Where the campfire is lit and the food cooks over. Wherever the stage rises, and the coins dance. Wherever Surrilo demands a lot from me, and Alessi gets all the attention. Wherever Gribble snores, and Haweth chews straw. Wherever Della Gianna picks apart performances of her train. And where the others do what we do to succeed in our chosen life.

One of my costumes is teal to match the sash that goes around Surrilo's waist. Made from the same material. That's the one I wore last night. The one with a sash around my waist that matches *his* outfit. My dress is made with a pair of trousers of the same material covered by strips of material that move and shift. Next to Little Benji in his outfit, we look like a matching family of entertainers.

The other costume is almost an exact match to Surrilo's, and when I wear that one, he wears *his* opposite, which is almost an exact match to my teal. So basically, we match no matter what. But he likes us to balance out the colors. And we switch every night.

I put the gold ornaments in my hair to match the double-chain necklace, letting my dark, lazily twisting locks stay only half pulled back tonight, though I may consider pinning my hair up more often now that I have to handle fire.

While I work on arranging my hair, Alessi primps and perfects her flower crown, shifting the flowers so they rest just so. Pink tonight.

Bright pink with lighter pink highlights. The flowers ring her head, and she leaves her curls only half up too. She props the hand mirror on a trunk and pins and twists until she's satisfied with it.

Then she fluffs a curl here and twists another there, adjusts her quadruple-chain, choker necklace with the net-like pattern, smiles at herself, slaps the mirror down on the trunk, and crawls out of the wagon, with light airy movements. With the wooden contraption around her waist, she has to turn to get out of the wagon, or it'll catch and potentially break, so she pulls handfuls of the dress around her and whips it out behind her to settle the way she wants. Then she climbs down using the little ladder Surrilo made for her. As soon as her feet hit the ground, she fixes the dress again to make sure the skirt drapes the way she wants and moves away. I hear Little Benji calling out to her.

The sun glazes the sky in a yellow-orange glow as it dips behind the line of trees in the west. The stage is set; the company is ready. And as I get down out of the wagon, I see many of the townies already piled together to see tonight's show. From here, their words sound like a muffled rush of wind through tall grass. Or the chattering of creek water over stones.

"Whistle," Surrilo says, catching sight of me and gesturing me over.

"Are you sure?" I hear someone ask as our kin lean closer to hear Della's news.

I don't hear her reply, but it seems somewhat urgent, so I hurry over to hear what appears to be an interesting tidbit.

"That's what they said. A Chelees heard tell that the entertainers were in town and has come. He's taken rooms in the upper houses in the square, so he can watch from the windows."

"Let's hope he's generous with his coins," Braun says, and several of the company nod in agreement.

A Chelees is a name for a noble of the land. Ranked by the king and by money, there are first-tier Chelees, second-tier Chelees, and third-tier Chelees. The female term is Cheleesai, and such women might have different ranks than their husbands depending on circumstances.

"What rank is he?" Alessi asks breathlessly, her smile wide and eyes bright.

"Second tier," comes the answer. Alessi giggles with delight and fusses with her dress, necklace, and hair again. She looks around at the windows as if trying to spot the noble. I've no doubt that if she caught his attention, her attachment to our lifestyle would diminish rapidly. She might make it happen, too.

"You'd better be at your best tonight," Della warns with her knobby knuckle bent around her cane. "The money could help us through the winter, and if we please him, he may invite us to his castle."

An invitation to play for a Chelees would do wonders for us purse-wise. And reputation-wise, which would in turn help our purses. He may invite us to play for his parties, where we'd be introduced to other Chelees, perhaps first-tier. From there, more parties, and we just spiral upward, eventually playing before the king. If the king finds our performances desirable, our services could turn into permanent positions.

We'd not be so embarrassing for the populace to talk to then. We'd still be entertaining folk, but more on the level of artisans. Sought for our talents rather than shunned for our lifestyle.

Surrilo takes my arm and pulls me aside.

"You know what this means?"

"Rooms in the castles. A bed made of gold," I say. He chuckles.

"Not yet. It means we have a performance to do, and we must absolutely enthrall. I believe your fire dance can do that, but you have to relax and also do well. No pressure."

"Thanks," I answer sarcastically.

He blows out a breath and bounces on his toes as if shaking himself out. Preparing to be the charismatic spokesman. Why not just send him out to meet the Chelees? Surely he'd procure an invitation within a half hour of meeting the nobleman.

Surrilo rolls his head from side to side, and the rest of the company prepares as well, shaking out their hands, stretching, humming, or tuning their instruments as the case may be.

Alessi's eyes still roam over the curtained windows of the upper rooms. I'm sure when the Chelees finally appears, her focus will be on him. She's not the only curious one watching for his appearance. Letta's eyes dart towards the windows, too, and Little Benji hasn't stopped staring since he heard.

For a brief moment, I wonder if the stress of his watching us is worth the potential rewards. He may not like our performance enough to advance us to a party circuit with his noble friends. It's just a fancy. A fancy we all share, apparently. It's like we've come to this moment, prepared for it all our lives.

And as the sun's rays die on the horizon. Surrilo makes his final checks with us all and then moves off to the stage with the rest of us trailing to our positions. He commands the stage as he announces our readiness to begin. His voice rises over the cheers of the crowds, and his gaze keeps moving upward to the windows where the curtains remain closed.

Then he does something I didn't expect.

"I hear that tonight we entertain a Chelees, and that his rooms are just up there. Is this not so?"

The people cheer in assent.

"Perhaps we cheer louder to let him know that the show has begun," Surrilo calls out. And the crowd howls louder, stomping their feet too. Finally, the drapery is whisked back, and a peasant opens the window. He goes to the next and the next while we wait to see the nobleman peer out.

"We welcome the Chelees to our show tonight," Surrilo says, not knowing for sure if the man can hear, but he's done his best.

He invites Alessi onto the stage with him, presents her to the crowd, and as she warms up, the musicians strike up their song. She launches into a powerful tune with a storyline of love and loss. And her notes carry to the windows, but still, we see no one there. Perhaps he doesn't want to be seen?

I suppose that makes sense.

And with that, my fancies fall back down to the mud from which I feel I should never have let them rise. Of course, this was not a means to fame and fortune. But I'm only half disappointed. And feel less pressure because of it. If he's not interested in seeing Alessi, he'll not be interested in seeing me. And there's some relief to that. Now it doesn't matter as much if I mess up.

So, as she and the musicians sing another and another, I sit back and watch, my delight growing in light of the fact that tonight might not be any different than any other.

Hmm...I may be afraid of success.

Alessi pushes herself, digging deep into her repertoire to find the most difficult songs she knows, presenting them to an empty, open window with candlelight as the only recipient of her immense talent.

Finally, her act has come to an end, and she bows graciously to the crowd, holding out her hands to touch the rain of gold and silver coins, laughing appreciatively, and ducking her chin into her shoulder coyly.

Then Surrilo makes his appearance again, shooing her kindly off the stage so the show can go on.

She bounces off the end of the stage, still glancing at the windows as if the man might appear now.

"You sang beautifully," Letta and Lalina assure her.

"At least the Chelees heard me. He must have heard," Alessi says. "I nearly sang the stage apart."

"I'm sure he did," Della assures her. "And what an act to start with tonight."

After Ollio's magic tricks, the man still has not appeared. I don't think he will. Even people in the crowd look for him, so it's not just the entertainers who are perplexed by his absence.

Surrilo has given up on him, too, no longer casting glances at the windows. He gestures for me, announcing our act. Reaching out a hand as soon as I leap onto the stage, he lifts me into the air, so I can grab hold of the smooth, rounded wooden bar overhead. Immediately, I swing my legs up and hook the backs of my knees over the top of the bar between my hands. Then I let go with my hands and hang free, whipping out my whistle and playing a short, trilling tune upside down. Then I tuck the whistle back into the leather holder and reach for Surrilo. He pushes his hands into mine until we find where we can balance like this, and slowly, achingly slowly, I lift one leg free from the bar and then the other until Surrilo is the only thing between me and the ground. Only his hands pushing against mine. Then with the slightest wobble, I fall.

The crowd gasps as Surrilo moves to catch me, and I twist around to land in his arms just like last night. They clap now as Surrilo lets me down, stretching out his arm as if presenting our trick. Then he gestures for the torches again, and Haweth brings them. Cheers explode from the audience as Surrilo grins, holding the unlit fire sticks out. Then he gestures for the whistle and trades me. He tests the whistle while I position the torches in my hands.

Just like we rehearsed. I can do this.

Then I glance at the crowd to assess their excitement for the fire dance. And there in the back, just like last night, is the man in the black cloak. The same orange glow of torches glittering in his eyes, the same light bouncing against the stubble of his beard. Arms still crossed. Figure still and foreboding.

But I can't let him distract me, so I turn to Surrilo to signal readiness, and he begins to play. Letting the music wind through my ears and into my mind, I allow the lilting tune to remind me of the movements we practiced earlier. Matching each one to the moment, I let the torches play, twisting and flipping them under my arms and back, twirling them around, and attempting the catch-behind-the-back trick. A little clunky, but it still works alright.

And the whole thing goes smoothly enough that I'm not as afraid when Haweth comes to light the torches between songs. I breathe evenly, preparing mentally for the heat and the snap and crackle of fire. I notice a transparent space between the wood and the flame. Staring at it, I wonder what causes that, and if I could dive in and live there.

Shaking away that strange thought, I wait for Surrilo's cue. But as he starts to play, I find I can concentrate better on the fire and the heat if I close my eyes. Deleting sensory input other than the whoosh of movement and the warmth. I can picture exactly what it looks like and where it is at every moment. The images are stark, contrasting against the haze of normal thought.

Opening my eyes, I note that the fire is exactly as I saw it in my mind. Even as I move and dance. It's always where I expect it to be. And the heat has lessened on my skin. Not as if it will burn me now. But more like a comfort. Twirling and twisting, I find now that it's the torches that are in the way. They keep me from feeling it as powerfully as I could. Keep me from touching it-

And with that thought comes a sudden feeling in my chest as if the fire speaks, and a tingle starts over my arms.

And the fire seems to leap then from the end of the torch, sending a small plume of fire flicking and snapping into the air like a whip curling around itself as it longs to dance with me. To be one with the music. To be alive.

Surprised, I hesitate as the crowd 'oohs.' Those in the front rows step back. I keep dancing because every single one of us entertainers knows that even through mishaps, one must keep going. And I'll not let a poorly made torch ruin the act. It's just one issue, *and* it's over. I can push through.

I'm only being fanciful anyway. Fire isn't alive. It's simply a...thing.

So, I keep dancing, relaxing, feeling the motion of the music, and sinking deeper into it. I let it sway me. Syncing movement and sound so that it's seamless. And as I do, feeling the tones within my chest, the fire of the torch on the right arcs towards the one on the left as if attempting to link the two. It acts like a chain or a sash one might dance with, curling of its own volition even as it reaches out, pulsing with heat and with the strains of melody.

Jolted, I pause, and so does Surrilo. In response, fire retreats back to the torch ends, becoming inanimate...or seemingly so. Of course, it still bobs, but it acts normally. Like fire should.

Strange sounds rise from the crowd now. Not the usual cheers, but as if this is something surprising and undesired. I hurriedly pick back up where I left off, getting back into the flow of the song and drifting away again, keeping the feelings of complacency at bay this time. And the crowd begins to trust again. Surrilo's shoulders slowly relax as he plays, but I catch his gaze and the flick of his brow as if wondering what happened with these torches. I wonder where Haweth got them and why they keep acting up. Is there something extra potent in the flammable mixture?

No time to fix it. Just keep dancing, just keep going. The tune ends, and I give a curtsey to the crowd, who clap and cheer now that the danger is over. Relieved, I turn to Surrilo, playfully suggesting we get new torches. Without hesitation, he motions to Haweth, who brings fresh ones. He takes the old ones. Relieved to see them go, I relax into these new ones. Getting a feel for the cold wood in my hands and the warm fire weaving an entrancing spell on the ends.

Much better. This should be fine.

"Ready now?" Surrilo asks, and I nod with relief. The audience shouts their approval and desire for more, so Surrilo begins a new song.

This one is a little quicker, so I move, bend, and keep up with the tilt of the notes up and down, and with the beat of the drum on the edge of the stage.

Delighted now and easy with the dance, allowing it to unfold and be what it is. Feeling freer and a little giddy, I let the fire mingle with my mind like a warm hearth, feeling it on my cheeks and forehead, sinking into my skin, wending through my chest, and feeling the smoke in my nose.

And then I feel the fire shift again. This time wrapping around my torso and winding around my arms, like the curl of a cat's tail. It flicks as it moves around me, then presses outward as if directed by my very breath.

In an instant, I drop the torches, batting at my clothes, but there's no need. The fire dissipates as if removed from its source of burning, dying like a whisper on a breeze.

Surrilo quickly extinguishes the flame before the stage catches light. Stamping them with his feet, he stares at me with terror in his eyes as if unsure what to do next. I don't know either. But it's *his* uncertainty that scares me.

Unfreezing, I search for burn marks on my clothes, but there are none.

Why would fire act like that? Why didn't it burn my clothes? Why didn't it burn me? I barely felt the heat of it.

Slowly, I bring my hands down to my sides while Surrilo quickly takes control of the situation.

"Whistle's Fire Dance," he re-announces, urging applause as he touches my shoulder lightly in a gesture that I should remove myself now. I do.

"What happened?" Letta asks me, and I stare at her for a moment, unhearing. Until I shake my head.

"I don't know."

Then I break through the throng of my adopted family and head to the wagon for some space, time, and air.

CHAPTER 3

Sitting in the deepest part of the wagon surrounded by trunks of costumes and accessories, I breathe deeply and let my mind carry me away from what happened on stage. It helps to not be there physically. The distance. The space. Gives me a bit of clarity. As much clarity as I can have right now. I still have no idea what happened.

I don't know what to think, so I've avoided it. Because if I do, I may come to uncomfortable conclusions. Deep down, I already know where this leads...There are very few explanations for what happened on that stage. No...there aren't 'few' explanations. There's *one*.

More than that, I *felt* it.

Curses. This is why I was avoiding thinking about it.

But the show must go on. I'm not done with entertaining tonight. Or more specifically, it's not done with me. Hurriedly, I change into my costume for act two of the play, pretending that the quiver in my hands is just because I'm trying to be quick. I pretend that the extra time it takes to do up the laces is normal, fine even. That it usually takes this long.

And as I smooth down the costume and move to exit the wagon, Surrilo's voice calls to me through the canvas. The music for the tumblers reaches from the stage, so I suppose he's taking a quick break to check on me. How embarrassing that he feels he has to.

"I'm fine," I call out, hoping he doesn't come closer. But I know I have to face him sometime. I have to face them all.

Gritting my teeth and steeling myself, I grab hold of the wooden poles holding up the wagon cover and stand in the open air as if waiting for a bolt from a crossbow to strike me. I must make a pretty easy target right now in the cream-white dress, trying to be someone I'm not.

He hesitates when he sees me, and that hesitation burns in my chest. Denial won't hide what we all suspect just happened. And an entire city of people saw it. There's likely no explaining this away like Ollio's tricks.

"We can dress it up," he says, "Try to salvage what happened. I've already mentioned that Ollio's flash powder got on the torches and your clothes, and that's what caused the fire to act out."

"You know that won't dissuade them. That looked nothing like flash powder," I answer. "I'm lucky they haven't come for me already." And in saying it, I feel the heat in my cheeks, knowing it's true.

"Did you know?" he asks, and his cheeks lift into his eyes as the corners of his eyes pinch because he, too, knows what this means for me. For all of us potentially.

I climb down from the wagon to give myself more time to think. More time to reflect on the past. Has anything like this ever happened to me before?

"No," I reply. "I didn't know." And it's true. I've never had that feeling, that pull, that touch with fire before.

He could lie to me and say that fire is one of the rare abilities and that perhaps no one will believe that a fire-conjurer exists. He could lie and say it's likely that magicians are extinct, as we believed. He *could* lie...but he won't.

I've just ruined our lives.

"Stay in the wagon tonight," he responds. "We'll have someone take your place in the play. We'll say you were burned and need to recover."

"There are no burn marks." But he already knows that.

"No one needs to know."

"Our family will see I'm not burned."

"No one wants what comes if this gets out."

"We can't keep it silent."

"You're not even trying," he says, taking another step towards me.

"There are hundreds of men, women, and children out there. Do you think not one of them will relay what's happened here? Whether the Chelees was watching or not, we can't keep this hidden."

He lifts his hands to plop them on his head while he blows out a breath. His Adam's apple dips as he swallows and thinks of what to do.

"Just...give me a chance to smooth it over. Let me do what I do," he says, raising his brows as if half-telling, half-waiting for my assent.

"Okay," I answer, knowing nothing will come of it. But he drops his hands and nods, his brow set now.

"Stay in the wagon," he says, turning on his heel and moving back toward the stage, the crowd, and our family.

I want to believe him.

I want to.

Why not let him? I understand how helpless he feels because I feel the same way. We're mice cornered in an alleyway waiting for the cats to come.

I climb back into the wagon. I'll stay. I'll pretend. And I'll watch his plan fall apart at his feet without even saying 'I told you so.'

I smooth down the dress as I sit once more amid the trunks and costumes. But white is the color of surrender. So, I change into my fire costume once more because when I'm taken, I'll be taken as I am. As I was. As I am revealed to be. Defiant until broken.

Fire-conjurers, they call people who do that sort of thing. Play with fire. I don't even know how to conjure fire. I don't know how to control it. It has a mind and will of its own.

I know that now. How strange. After all this time...

What will they do to me? What torture awaits? Will they torture my family, too?

What if I run? Could I evade the guards, knights, and bounty hunters with their hounds?

Maybe, but I'd never forgive myself for leaving my family to whatever comes next. There's a chance, a small one, that they could convince the authorities that they didn't know about me and that there are no more sorcerers in the company. Maybe then they'd be set free.

Maybe not, though. And it's that possibility that keeps me seated where I am. Because I've been here before. With a choice like this to make. I chose wrong last time. Never again.

I pull my knees into a crisscross, rest my arms over my legs, and feel like I'm stuck in a catapult just waiting for it to be released. No effort at resistance will stop it. I just wait to splat against a wall. The stark sensation swallows me because there's nothing else to do now as I listen to Surrilo setting up act two of the play.

I lean back with my head resting against a trunk as I stare at the canvas overhead.

We all know the tales of the dragons who used to rule these lands. The secret is that they weren't some great winged beasts with claws and armor of tough scales. They were sorcerers who brought fire to burn the villages and contend with the armies of the kings. Bent on wealth and power, they wrought destruction, sweeping over these lands until the strength of ordinary people was finally able to overcome. They were executed. And ever since, sorcerers have been hunted and killed, so such a thing never happens again.

I smack my knee. Fire. It *had* to be fire. It may have been one thing if I'd commanded the wind or sunlight. But not this. Not fire.

And with that thought, I consider my life and if I'm ready to die. There's much I wish I could have done. Much I'd have done differently. I know most people don't believe they got a fair chance at life. If only it had been this way or that. Even the wealthy have complaints.

I have more regrets than I can even call to mind now. But I recall the worst of them.

Before my family took me in, I lived on the streets. Banded together with some gang or another of other children who also lived on the streets or under bridges. It was hard. There were a lot of hungry days and nights when I couldn't steal enough to feed myself. And often, my dirty, snot-nosed, childish face couldn't summon enough mercy from a stranger for a coin or a heel of bread. In the gangs, we *did* share. But most times, the leader got most of the food and divvied the rest according to his desires.

That is, until Atiene. He was a little bigger than the other boys and had a way of talking, a way of leading by how he moved like he had nothing to hide, and everything was open. They trusted him because he was trust*worthy*, spreading all of the food between us, letting the smallest eat first, and making sure everyone had enough before he ate. Everything was transparent. And since I'd been the smallest then, he'd often looked out for me first.

He was clever about how he obtained food as well, and though we didn't know how, he got out of situations with bakers, butchers, or other merchants that might have had him in stocks.

But his prosperous reign was cut short.

One night, I'd followed him to the baker's. Whether he intended to steal or not, I didn't know, but I wanted to see just in case I ever had to resort to his tricks. He kept low and in the shadows. The closer he got, the slower and more carefully he moved. And at one point, he looked around to see if he'd been followed. But I was pretty good at hiding, so he didn't see my small frame behind the pile of empty crates.

Finally, he entered the baker's shop from the back door. And I followed, keeping low, crawling on hands and feet, silently, slowly. I peered inside, watching as he swiped a few loaves and tucked them into his jacket.

Then the baker jumped out from behind the door, slamming it shut, so I couldn't see what happened next. But I heard the baker's angry tone. Something wooden crashed to the floor, and Atiene cried out. Afraid for him, I rose quickly, throwing the door open, my whistle out like a weapon now despite how precious it was. My abrupt entrance was enough to get the baker's attention. Atiene kicked the man in the shin, shouting for me to run, but I refused to leave until he could get away too.

My obstinance only led to the baker getting ahold of us both with the help of his wife. To remind Atiene not to steal, they whipped him across the hand twice. Two cuts blossomed blood crossing the back of his right hand. I'm not sure they meant to cut him like that. I think they only meant to cause a welt that might disappear in time.

But the damage was done. Atiene held in the pained cries, but I saw them twisting his face. His hand shook, and blood dripped onto the counter. It made me angry. Wriggling violently, I freed myself from the baker's wife, so I could get to him. A candle was knocked over, and the shop caught fire...

...in a blaze that raged far too quickly and violently.

Oh...I *have* seen this fire trick before.

I let that sit for a moment, staring at the cover of the wagon as if it had known all along and kept this secret from me.

Traitor.

I sit back up, shaking my head and rubbing my eyes. I recall what happened next.

In the shock of it all, Atiene grabbed me, and we ran from the shop and into the alley. And I saw the blaze of the shop, the smoke rising in the air. The smell of it, the thick billowing of it as flames poured out of the windows and the door. It was too late for the bakery.

The proprietor barreled out the door and grabbed Atiene before he could get away. The boy pushed me and told me to run, promising he'd be okay and that he'd find me.

He said it was okay. And I believed him. He was the leader after all. Usually, when he said things would be okay, they were.

So, I ran and left him to his fate like a coward. I hid in the trunks of a wagon passing through town and fell asleep in the dark, waiting for him to come find me. Later, I woke from the jostling, and a big man with straw hanging out of his mouth pulled me out of the trunk. By then, we were far away from the town. Far away from my friend.

How could Atiene have been okay after what happened? As a child, I believed he'd pull through. As an adult, I don't. What did I leave him to? I've tried finding out. My family has been back to that town since, and though the old haunts aren't empty, it's not the same. The baker's shop was rebuilt. But nothing remains of the boy.

I'll never know what happened to him.

And once again, the fire is out of control. It's my fault. But I've already been buried with guilt and regret over leaving a friend. I'll not do it to my family.

CHAPTER 4

Final applause patters like rain on the canvas as the curtain falls on act two of the play. The company take their bows as Surrilo announces who played which part and invites the actors back on stage to receive their share of the approbation.

I follow their progress in my mind. How they'll each have their turn to bask. Seeing the joyful faces and the coins raining down. And perhaps the cloaked man is still there. Turns out he's the least of our worries. Unless he's the one who tells of the fire dance...But even a child may spread the word of what happened, and who'd blame them?

By the sounds, I can tell that camp begins to liven as the stage dies. When will the guards come? Or has Surrilo really held off the townsfolk for now?

Alessi throws back her hair and climbs into the wagon. Then she stands, hand on her hip, head cocked as she stares at me.

"They believed him," she says, and I feel like I've been submerged in a cold spring with water rushing over my face and down my body, but also like I can't breathe because it's not over.

"Word will spread," I say. She nods. She's no fool.

"Aye. And they'll come for us all," she answers, but there's no malice or accusation.

"Might be time to run off with one of those young stags," I say.

"Or the Chelees if he'd cared enough to show his face," she tosses out, rolling her eyes as she moves to the trunks to begin dressing down for the evening. "Della wants to talk to you."

"I'm at her disposal," I say sarcastically, and scoot to the edge of the wagon, catching Alessi's smile as she rummages through her trunks.

I drop from the wagon, finding the fire with the troupe already banded around it, still in their costumes which clash with the weight of the moment. As Braun catches sight of me, he gets Della's attention, and several heads swivel to me. Taking a breath, holding my head up high, I move toward them now, wondering what they think. Are they afraid of me now?

I would be. I *am*.

I step into the firelight's glow, watching the cast of its glow bobbing on the faces of my family.

"Casting you out will only divide our family. And it won't save the rest of us," Della cuts the silence. "Surrilo says you didn't know." That last part is more of a question than a statement, requiring an answer.

"No, I didn't know."

"Mm hmm," she says, nodding, her thin lips pressed tightly together. She doesn't yet know what to do with me. The pot over the fire begins to pop and bubble, so Letta breaks the stillness, swinging the pot away and stirring it so it doesn't burn.

"It's not black and white," Della says. "Looks like magic. Can be explained away. No one's quite sure what they really saw. Surrilo did his job well."

Where is Surrilo? I look around at the faces here, but he's not among us. Is he still clearing things up with the locals? I must have created a lot of work for him.

Letta ladles food, softly encouraging the others to eat. They settle into the meal. Quiet.

But then the clank of armor and the tramp of many feet echo through the square.

My heart sinks as I bite my lip, turning to face the threat.

That was fast.

A wall of knights, five across and five deep, slowly advances toward us. Some hold torches to throw light, while others carry spears. A cloaked man rides alongside the soldiers on a large, black battle-horse. The same man from the audience? The slope of his shoulders is very familiar. The light of the torches still lands on his face the same way. Turns out he's a trouble-maker after all.

"Entertainers hold steady," the cloaked man calls out. Those around me flinch, moving back as if ready to run. I step towards the knights, though. One step. Two steps. Hands out to my sides to show that I've no intention of conjuring, and then I stop, so they don't assume that I'm advancing on *them*. To make them feel safe.

"Just me," I say. "Don't take them. They didn't know."

"Halt," the man calls, and the knights stop with a loud, final tromp. Then he pulls back his hood. He has dark hair that falls a little unruly around his ears. His beard is trimmed close and neat, and he stares at me for a moment, as if ascertaining how much of a threat I pose. Then he takes in the troupe behind me as Della moves with alacrity

I've never seen in her old frame. She grabs my arm, pulls me back, and puts her body in front of mine.

"Cease this at once," she says, standing as tall as her tiny stature allows. "Whistle is one of us."

"That's why we're taking you all," the man says, as the horse he rides flips its head, fiddling with the bit in its mouth.

"You'll not take us," Della says with a finger wagging at him as if she can hold him off with it and the commanding in her tone.

Then another man on horseback approaches. This one also wears black, head to toe, his hair cut and styled with intention. A slight curl at the ends as it sweeps over his stiff collar. Even in the dark, I can see the droopy quality to the underside of his eyes as if they've begun to melt, a strong feature of the noble families. His brow is strong, his nose prominent like the cloaked man's, but overall, his complexion is paler. Perhaps the absent Chelees?

And the cloaked man confirms it with an acknowledging nod of his head, as the noble pulls his horse up next to him. The first man must be the captain of his guards, then.

"This is them?" the Chelees asks him.

"Yes," the captain answers.

"That's her." The Chelees points casually at me.

"Yes."

"Then what are you waiting for?" he asks, flicking his eyes over me and then over the troupe. We're no threat, and he knows it. The roll of his head on his neck suggests boredom rather than the danger of the situation. At least for us.

"No," I say, "Let them go. They knew nothing about this. They have nothing to do with it."

"Shut your mouth, fool girl," Della warns.

"Look at her," I say to the men, pointing to the fierce little woman. "She's old and frail. She's no threat to you. Let her go. Let them all go."

"That's not an option," the captain says calmly, as his horse stretches its neck, tongue working over the bit as if trying to spit it out. "You're all coming with us, and we suggest peacefully."

"We'll not just give ourselves up to our deaths," Della says, shaking her knobby fist at him.

"Very well. Bring the prisoner," the captain says to his men, and from the alley, two knights drag Surrilo between them. Blood spills from his nose and onto his tunic. His face is angry, but he doesn't fight them.

My hands jump to my mouth. Della's stunned indignation stumbles over slurs and curses, demanding her grandson be returned immediately.

Clearly, she doesn't understand this situation. We're at their mercy. Or lack of it.

The captain looks from the old woman to me. "Do we understand one another?" he asks, still calm.

I nod and slowly, steadily put my hands together, holding them out as if waiting for the binds that will inevitably keep them this way. He dismounts and moves forward to accept my surrender. The knights spill out of formation, moving towards us. Della shouts at the captain, batting at him with her scrawny arms and fists. One of the knights removes her from his path as if she's merely a gnat and not the force of nature she dubs herself.

"Be gentle with her, please," I say, watching the fierce woman being dragged away.

She's still delicate.

"Check the wagons. Make sure we've got them all," the captain calls out as he steps forward, taking a leather cord from his belt. Standing directly in front of me, he wraps it around my wrists. His gaze is on his task. *My* gaze never wavers from his face.

Look at me. See what you've done. Acknowledge that this is wrong. See that we do no harm to you. Do you not care that we'll all suffer for nothing?

But he doesn't acknowledge any of that. Instead, his eyes seem to have a tired quality to them, and his movements are steady as he ties off the cord, sticking his finger through the loops, testing the tightness. I note too that he's tied the leather around my leather cuffs and not the skin of my wrists.

Strange...

But bound now, I motion to Surrilo.

"May I see to him now?" I ask.

"No, the knights will see to him. You'll remain here." Then he turns. "Bring up the wagons."

The rattle of wheels and clank of chains against wood accompany the appearance of several wagons with bars on the windows from down the street.

My heart drops in my chest, and my eyes flutter at this new sight. It's getting more real. More inevitable. The bars, the chains, the metal things that will trap us. Hold us bound when we, with everything we are, long to be as free as the creatures in the forest. As free as the howling wind or crashing sea. Cages, to us, are death. Living buried with only the animalistic urge to claw until free.

If this doesn't kill them, they'll wish it had.

"Please," I say to the captain, shifting my feet, looking from the wagons to him in pleading. "They've done nothing wrong. Let them go."

His tired eyes turn back to me, moving between mine. His face softens in thought, but the thought doesn't soften his resolve. He shakes his head and walks away, leaving me standing alone in the chaos.

Torchlight bounces off the shiny armor of knights threading in and around us, corralling, herding. My family being dragged together, wailing, shushing, comforting one another.

Alessi's head falls a moment as she gazes at the hands clamped on her wrists, and then she looks at the men around her as if wondering if she can flirt her way free.

Della, glaring, muttering, and pulling Little Benji to her bosom, holding his head to her neck as her chin rests on his hair, daring the knights with the flint in her face to come closer.

Braun rubbing Letta's arm as she sniffs and presses her face into his chest.

Surrilo watching all of this, with his jaw tight. And then his gaze catches on mine. His brow draws tight, and his mouth presses into a line. He doesn't say a word. He doesn't have to.

And a shiver of rage shakes my frame, my jaw clenches, and I twist my hands slowly in an attempt to loosen the bindings, so I can slip free. But even if I could, what could I do? I'm just one against many. Even if I could do something with fire, my family intermingles with our antagonists. They're in the crossfire.

This wasn't how our sojourn in the city was supposed to go. This was meant to be our triumph. With the attention of the Chelees, we were to be propelled towards glorious heights or at least get a few more coins than usual. It was *not* to be where we ended.

Letting the feelings accumulate as wetness in my eyes, I can't force it back. But I'm just stubborn enough to not let it fall. Chin high, feeling that hollow-cheeked pride I get when especially obstinate, I stand strong before the knights. Sorrowful and penitent for my family.

They're led to the barred wagons, the knights separating out who goes where. And the captain moves to his horse again, where the beast stands, held by a knight. The Chelees has long since left. Bored, I guess, with the tearing apart of lives.

"What do we do with their possessions?" one of the knights asks the captain. He looks around at it all and then at the knight. He says something I can't hear and then mounts the animal.

The knight moves away with his torch fluttering. Temptation tugs at my stomach to reach for the fire, but I turn away from it because even if I could reach it, I don't know how to control it. And one of the knights moves to take my arm. I shoot one more glance at the man on the horse. Hoping to see some semblance of mercy there. But I see nothing of that sentiment.

I'm led to one of the moving prisons. Placed exclusively with women: Alessi, Letta, and Lalina. And the door closes on us, signaling the end to freedom with the finality of the lock clanking into place.

Chapter 5

None of us say a word, as the box creaks and chains rattle, bearing us to the outskirts of the town. Outside the city wall.

A bench lines each side so we can sit, thankfully, but the chains rattle ominously around our ears. Not used on us, but the fact that they're *there* is unsettling. The wagons aren't that big, but the four of us fit as comfortably as we can in such circumstances.

Alessi lies down on the floor, stretching out and leaning against the wall. She curls her hair around her finger, her eyes moving from one barred window to another.

Letta and Lalina sit on the right side, with their arms around each other, sniffling and bending their heads to touch.

I'm not sure where Della is. She must still be with Little Benji.

I sit on the left side of the wagon, twisting one hand in the leather bindings still on my wrists. Then I relax that hand and twist the other around, fancying that I feel a little more looseness. I stay as still and small as I can to keep the illusion of space alive. Breathing slowly and calmly to force fear into the pit of my stomach, burying it with schemes for freedom, and staring out the window at the night sky as if drinking in the stars can save me. If not from this moment, then at least from debilitating panic.

How can I possibly reach the lock on the wagon? From the sound of the heavy metal of the mechanism clanking as we moved, I know it's placed low. Probably on purpose. Captors wouldn't want people reaching through the bars and fiddling with it. My arms aren't long enough. I don't even have to try reaching through. The windows aren't aesthetic. They're just holes in the box to keep the caged creatures alive.

We *will* get free. That's the conclusion I've come to. Somehow.

We're not in the middle of a town, surrounded by a wall and by hundreds of citizens now. All we have to do is get loose and hide in the woods. Not all of us together, but two or three of us, going different directions. Finding different villages to settle in?

Letta and Braun will obviously go together. Haweth and Gribble have a grandfather-grandson sort of relationship. Perhaps they'll stick together? Alessi will be accepted wherever she goes, so I don't worry about her.

Della has a reputation…so does Big Henri, so it'll be harder for them to hide and then assimilate themselves. And Della has said many times she'll die on the road. She'll never settle down.

Surrilo will feel smothered in any life where he can't entertain. Perhaps playing in a tavern will work for him. Though it's a step down from traveling entertainer, the consistency will eat him alive. No, he'll want to travel. But the more he's known, the more likely it is he'll be recognized.

None of their options are ideal. And the question becomes whether they want to live or be free. How does one make that choice? We know the lengths people will go to when faced with death. But there are lengths people have gone to when faced with a cage. Death is one of them.

Thinking of them distracts me from myself, because there's no way *I* survive this. Where would I go? Where would I be safe? Rumors will spread. Drawings of my face will be posted in every village. The bounty on my head will be high enough to tempt anyone. Until the nobles find me, I'll never find peace.

Unless...I start again somewhere so far away, no one's heard of me. That won't be possible on the islands. But across the sea...?

Something to consider, but perhaps not the best use of my time right now. Escape first. Survive later.

Alessi rises and paces to the back of the wagon, holding her hands to the bars, and staring out.

"Gribble?" she calls out, "Surrilo? Della? Ollio? Haweth?"

Someone answers back from far away. It's muffled, and I don't understand the words, but it's something.

"Quiet," a guard warns Alessi. She flinches but keeps her face pressed to the bars as she turns her head to see the guard more clearly.

"I'm awfully thirsty," she says as if apologizing, "Can we get something to drink in here?"

"In the morning."

"Can you tell me where we're going? What's going to happen to us?" she sounds half-afraid and half-kindly.

"You'll find out when you get there," comes the reply. And with that, she falls silent. I see her mouth screw up in thought, and then she bites her lip as if wondering what she can get away with.

She decides to be done for the moment. Her hand drops from the bars as she moves slowly across the wagon. The soft soles of her boots pad with what would normally sound quiet, and yet at this moment, it rasps against my ears like a physical thing.

Her fingers tap lightly against the metal over my head, and then she puts one boot on the bench next to me, pulling herself up and staring out of the window. She heaves a sigh, and her fingers play over the metal as if playing an instrument.

Birds and cages. Especially hoot bobbits...It's said that if a hoot bobbit is caught and put in a cage, the opalescence of its feathers fades into dull gray. In a strange way, I really hope that doesn't happen to Alessi. And in my head pops an image of her sitting by the community fire a few days ago, fixated on a bit of dress she worked over, stabbing the fabric with her needle over and over. That defiant streak is what I like about her. Not letting the world decide for...that spite...that's what makes her tolerable.

Letta asked her once if she wouldn't prefer something with style.

Alessi had simply replied, "When everyone goes one way, the answer to standing out is to go the other way. Fashion goes in a circle, and what is out *now* always comes back around. So, am I behind the times or am I ahead?"

At the time, I'd almost wanted to congratulate her.

She's smothered here. Wouldn't it be great if she could transform into one of those small birds and just fly away? Unlikely. And still leaves the rest of us caged.

I have a knife I always keep on me. And a set of lock picks. The lessons of street life have not left me. The knife is in my boot. The lock picks...scattered about my person since one never knows. A couple hidden in the gold ornaments in my hair, one underneath each leather cuff on my wrist, a set in my belt, and one in each boot.

That's not paranoia. That's preparation.

I just need to be able to reach that lock...Or attack when the guards open the door. Unfortunately, they'll be ready if I try anything then. And they're trained for this kind of thing. It's my first time.

And escape only works if we can all get free at once. No one must be left behind, or else they'll have leverage over us all.

They know that. Or else they wouldn't have taken Surrilo.

And that's the next step. Finding out where everyone is kept. I assume in the wagons, but who is in which ones? Can they *also* pick locks? For example, can Surrilo, Gribble, or Haweth pick the lock of another wagon at the same time as me and thus speed up our escape? Communicating the intentions won't be difficult once everything is underway. We just need some cover from the guards.

How many guards are there?

I get up from the bench, turn, and join Alessi at the window. From here, I can't see much, except the woods beyond. But I assume the guard who spoke to her is somewhere close by.

I get down, grab the knife from my boot, flip it in my hands so the handle is in my palms and the blade between my wrists. Sawing awkwardly at my binds, I keep the blade tight against the leather until it snaps under the pressure and falls to the ground. Then I pick up the cords because they might come in handy. You never know.

Replacing the knife in my boot and looping the cords through my belt, I move to the back now. Staring out, I listen for any signs of knights, the shine of armor in torchlight, metallic sounds of shifting, even breathing or snoring if they've fallen asleep. I need to be familiar with their locations and routines so we can avoid them. A few can be overpowered. But not as many as came last night. Will they all be traveling with us? I suppose it depends on the Chelees and his plans for us.

I know there's one somewhere near us, the one who spoke to Alessi, but I can't see him. If they're smart, they'll have guards on each wagon. But how many? I can only see the slightest hint of a shape behind the wagon immediately in my view. I hear another sneeze from farther away.

The night guard seems sparse enough. We might be able to escape at night if we can get out.

Still, we shouldn't be rash about this if we intend to succeed. A distraction then? Perhaps, I could create a diversion with fire that lures them away from the wagons? But if I do, they'll know it was me, which means they'll suspect and may coalesce instead of moving off. And I'm not sure I can control the burn. What if it gets out of hand?

I move to the side where the chain is locked, knowing *I* can't reach *it*, but maybe there's something I can do to make *it* reach *me*...changing the circumstances just requires a bit of creativity.

The whole back door of the wagon is designed to swing outward. It's unlikely that the chain goes across the whole of it. And I gaze in the dark towards the shapes of the other wagons, trying to see how they're locked, but they're turned in a line, so I can only see outlines of chains and locks. I press against the door, noting how it doesn't wiggle or give. Latched, probably, and the chain added for security, which means we have two problems to contend with.

Then I stand still for a moment, waiting out the silence as if it's a game to see who'll flinch first: me or the night. When all is still for a while, I reach my arm through the bars as far as I can. The windows are higher than my shoulders, though. With the awkwardness of the angle, I can't even touch the side of the wagon. I press one foot against the bench I'd been sitting on (and on which Alessi still stands). Pressing the other foot into it, I'm lifted and tilted towards the back of the wagon, my side pressed against the door.

I hear Letta say, "Oh, Whistle, don't-"

"Shh!" Alessi warns. And then they all fall silent. I reach as far down as I can, but as predicted, I can't reach the lock. The tip of my finger grazes the top of the latch. It's something. I press harder against the bench behind me to crunch myself against the bars, reaching as far as I can. The cold metal presses hard into my armpit, but I keep straining, and my efforts give me enough reach to tap the metal loop around which the chain is wrapped.

That's it. No farther. Progress at least.

What if I let down the leather cords, hooked them through the chain? They may not be strong enough to hold the weight, but if I can lift the lock-

"Is this what you're after?" a voice asks as the lock plunks solidly into my palm. Gasping, I pull my arm back through the hole quickly.

Fool! Part of me thinks. *You had it.*

Stay safe and keep your arm, says the other part.

And my heart just thrumps wildly in my chest as if it's trapped as much as I am. I stand silent and still, waiting for the captain to speak again.

"I thought you might try something," he says, speaking evenly, and despite the night and the call for quiet this time usually elicits, he's not whispering.

I don't respond, but I do peer through the bars to see him now. He knows it's me. No use in hiding. I want to feel venom for this man. But the way he looks so casually as he leans against the wagon, snuck up silently so we wouldn't hear or see...he's good at what he does. It's unsettling.

Still, he holds us all hostage for unfair cause, and that's worth some venom.

When I don't reply, he says, "It's my goal to transport you and your family as safely as possible. We've quite a way to go until the castle. If we can get there in one piece, you and I might negotiate your family's circumstances moving forward. If not, your partner will be beaten every time you step out of line, and your family will be sold as slaves. Understand?"

"Why are you keeping them at all?" I ask, wondering if there's some sort of negotiation I can make *now*.

"You know what happens to those who harbor sorcerers?"

"Yes."

"Then you know why I'm keeping them."

"You've used them as leverage so far. You don't have to. If you let them go, I'll go peacefully, and I won't try to escape."

"You'll go peacefully *because* I have them." It's a statement, not a threat. Delivered plainly. "There's a reason I do what I do. Once you accept that, we might get along."

He pushes off the side of the wagon now, straightening. "No more escape attempts if you care about your sandy-haired partner."

He makes no attempt to muffle his steps now as he leaves. I wonder how far he's gone. And why he's still on watch at this time of night. He could trust his guards with this, no? Otherwise, what's the point of having guards?

I smack the wood, as shame bubbles in my insides and blazes in the back of my neck. I lean my head against the wagon wall now, my nails pressing into the wood. How is it possible that this thing that can be cut with axes and burned with fire, shaped for human use, is now blocking me from freedom?

But all of that is to distract myself from how easily I was caught. Perhaps the lessons of the streets are farther away from me than I thought.

And this all leaves me with the uncomfortable feeling of being watched, bested, and controlled. Not to mention that now if I do something wrong, someone else gets punished. Not just *someone else*, but Surrilo.

Does Surrilo know about the threat?

If I'm compliant, he'll never have to. If not...

I turn, leaning against the door of the wagon and sliding down until my bottom hits the floor, and my knees bend. I cradle them to my chest.

"Could have been worse," Letta comforts me.

"Could have been better," Alessi says, turning and peering through the bars and into the night.

CHAPTER 6

Morning hits bright against the shade of the wagon, and I stretch the stiffness out of my limbs. The wood is hard to sleep on. But I dozed a little. My eyes feel heavy, and my head feels full of wool. But through the foggy haze of sensations that don't quite make it through to my consciousness, I understand that we'll get a small break. So, I breathe in deeply, hoping that it'll help clear my head.

"Stand back," the knight says as he removes the lock, and the unwinding chain clanks through the loop.

Alessi chooses this moment to shine. She's already primped her hair and fixed the flowers in her hair. As the door swings open, she flips her hair and smiles, reaching down for a knight to assist her as if she's not a prisoner at all.

They do assist her, and her eyes crinkle in delight. She moves aside, shading her eyes against the morning sun, not moving too far away. I've seen her enact this ploy before with men, making it look as if she's merely waiting for us, when she's basking in the small victory and pushing her influence as far as it'll go. The opposite of 'leave them wanting more.'

I let Letta and Lalina go next. Letta looks for Braun, and when she doesn't see him, she asks the guard where he is. The guard merely points towards one of the wagons where some of the men are being pulled out. She and Lalina move that way, holding hands.

Then the knight reaches out to help me, too, but hesitates, I think recognizing who and what I am. But then, determined to do his duty, he reaches out, his gloved hand unwavering now. I stare him in the eye as if to say 'coward,' and then get down myself.

I follow the others to the clearing where the guards let us stretch, eat, drink, and be human for a moment before starting the journey.

One of the knights hands out crusts of bread and cheese that had been left out from our camp in the town square. I can tell because they didn't wrap it up. It crunches now, as I squeeze it in my hand, watching crumbs fall into the long grass. A bucket of water is plopped on the grass, water sloshing over the side. The knight drops a dipper into it.

Letta doesn't eat. She's wrapped up in Braun's arms. Little Benji looks dazed with swollen eyes as if he's been crying. Ollio is quiet as he pulls his bunny from his cloak and soothes the animal as he sets it in the grass to eat. I don't see Riccard or Theliane. Did they get away last night?

Surrilo still has crusts of blood on his upper lip and chin. Traces of it mark his clothes.

"Are you okay?" I ask, knowing that whatever happens to him from this moment on is on my head. For all of them, really, but him more so.

"Bad night for entertaining," he waves off. He crosses his arms, leaning back a little as he surveys our little family.

"Where are the tumblers?" I whisper so the guards can't hear. He shrugs and gives me a look full of meaning.

"Where are you taking us?" Della asks imperiously as she moves stiffly, legs wobbling as she holds onto Big Henri's arm. He keeps a slow pace so she can walk with him.

"Merincillo," one of the knights responds. And several of my kin make noises as if surprised. Obviously, we've all been wondering where we're going now and what happens to us when we get there. Merincillo was not a place I'd have guessed. Seems the others didn't suspect it either. I'd have guessed somewhere closer to the king's castles or his enormous palace.

Merincillo is a castle along the cliffs and wooded areas of the southwestern coast. None of us has ever seen it, but we've been to the villages and cities nearby. Warmer and balmier there when I prefer the cold. We don't know much about the Chelees who owns the castle, but it must be the one from the night before.

What is he doing all the way up here? Business, of course. I guess the kind of business hardly matters. Finding a fire-conjurer must have been worth far more than what it cost to come here. Right place. Right time. For him, that is.

We must be several days' journey away from the castle. I breathe, closing my eyes for a moment because I'd like to remember the roads between here and there. I don't remember much, unfortunately. Travel is boring, often prompting me to distract myself from the monotony. Hence, the tile game. Haweth would know the route, though. In fact, all our drivers would know. But how do I ask them without the guards knowing?

I look around at the guards, noting where they are, how many, and who they watch. They ring us in the meadow, four keeping track of me, while four more keep track of Big Henri. Seven scatter where the men are grouped, but the women don't seem to be much of a threat to them. That's our 'break through' spot.

Surrilo taps my arm in farewell and then moves to speak with others in our troupe. Alessi's found Gribble, and they stand apart as Surrilo joins them. Then Haweth joins them too. The wagon mates of mine for years. And for a brief, panicky moment, I feel slightly estranged. Not because they intend for me to feel that way. But because I'm punishing myself.

This is my fault. Not entirely. It's not entirely on my head. And I refuse to take responsibility for this situation beyond what I ought. It's shoddy laws, indoctrinated knights, and erroneous authority wielded dubiously. Wrong time. Wrong place. For me, that is. For them.

Where does my responsibility for this situation end, and that of errant rulers begin? Though that might be a dumb question, considering they don't take accountability for their ignorant actions.

Still, I must act within the bounds this world has set. And it has set some pretty stiff bounds. Fine. I'll work within that. They'll do their worst. I'll do my best. And I'll not go broken to the end.

Soon enough, the captain appears on his large battle-horse, which prances and flips its head, batting the air with its mane and flicking its tail.

"Prepare to move out," he orders, and the knights gather us back up, herding us like sheep towards the wagons. Braun assures Letta that they'll be okay, but the knight still has to pull her off of him. The knight holds her upper arms, pushing her along, while her body rebels, bending toward Braun.

I resist the knight's 'help,' climbing back in by myself. Once we're all inside, the door swings closed, cutting off our easy access to sunlight and each other. The chain clinks into place, and the lock engages.

This is going to be a long journey.

Four days into our journey. Four days of rattling from side to side in the wagon, getting breaks at night and in the morning. Four days of crusts of bread and cheese for food. Only water to quench our thirst.

And we're undone. Not with fear, but with helplessness.

The initial shock wears away under the grinding of our minds against harsh reality. Once afraid for our lives, now chafing in the wagons that hide most of nature from our views and only provide peeks through unbending metal frames. Except for the breaks, outside may as well be a painting.

Some of my family go numb. Some get angry. Some weep. Some, though trying to stay collected, show signs of anxiety. It grows each time we see each other. The four of us in the wagon stare at each other, the wooden walls, and the faraway views of nature.

My skin tingles and itches. Lalina just stares. Her eyes have gone dull, and she seems somehow paler, and her cheeks sink as if she's not eating.

Alessi sighs, fidgeting with her fingers, pacing, arranging, and re-arranging the fabric flowers in her hair. Occasionally, she goes to the window. She presses her face against the bars as if she can somehow squeeze her way through. But when that doesn't work, she stares at the trees and whistles a tune to the birds. One seems to answer her with a clear call, so she whistles again. The same tune.

And it calls back again. She sings a few notes. But we're still moving, and the bird is not, so it's left behind. And Alessi is left trying to make new friends with the new birds along the way until the guards get tired of it and tell her to stop.

She rolls her tongue and hops down off the bench. Her shoulders tense as she moves to the middle of the wagon, swaying with the bumpy movement of it, and the fiddling with her fingers starts again. Her movements seem to suck the air out of the wagon, even though we have three windows. It takes up the space, making my skin feel more itchy.

This isn't like traveling in our wagons. Not that ours were much smoother, but they were better. At least we could stretch out our blankets and pillows and nap. Or we played games, talked, and told stories. We could even switch wagons if we wanted to, changing up our company.

Now we're just...stuck.

And the constancy of the movement without the option to stop provides a sensory assault that is hard to bear. Especially with the sounds of rattling wheels, rattling wood, rattling chains. Rattling. Rattling. Rattling. The sunlight through the trees casts sprinkles of shadows that shift, blink, and blind us. I'm not sure a pattern would be preferable to the randomness. It's all annoying, and it doesn't stop.

I want out.

That desire, the sensations, the monotony, and emotions of myself and the others rub against my consciousness until I'm raw. But there's no balm.

The only refuge is the mind. So, I sink down on the bench, down into nothingness, begging sleep to carry me away from this awful place. But everything pokes, prods, and taps, demanding attention, scaring sleep away. And lying on the bench only makes the motion worse. Makes the wood jab my ribs more.

Biting back a sigh, I rise, taking Alessi's place on the bench with my face pressed against freedom I can barely taste if I stick my tongue out far enough. Closing my eyes, though, I call up reveries. I conjure the image of standing on the stage in front of the crowd while they awaited Surrilo's daring act. The feel of the torches in my hands. The heat licking over my hands, even pressing through my sleeves. And how it had sunk deeper, expanded more, become something else. Something not as physical but almost tangible. Comfort in my chest and against my cheeks. And the terror and fascination of it coming alive. Afraid as I was when it touched me, it was almost like a blanket or like a pet asking to play. Had I not been scared of it, of what it meant, and of being seen, what could I have done?

What could I have been doing all along? I've no interest in power, but I like the way fire dances. And it seems to enjoy bobbing and weaving with happy little crackles and pops. Sharp snaps and spitting ash, but bouncing, ever bouncing, reaching as if determined to spend each breath of life to its fullest. And that's the point, isn't it? To burn bright while it can? Until its end?

Isn't that my purpose too?

The brighter it burns, the faster it dies.

And its physicality is built from...Well, built from what exactly? I guess I'd never really thought about it. Air, certainly. Wood or something to burn. Spark. Devouring. Spark comes from something, from somewhere. When it catches, humans are careful to nurture it until it can spread and survive on its own, upheld by that source. Springing from a base. Fire can't just exist in nothing. Maybe that's why it disappeared when clinging to me, detached from the torches, from its source of burning. But then why reach for me in the first place?

I don't pretend to understand the nature of magic. But I know it has one. So...the mystery must be unravelable. And fire must continue to be a physical element, considering its relation to the physical world? Or does it become somewhat untethered when controlled? What would that mean?

What are the limits? How far can I push them?

Because now that everyone knows I have a gift, it won't matter to the knights, Chelees, or King that I can't conjure or control fire. Either it makes me look incompetent or makes me an easy target.

No, not knowing how won't save me or my family. But using it might.

CHAPTER 7

The trick is to learn how to conjure without getting caught. That will be difficult, considering I don't know how it works, and fire announces itself through sight, smell, sound...feel.

That being said, utilizing the torches at night to learn how to *connect* with the blaze is the best option, but *conjuring* will have to be tried during the day when it's less likely to be seen or heard by the guards. That means inside the wagon...which puts us all at risk if it gets out of hand. But outside the wagon will definitely be seen.

If I do end up conjuring it, it'll be in the front corner, so we still have an escape route if the flame catches on the wood. Assuming the guards let us out...

I'm being foolish...even considering it is a fool thing to do. Especially because even if it goes well and we can stamp out the tiny spark before it catches, the burn marks could be seen by the guards, and Surrilo will be beaten.

And what do I even use this skill for? (If I manage to turn it into a skill that is.) Spreading fear? I've never actually hurt someone with fire, but as my mind conjures the memory of the baker's shop, I have to add 'intentionally.' I've never *intentionally* used fire to hurt someone.

The problem I keep running into in all of this is that if I plan an escape and fail, *they* pay the price.

As the sun sinks toward the tree line, we hear the drivers calling to the horses to stop. Thankfully, the cacophony ceases, and we crowd the door, eager to be out of here. As it swings open, we follow the established routine of grouping together, eating, drinking, talking a little, feeling solid ground beneath us, and enjoying each other's company for the moment.

Della sits in the middle of us next to Big Henri, who passes the water bucket across the circle we've created. Braun sits leaning back with his arms stretched out behind him. Letta's head rests against his shoulder. Some of our family don't sit, though. Alessi paces to feel the freedom of movement again. Then she stops, stretching her arms out to the sky. She pins the stars with her gaze and then takes a deep breath. She belts out a beginning note like bidding it to be free in the world. Expelling it with a wish of good fortune.

Surrilo joins in, harmonizing an octave lower. Then Gribble adds his own melody. Lalina passes the water bucket back to Big Henri, who knocks the dipper against the side and top to create different sound beats. Braun and Letta keep time with their claps.

And I pull out my whistle, touching the detailed and worn engravings, blowing a tune, and working my fingers over the different holes to catch the different notes. I follow Alessi's melody because her pitch works better for the little instrument.

Della's old, craggy voice contrasts with Alessi's, creating a round here or an echo there. If I close my eyes, I can picture the campfire in the middle, my family all around, and the possibilities of a new show to look forward to. And I think that's the whole point of this. But here they are around me, and I should soak this in while I still can. So, I open my eyes, peering around at them.

The captain joins the guard to see that everything's done. He's a little road-worn, his cheeks darkened by days in the sun, his beard grown out a bit more, and his hair still unruly.

"Should we tell them to stop?" a guard asks him, but he shakes his head, and then his eyes flick to me.

Surrilo comes to my side, grinning as he drops his notes.

"Dance," he says, holding out his hand to take the whistle from me, while several of my family move to make a 'stage' for me. Surprised that he'd ask me and not Alessi, I hand him the whistle. But then she is the better singer. Her talents serve best where she is.

Surrilo takes some liberties with the tune, adding his own embellishments. And as Braun and Haweth add vocalizations with depth to anchor the song, I move to the center of the 'stage' and feel the music all around me.

If we're to have one last night, let it be a joyous one. Freedom in the face of captivity in the form of song and dance. In the form of pulling together to create something beautiful. Something that will never last because the song will fade into the night, and there'll be no remembrance of it but ours. And not a single memory of this night will be the same from one to the other, so each is unique and utterly our own. But right now, we share it. The night is our secret-keeper. The woods silent and still. The captors...almost non-existent.

So, I move with the music, letting it flow through me. Letting it have a new voice, one with twirling, tapping feet, with hands high above my head, moving this way and that, swaying, dipping, curling, extending, swishing, twisting, and jigging by turns.

Right now, I'm free. And *we're* free. As unbound as we can be under a canopy of stars, with the torchlight ringed around us, and the guards as our unsuspecting crowd. Though it is exhilarating to not care if our audience likes it or not. Pure creation for creativity's sake. To release *ourselves*. And this. This is the true value of what we do. It's not about the esteem or the money. It's about freedom of our bodies and minds, even in the midst of all the terrible things life has to throw at us. It's expression in the void. The spark of creative light and life in squelching darkness.

It's harmony and connection with my family.

So Alessi leads into another song, and the others catch on in their own ways, and I find the new rhythm of this one, and we continue. Some laughing now.

Thrilled with ourselves for creating something beautiful from a rough canvas of silence. We decorate our cages with musical notes wrapping around the wagons. And they reach upward in the night as if borne on the back of the torches' glow. Stretching and expanding time with feelings other than terror. We are alive. And every bit of my body feels it. And it feels good as it works through, expelling the fears and the stiffness of the wagons and the aching for life. Ridding ourselves of the cage, at least for the time.

I already know that tomorrow, when the monotony continues, this is the memory I'll return to. I wish I had fire now to see what we could create together. What would that look like?

And in my twirling, I catch sight of the captain through the waver of the torchlight. Watching us. Not *us*, watching *me*. Not with interest, but with thought. Or perhaps as if I might call the fire to me now. What would he do if I did? What would any of them do?

His gaze doesn't waver.

Neither does mine. At least for the moment. And half a smile tugs at my mouth as if to say, 'Try to snuff us. We'll keep burning. It's who we are.'

Part of me wishes I were a dragon. I'd burn until we could be safe again.

All too soon, we get tired and realize that it's come to an end. To keep from being cut short, we let it just die by itself like embers blinking out. Silence stretches like snow overtop of us as the exhilaration fades and dissipates. And we release it. Surrender it to the night where it belongs. Wrapping it up like an heirloom to keep safe. As delicately as I take the whistle from Surrilo, rubbing the old carvings. My pinkie touches the little 'A' on the inside out of habit. I slide it back into its holder. Aware that I'm being watched, my eyes flick up. My gaze tangles with the captain's, and I'm not particularly happy that he saw a tender moment between me and my most prized possession.

He turns his head. And that's something. Maybe he'll forget.

Finally, the captain gives the order, and the knights move into our circle, pulling some up by their arms, murmuring 'let's go.'

Packed neatly away, I wait until the lock clinks into place before standing on the bench and watching the torches that the knights haven't claimed or put out yet.

Gazing into the depths of the fire, I recognize that bob and weave. The desire to be ungrounded and loose in the world. And as I feel something warm open inside my chest, the flame stutters. Following the feeling of warmth and recalling the way it felt to dance with it before, I let that wash over me, combining that with the exhilaration of dancing tonight. And the blaze burns a little brighter, a little higher, fluttering toward me like a delicate scarf.

Yet, the air is still. There's no wind to cause the torch to behave that way.

Smiling, I get down from my perch, settling with the others, trying to get comfortable for the night.

Oh yes. I can be a dragon.

CHAPTER 8

The afternoon sun drenches the land as we move through the trees that press on either side of the road. We're close to Mercincillo, but we don't know how close. Equal parts relief and fear mix in my stomach, turning it sour.

At least the end of the road is near. No more 'living' in a wagon. But what are we walking into?

Letta is at the window, and Lalina touches her shoulder, half in a gesture to hold Letta steady, half in comfort for herself.

Alessi and I stand on the bench on the other side, trying to see as far ahead as we can.

This is so dumb. We'll get there when we get there, I think to myself. But I'll need to know how to get us out of here when the time comes, so I keep watching for places we might hide. Though staying by the road will be a bad idea.

And I give up...a few times. *And* keep coming back to the bars. *And* find myself pacing by turns like Alessi usually does. As I step back up to the window *again*, she sends a side-eye glance at me with an amused look, despite the inevitable destination that the steady plod of horses drags us towards.

"Nervous?" she asks.

"Not at all."

"I can tell."

"He said we can negotiate if we all get here safely," I say half to her, half to myself. "Maybe he'll let you all go."

"Don't hold your breath," she answers. "It may not be up to him."

I don't answer, because a cream-white tower peeps over the trees in the distance, and my heart drops into my boots.

I don't want to see. But I need to.

Before I can get enough of a bearing over the tops of the trees, the wagon turns, and we're headed directly towards it. Our views of the castle now blocked, we take in everything else as the trees fall away and give way to a pretty iron gate and a wall which is also cream-white and smooth.

Then we're in a courtyard, partly cobbled, partly with grass and nice gardens. The land rises up and away from us. The wall seems to curve around and disappear in the distance with blue sky beyond. I hear seagulls calling, as several fly overhead.

The prison cart halts abruptly. As we wait for the door to be opened, I see the other wagons pulling up next to us. Familiar faces also pressing to the bars to take in everything they can. We exchange glances of surprise and questioning as the guards filter to unlock the doors.

Alessi takes the lead, pouncing at the exit, eager to see the castle and everything else. When the door finally opens, an expanse of road and a circle of garden greet us. Alessi lets the knights help her down, but quickly lets go of them, prancing to smell flowers in a bush. Her nose buried in the petals for a moment, and then her face turned up towards the sun and the castle, soaking it all in. The view, the novelty.

I'm no less eager, especially after seeing her reactions, but I wait for Letta and Lalina to go next, and Letta moves to grab Braun's hand while they're herded towards the castle between the wagons. I hop from the back landing lightly on the cobblestone, following them through the parked cages, making sure all my family is there and accounted for as I follow, standing on tiptoe to see over some of their heads, looking around Big Henri to see that Little Benji and Ollio are there as well.

They're all here.

Surrilo catches sight of me and sidles up.

"Not bad for a prison," he whispers as we herd like cows from between the wagons into the open, "Ladies and gentlemen, our fate." We're standing on an open loop of a road before the castle. It's modern in design with several large, rounded towers connected by boxy sections, sprawling and relaxed looking for a castle. More like a really nice home. The roof is red-clay tile. And behind the castle is blue sky, so I'd assume it's on the edge of a cliff.

The captain dismounts and passes his horse off to a servant, as he removes his left glove, pausing then as if he's forgotten to remove the other.

"Has Ilano arrived?" he asks another servant.

"No, he hasn't," the servant replies.

The captain nods and then turns to his knights, who await his orders. We wait too.

His eyes sweep over us until he finds me in the back. "You. Come with me. The rest will go with the guards."

He turns away as the knights shift to carry out his order. Surrilo grabs my arm.

"We'll stay together," he calls out to the captain, "We're still family."

The captain turns back, popping his leg out and tapping his glove against it. I sense that this is not the time to test him. He must be as road-weary as we are.

"If you're family, then you'll comply to keep the others safe. Whistle has stayed in line because if she steps out, *you'll* be beaten. Now consider the reversal in effect."

Surrilo's hand drops, and he gives me an apologetic look.

The captain nods. "Very well. Move out."

The knights separate us, one of them reaching for me, but I glare and pull away, following the captain without needing to be pushed or dragged. And as my family drifts one way, I go another.

The captain goes up one side of the stairs that curl away from the door on the left and right, so one might choose. Flanked by two guards, I go too, and at the top of the steps, a guard opens the door. He gestures for me to enter ahead of him.

I do, my eyes at once taking in the light, airy room with marble pillars and peach tapestries. Here, too, two sets of stairs curl away from an entrance above, and just below is an entryway that leads underneath into another room. Also, well-lit with a large window.

Taking it all in, my head swivels one way and then the other as the captain moves around me and bids me follow. We pass underneath the stairs and into the room beyond, which appears to be a hall like a king might have for gatherings.

"Where are you sending them?" I ask, hearing my voice echo back at me from the stone walls.

"To rooms in the servants' quarters for now."

"You said when we got here, we could negotiate their release."

"I said we'd negotiate their circumstances moving forward. Not their release."

A fire burns in my chest as I feel lied to, but there's no way to verify what he said. I say nothing as he gestures to a door, indicating that I should go in first. I do, and he dismisses the guards as I take in the room.

It's a study of sorts with shelves of books, scrolls, and loose parchments. The table is neat with writing utensils, and the chair is nice. But it's the window that draws me.

It's large, and the view it holds is like nothing I've ever seen. I feel like I'm standing high up overlooking the sea that laps in blue and white foam. I go to it, pressing my face to the glass to see where the ocean meets the shore. Below is a small stretch of sandy beach, ringed by large boulders and rocks that build into cliffs on either side. Looking from side to side, I can see the wings of the castle stretching out on either side of where I stand. It's a bird about to take off over the sea. At any moment, we might rise into the sky and kiss the sun.

"Beautiful, isn't it?" he says, stepping up beside me.

I don't answer. Instead, I step away from the window, peering around the room once more. The dark wooden door is closed now. Shelves line the wall opposite the desk, and the wall has some sort of decorative plaster, like leaves and vines curling. Painted, too, in plums and golds, while the bottom of the wall is peach with a strip of white separating the two designs. But that's just one wall. The others have a dark blue underneath the shelves and hold the window in place.

He lets me wander as he crosses to the table, letting me explore.

I don't like his nonchalance, so I interrupt him.

"If you will not release them, what options do they have?"

"First, tell me your story," he says, unbuttoning his black overcoat. He slips it off his arms and lays it over the back of his seat. His clothes are simple: a black vest over a white tunic. It's stark against the soft colors of this room. Of this whole castle, really.

He gestures to a chair where I may sit. I glance at the very comfortable-looking padded thing with etched wood and arms. Then I return to the bench under the window and sit there instead. He makes no indication that it bothers him as he sits behind the table.

"I'm a simple entertainer," I answer.

"And when did you first discover you could manipulate fire?"

"I didn't know I could until that night that you were there in the back, watching us," I accuse, waiting to see how he'll take it. I know enough not to push him too far. But where's the line?

"You had no indication before that night?"

That memory of Atiene surfaces, and I turn to the window without really seeing beyond the glass.

"There was a time before that, it may have happened." I turn my gaze back to the captain, locking eyes. "But I didn't *know* until that night I told you."

"What happened the first time?"

"I was just a child," I answer, not wanting to get into that with a stranger. Not wanting to share that piece of history with someone who won't hold it as carefully as I do.

He waits, watching. His hands clasped on his stomach as he leans back as if he'll wait me out. So, I scowl and rise, turning away and pacing to get some distance.

"I was angry. A candle was knocked over. The blaze got out of hand," I say stiffly, turning back to him now as if daring him to ask more. He doesn't know, and I don't have to share it.

"You were angry," he echoes. "And that night at the festival, you were dancing."

"Your point?" I ask, shifting to the seat he indicated. I settle myself, though the arms around my sides like captivity reinstated.

"Seems it may be tied to your emotional state. Probably best there are no candles here now."

Is that his attempt at humor?

I answer nothing, mouth pursed, waiting. He muses, staring back.

"Why were you angry?" he asks finally.

I look away now. "My friend was in danger."

"What kind of danger?"

"I'd rather not talk about this."

"If you want your family to get the best possible deal, you'll answer my questions."

Setting my jaw and lifting my chin now, I look him in the eye. "He'd been caught stealing bread. I went to help him. Then they caught me, too. The baker hurt him. That's when the candle got knocked over."

"And the fire saved your friend?"

"No," I admit, my gaze falling.

"Then why?"

"I didn't do it on purpose. I didn't know how to control it. It just happened."

"Do you now?" He shifts in his seat so that he's still leaned back, but his elbow is propped on the chair's arm now, his fingers pressed into his cheek.

I wish I could lie and tell stories like Surrilo.

"I have...theories," I respond strategically.

"Not knowing can be more dangerous than knowing," he says evenly.

"It'll hardly matter when this is over," I exhale tiredly. "Can we talk about my family now? I've behaved. We're here. I answered your questions."

"What happened to your friend?"

And that question feels like a stab in the chest. On purpose. He knows I'm upset by the story. I don't see how that information is relevant to here and now. But if I don't answer...

"I don't know. We got separated. I ran like a coward instead of staying and making sure he got away. I never saw him again. There. Does that satisfy you?"

His gaze drops for a moment, and then he shifts, so he's sitting straight, his eyes pinning me.

"Laws demand that people like you are to be turned over to authorities. Chelees or kings. Those who harbor people like you can be punished to the full extent of the law, which includes execution."

"They didn't know."

"Your story indicates that. So does Surrilo's. The rest will be questioned. From there, I'll ascertain the truth and decide what to do with them."

"What circumstances will you place them in if the story lines up?"

His eyes are steady, and his left hand fiddles with a pen now. "You seem to be overly concerned with them instead of yourself."

"I know my fate," I counter. "*They* still have a chance."

"You seemed to think *you* might have a chance when I caught you trying to escape."

I cock my head at him. I'm no fool. I'll not reply to that.

He doesn't seem to need a reply. He simply gives a 'hmm.' Then he plunks the pen back into the golden holder.

"The guards will show you to your room." He rises and walks to the door now, opening it and indicating that I should leave. I rise, step to the door, watching his face for any sign of what comes next for my family.

He calls for a guard to receive me into their custody, and they do. Then he watches as we leave.

After a moment, I hear the closing of his door echo on the stone, and I'm left agitated and with prickly skin as we journey through the beautiful castle.

Down in the servants' quarters is a long corridor with several doors on either side. Letta holds Braun's hand as the servants and guards direct them, and it's quite tight down here with the extra bodies. Lalina walks behind one knight, holding a basket of clothes. She ducks inside a room while Alessi's singing can be heard from inside another. Surrilo then comes through the door on the other side of the corridor, catches sight of me, and waves.

He waits for the guard to deposit me with the others before asking what happened with the captain.

"He questioned me about fire. He's going to ask everyone else to see if their story aligns with mine, and then he'll decide what to do with you all."

"What about you?"

"I didn't ask," I admit. "He said he already questioned you."

"Yeah, the night they caught us," he replies, shifting as a servant passes us. The sight of his bloody nose pops into my mind, and I shiver.

"I'm sorry," I say, leaning against the wall, with my hands behind my back.

He shrugs, crossing his arms and leaning next to me. "We wanted to impress a Chelees, so he'd take us to his castle. Seems we *over*did it."

I laugh, and he casts a look at me.

"Well, we're here," I say. He laughs, and his Adam's apple bobs with it.

"You're in here," a guard says, pointing me to a room next to Lalina's. I nod and enter to inspect it. It's small, simple, with two mattresses on the floor, a window, and a small table with a chair. Alessi stands at the window, singing, twisting a curl around her fingers, and watching the servants in the courtyard.

"You're not to leave without a guard," one of the metal-encased people says to me. They seem less and less human all the time. More like functions. I'm guessing there will always be one stationed just outside the door.

"Well then, now that we're all moved in and settled..." Alessi says, waving to the scant room and lack of possessions. "...shall we explore?"

"Go without me," I dismiss as Surrilo says he'll go. Gribble meets up with them, too. Alessi hooks her arms in theirs, and the three troop off with a guard following behind as if they're guests here and not prisoners.

I guess that's something. In the realm of prisoner to execution, there's territory in between for 'slave ' and 'servant.' So 'guest' is a step up. Not that we know for sure what we are. We're just testing borders.

At the very least, we can be entertainment for the Chelees.

I slump against the wall, still agitated over having told the captain so much about a past that still haunts me. My enemy shouldn't have a right to that information. In fact, he *doesn't* have the right to it. He only got it through coercion.

He doesn't know the most important parts, though. That's still mine.

I take out my whistle, gazing at the markings I've seen thousands of times over the years. They make me smile. A young boy's attempt to make me feel better about having no home or family. To brighten the dreary life on the streets. He wasn't particularly skilled with carving, so the etchings are a little jagged, but he tried. The swirls and flowers have faded with time, and my habit of rubbing my fingers over them. I've oiled and cleaned the whistle with care for many years. And like Letta's cap, I refuse to give it up for a new one because of what it meant when Atiene gave it to me.

It was a chance for me to make money on the streets. To live without having to steal. To grow a talent and be noticed and appreciated by the townsfolk instead of being a beggar and a nuisance. He taught me to play a few songs on it. His fingers played over the little instrument, showing me the sounds it could make. And then he helped me position my own little fingers on it, practicing until they didn't feel so wooden.

Then we went out on the streets together, and he played first to show me how to attract people. Taught me to collaborate with the merchants, so we could set up near them to play. We drew in customers for them, and they gave us a coin or two at the end. I loved watching him because he knew how the world worked. And I needed to know too.

I remember finding the little 'A' carved inside the whistle for the first time. I laughed, and his eyes twinkled as his nose wrinkled. He seemed embarrassed and told me that artists usually sign their work, so the world knows who did it. It was a flimsy excuse. A lie. But I accepted it so he wouldn't feel embarrassed about it anymore.

Atiene gave me my name...

As guilt floods my chest, I thumb the smooth wood. How could I have been so cowardly as to leave him? His fate should have been mine, whatever came after the baker grabbed him again. He would never have left me.

I flop back on one of the mattresses, holding the whistle against my stomach.

Whatever the captain knows about my friend, whom I abandoned, he doesn't know this. He doesn't know about *how* deeply I feel. It can't be corrupted by him. And it can be kept pure and protected inside me. Because wherever he is and even if his life is merely a memory now, Atiene deserves better than that.

CHAPTER 9

Night falls slowly, and I feel stagnant in the room, so I peer out the window. When I see the bonfire in the courtyard, and some of my family around it fiddling with instruments they must have found in the castle, I can't help thinking they're being a little *too* brave.

Rushing from the room, I find my way to the courtyard. How they got the guards or servants to agree with this, I have no idea. But Surrilo grins and waves me over. I join, noting the stash, laid out on a blanket. Gorgeous instruments of various types and sizes. Shaped with care. Some new, with glossy finishes which shine in the glow of the fire. They don't belong out here, and I'm afraid to touch them myself. I don't feel worthy or clean enough.

"They let you bring these from inside?" I ask.

"We didn't ask permission," Surrilo replies. "If you ask, they can say no." Then he taps his head as if sharing a piece of wisdom.

"So, did anyone try wandering outside the gate then?" I ask.

"If we had, you'd have heard about it," Della says, sitting on a nice chair that was also brought from the castle. Does the captain know about this? I can't imagine he'll be happy with it. Who will he blame? Who will he beat?

Surrilo holds a handheld stringed instrument, tuning it while he hums. Then he leans in close and whispers, "Haweth found a way out of here. He knows the waterways and where we can hide until we can get a ship to the mainland. We're going tonight, but we figured the guards would be suspicious if we lay low. So, we're...laying high."

My brain dismisses that and clamps onto the 'we're going tonight' part. I stare at him, forgetting to breathe. My hands feel disconnected from my body.

I wasn't the only one looking for a way out. That takes some of the pressure off at least. But on the other hand...

"If we get caught-" I whisper back.

"Isn't a potential beating worth freedom?" he asks. "Don't tell me you're too scared to try."

I hesitate, snapping my mouth shut. Because while freedom is exactly what I want, I...

"Don't worry. We have a plan. Just like any performance, follow my lead." He winks and starts strumming and tapping his foot to the beat, bobbing his head as others join in now.

Alessi takes a timbrel and shakes it while she sings. Lalina and Letta clap their hands and join in. Big Henri pulls the drum closer and pats and bops it, creating a different sort of beat, and Surrilo nods appreciatively, his grin widening. But somehow it feels stiff and forced. As if we're all just holding our breath, stiff and waiting on the edge of a precipice. Muscles primed and ready to spring. And once we jump, there's no coming back. For better or worse, once we make this move, any negotiations we could have made are done.

Gravity only works one way.

And though I hesitate, I can't let them do this alone. Of course, I'm going with them. I suppose I'd better help them keep cover rather than stand here looking terrified, so I pull the whistle out of the holder and blow a few notes to add a bit here and there, sounding more tittering and unsure than usual. And Surrilo can tell. He casts a raised-brow look at me as if simultaneously asking me what's wrong and telling me to keep calm.

I can't. I don't know the plan. I don't know my part or lines. I *hate* it when he does this.

It's very hard to sink into the music.

A loud crash and a flash of light call my attention, and from the other side of the courtyard, hidden from our view by the castle. A curl of fire unfurls towards the stars as if trying to become one with them, but its reach can't quite extend enough, and it falls delicately, leaving the belching of dark smoke in its wake. And immediately, the knights rush to see what it was, calling for aid. Only two remain with us.

Surrilo catches my arm, pulling me aside, as a crashing sound of hooves and skittering wheels comes from the stables. Loose rocks spray from underneath the carriage and the horses' feet as Haweth pulls on the reins, feet planted on the footboard.

"Halt," one of the knights calls, but Big Henri slams his meaty arm into the back of the man's knees. The soldier buckles, hitting the ground with a metallic crunch. Surrilo dives to tie the man so he can't get up or follow us. The other knight rushes the giant, but Big Henri seizes the man's spear, yanking it out of his hands. Then he snaps it over his knee and tosses the halves away, advancing. Surrilo sneaks up from behind and taps the knight to get his attention. The guard swings as he turns, but Surrilo ducks, and Big Henri grabs the man's upper arms. Surrilo works to tie him too.

Then Braun pulls up with another getaway rig. Big Henri scoops up Della and Little Benji while Lalina and Letta hurry towards the vehicles. Alessi reaches up, slapping her palm into Gribble's as it extends out of the side door of the smaller carriage. He pulls her inside.

"Prisoner escape," one of the soldiers calls as Braun makes sure everyone's loaded into his transport and then whips the horses to get going again. I rush toward the smaller one, turning back before getting inside to make sure Surrilo is coming.

"Go," he says, as he rushes to my side, pushing me inside. He hops in after, slamming the door closed. I collapse onto one of the seats as the thing lurches into motion.

"Ollio?" I ask, guessing that the diversion was him and his flash powder.

"Braun's grabbing him," Surrilo answers as he settles onto the seat opposite.

I've never been in a carriage before, but this isn't the time to marvel. I whip the curtain aside so I can see what's happening outside at least. Even as dark as it is, shapes are recognizable once we're turned around and headed towards the road.

"The carriages will be recognized, so we're going to ditch them and hide out in the woods," Surrilo explains as the gate passes by, and we're whisked beyond the immediate reach of the knights.

Something warm and energizing breaks through my chest. We're doing it. We're actually getting away. I can't wait to taste the salt air and breathe in the relief of leaving this place for good. I've never liked the idea of leaving the islands. Everything I know is here, but if it's no longer safe...

We can always build again on the mainland. We're used to making do with very little. And we have talents to help us.

Who knew our escape would be so soon?

But we're not quite out of it yet. There's still a chance this doesn't go well. They'll send knights to look for us.

As the transport careens down a turn, we're tossed inside. I reach out to brace myself against the wall. We hear a loud crunch as the vehicle dips hard and skids to a stop, balancing precariously for a bit until Surrilo throws his weight to the other side of the carriage. It lands back on two wheels, but we can tell one's busted.

"That wasn't supposed to happen," Surrilo whispers when the thing finally settles. He rams his shoulder into the door to pop it open. "We gotta run."

He pulls Alessi out first, then checks Gribble, who's holding his arm.

"I'm alright," the tumbler says, grimacing and flexing his fingers. Breath hisses through his teeth, but he gets out of the tipped thing, on solid ground again.

Surrilo reaches inside for me, clasping my hand, and he helps me out. Haweth soothes the panicking animals to keep them from bolting.

"Haweth, we gotta pivot. You coming?" he calls out, as Gribble and Alessi move off the road.

Haweth tosses the reins on the animals' backs and hops down from the driver's seat, following us into the woods. He pauses, looking around.

"This way," the old sailor says, leading us farther into the darkened woods. Off in the distance, horses neigh behind us, and knights call to one another. Surrilo jogs a pace or two backwards, peering through the trees to see where they are.

"They're going to find us," Alessi breathes.

Haweth shushes her.

"Run," Surrilo whispers, turning back around. He clasps my hand and then takes hold of Alessi's arm to keep us from getting separated, and he drags us after Haweth. Tree branches whip our faces and slap our arms and legs. We hurry over logs and around tree trunks.

"They're in the woods," we hear someone shout from the road, and Alessi lets out a tiny shriek. Gribble covers her mouth, his good arm around her shoulders.

"Keep moving," he says in a low voice.

Her eyes bulge, and she keeps tossing glances behind us, which slows us down.

Haweth is far enough ahead that I can barely see him now. The whip and shush of the foliage ahead still serve to direct us, though.

We can do this. We just have to stay level-headed.

Hoofbeats tramp through the foliage.

Curse.

On horseback, they'll run us down. Unless we can find somewhere to hide.

Where is Haweth? Can Surrilo still see him at least?

Alessi looks behind us again and trips over a log. She screams as she falls. Gribble and Surrilo try to keep her upright, but she collapses into the leaves. Sprawled on the ground, she groans and leans back on her hands as if trying to get space between her and the pain.

"I can't. My ankle," she hisses. "Leave me."

"Carry her," Surrilo says, but it's no use with Gribble's hurt arm.

"Just go," Alessi says, her nose wrinkled. She reaches down to her ankle with shaky fingers, touching it lightly. She bites back a scream, ripping her hand away.

"We're not leaving without you," I answer, reaching down to help her up. She shoves me away as the knights shout, pinpointing our location from Alessi's noise.

They're getting closer.

"Go," she whispers to us. "It's too late for me. Get away from here."

Gribble casts a panicked look behind us and takes off through the trees, still holding his arm.

"I'm not leaving," I reply, but Surrilo bends down and picks me up, so my body is draped over his shoulder, and he takes off.

Horrified, I freeze in shock and then come back to myself all at once.

"Stop it," I whisper harshly, smacking his back and kicking my legs. "Put me down. We can't-"

"Shh," he says. Still running and guiding himself through the trees with his free hand. I'm not sure he's the direction that Haweth went. Is he thinking we need to split up?

Alessi...

Someone will go back for her, right? She won't be left alone to be found by the knights?

After a minute or two, Surrilo stops running and deposits me where a fallen log meets a tree.

"Stay here," he demands,

"Are you going back for her?" I ask, turning and wanting to follow.

He doesn't answer as he melts into the shadows.

My heart flutters as hope spreads like a tiny fog in my chest, blinding the fear for a moment. And yet, fear is more like the light of the sun, burning holes in the ethereal mist.

My fingers fiddle with my sleeves and leather cuffs.

Coward, my brain screams at me. *Go back for Alessi.*

I can't possibly forgive myself if I don't go back. I don't care what happens to me now. We're family. We can't separate ourselves like this.

Where am I? Where is she? If I can get back...

I leap over the fallen log, but then pause, pushing my hair out of my face and listening for any sounds of knights or my family. Something to tell me where to go. But my breathing seems too loud now, so I shake out my hands and try to breathe slowly through my mouth.

They're out there somewhere. In all this foliage, my family is falling apart, and I'm stuck, helpless here. Lost and confused.

Then I hear Alessi scream, and men shouting.

No. No. No.

But I have a direction. I run toward her, pushing through foliage until something slams into me, pinning me to a tree. A person. Someone's body. But it's not Surrilo. It's not Haweth or Gribble. It's not anyone in my family.

My nerves spark, and I push him. But he's solid, and a glove lands against my mouth.

"Quiet," a voice hisses in my ear. The captain.

No. Why him?

Frustrated at myself for being caught, I struggle, shoving him and digging at his hand on my mouth. I twist, trying to break free, but he captures one of my hands and pins it between us, so my elbow is cocked funny, and my fingers squish into one another. Then he takes hold of the other, clamping down on my wrist, not terribly hard, but firm and unyielding.

Tears prick the sides of my eyes, and two traitorous drops slide down my cheeks. I have to get to Alessi. Surrilo and the others might have gotten away, but she didn't. And I won't leave again.

But I *did* leave. I left.

I try to scream through the glove or bite his hand.

"Whistle," he snaps, "Stop struggling unless you want the others to get hurt."

Shaking with rage, I settle against the tree, boring holes into him with my gaze. My jaw tightens with fury and disgust.

I will end him if he hurts them. I will burn his whole world to the ground. I don't care that I don't know how yet. I will find a way.

If I could conjure fire now, he'd be incinerated in an instant. Then I'd burn down this whole forest with his men inside.

He doesn't notice my ire. Instead, he listens to the night. Waiting...watching...For what? He doesn't call out to his guards for them to come. He doesn't move.

That's not right...He should be calling for backup. He should be dragging me back towards the guards or the castle. He should be claiming victory. Punishing quarry. Reveling in triumph.

He shouldn't be just standing here...

With a shiver, my hairs stand on end, and my arms tingle. The air seems suddenly cold and pricking against my skin as if it plays notes, playing lightly across my arms, neck, and face. My vision seems to expand as my body quivers. I can hear every sound, and my muscles tense.

The voices of the knights get farther away, seemingly leaving at least this portion of the woods until we are alone.

Why does he just wait?

What is he doing?

This isn't right. Which means it must be bad. Worse than I thought.

What does this mean for me? Perhaps I should have tried my luck with the knights. I still have my knife at least. I can't reach it right now, but maybe eventually, I'll have an opportunity. Patience.

Minutes pass this way: his head turned away, with me pinned to a tree with the scent of his leather glove in each breath. Finally, the forest feels completely empty, and the normal night sounds of the animals resume.

My body trembles with rage and fear in equal parts. Waiting...watching...

His head falls as he breathes a couple of times. Then he turns back to me, meeting my gaze in the dark.

"Don't scream. There's a chance they'll still hear you. *If* they hear you, they'll come, and then all of this is for nothing," he says, slowly removing his hand from my mouth, as if testing me to see if I'll obey. I would scream but for the strange tilt to his brow and mouth as he says, "I'm sorry. Are you hurt?"

I ignore the last part because what does he care?

"Sorry for what?" comes out as a soft breath because he's still too close. And because the apology could mean so many things that aren't necessarily good. I won't celebrate yet.

"That it had to be this way." He steps back, giving me space, but not enough for me to get away.

"What way?" I ask to keep him talking and distracted while I calculate the best way out and think of how best to get my knife without a struggle.

"I'll explain. You need to trust me."

"I don't."

"I can see that," he says, his eyes dancing from my tensed hands to my feet. "I can't risk this going wrong. Hear me out, or you will lose everyone you love."

"Because you take them," I spit back.

"No. Because the *authorities* will. Word has spread about the girl who dances with fire. It's long since reached the king, and he's making demands. Pulling strings and putting pressure on the nobles. He'll get what he wants. If he can't have the fire-conjurer, he'll have those who protected her. He's not a reasonable man."

"And you are?"

He stares at me for a moment, his eyes still tired, but with a little something extra that tugs at the corners of his eyes and creates a tiny line between his brows.

"Yeah."

"Prove it. Free them."

"If I let your family go, they get scooped up by a Chelees who'll trade them for standing with the king. They're safer here."

Anger pools like heat in my arms and fingertips, and I flex my hands.

"What is this? Why were you watching us perform? How did you know about me? *I* didn't even know about me. How did you mobilize so quickly to catch us? Why did you do all this if *not* to turn us over to the king? And what are you going to do with us?"

He nods, and his mouth pulls tight as he thinks of what to say. His eyes drop for a moment, and then he meets my gaze again.

"That boy you spoke of. At the baker's shop. He gave you that whistle that you carry. He carved it for you because he knew you liked those flowers that pop up in between cobblestones. They remind you that even in seemingly impossible conditions, good things can still thrive. He taught you to play. And he carved an 'A' inside, so you'd never forget him."

My mind feels compressed and stretched all at once. As if a jolt like lightning crashes into my spine, planting my feet to the ground. My arms go slack. I feel like I've been dropped from high up and collide with the earth. An unstoppable force meets an immovable object, and I'm between them.

My cheeks flame as I stare at the man who said these impossible things. How?

No one else knows about the 'A' and what it means.

A memory flashes of him watching me touch the 'A.' But he wouldn't have known it was there...

My heart stutters.

He *can't* know. No one knows. No one except...

"Show me your hand," I breathe, words barely above a whisper, and I'm not sure he hears me at first because it takes the space of two breaths for him to comply. He doesn't ask which one. Slowly, he pinches and pulls at the fingers of his right glove to loosen them. One by one. Then he tugs the covering off, showing me the back of his hand. Across the skin, two scars crisscross, marking where the baker's whip landed. Even now, I hear the sharp slap of it. See his face twisted in pain. And the blood...

My body trembles for another reason, as my hand covers my mouth and then presses into my chest to keep my heart from pounding through. I reach for the tree behind me to steady myself.

"Atiene..." I whisper, my eyes bouncing from the scars to his face, looking for traces of the child who saved me so many times. Is he really there? Somewhere inside this...person? "You're okay...you're alive. You're here?"

He doesn't move. Doesn't say a word. Just watches and waits.

"I'm sorry," I say, as my head hangs and the tears start. "I shouldn't have left you. It's my fault."

"No," he says, and steps towards me. His hand rests gently against my arm as if unsure what he should do. "It's not your fault. I made you run. Then I lost you."

"What did they do to you? What happened?" I ask, grasping the sleeve of his black cloak and tracing the scars with the tip of my finger, wincing as if it were my own pain.

"It doesn't matter now," he says, his eyes flicking from the scars to my face. And as my mind trips over this new information, I drop my hand from his.

The 'A.' The embarrassment he felt at the time. How he was always kind and took care of me. Not because I was the littlest in our gang. Because he cared for me. And then when he got free, and I was gone...

"Why were you there in the crowd?" I ask, needing to hear if what I suspect is real.

"I never stopped looking for you," he says, and his face tightens a little.

"Atiene..." I trail off, my hand resting on his chest, and the other finding my mouth again because I don't know what to say. I don't know who he is now. And he doesn't know me. And the pressure in my hand is as much to make sure he's real as it is to hold him back. Because I can't...

I need to stay grounded. Thinking. No. I'm not thinking. More like racing towards a ravine and unable to stop. Not knowing if I want to.

My circumstances snap back into place for me.

"Why do all this?"

"Because if I didn't do it, if I don't continue, the king will kill you. And I just found you. I had to make the arrest look real. For you. For your family, and for the king's spies. That's why I asked Surrilo to help me. So, I could talk to you out here where we're alone. Where we won't be heard."

"So...my family...they're okay?" I ask, daring to hope that Alessi might be safe, even under guard. That the others-

"I don't know." He shakes his head. My stomach drops.

"Surrilo knew about this?" I ask, feeling betrayed and left out. If I find him, we're going to have words.

"He's good at what he does. I knew he could keep the secret. Keep up the act."

"You hurt him. Or *had* him hurt. His nose."

"That was *his* idea. To look real."

"You both lied to me."

"Please, believe I didn't want to."

I drop my hand from his chest. Not welcoming. Not pushing away. I'm uncertain. Part of this makes perfect sense. And still stabs me because neither of them thought I should know. Until now, that is.

"We have to keep up the charade," he continues. "There are spies even in my castle. I'll need you to continue on as if you don't know me. As if you hate me."

"This is a lot," I reply, rubbing my forehead and collapsing onto the tree. The trunk provides a sort of support in the onslaught of information. I want to add, 'And I *don't* know you.' It's been years. We're not those children anymore. Instead, I just look at him again, trying to reconcile everything he's done. Everything he did. The boy and the man.

No other explanation makes sense.

"You've changed," I say.

He smiles. "So have you."

That's true. And I do believe Atiene would have done everything he could have to protect others. Even playing out a strange, terrifying whirlwind of a ruse. He's put himself between the king and my family. Between the king and me. What will the Chelees say?

So, I straighten, step closer, and reach up, placing my arms around his neck. My chin rests on his shoulder.

"Thank you for everything," I whisper as if saying to the boy I once knew, because I didn't get to say it enough at the time. And I recognize in that phrase all that I owe him. For my family and for myself *now*. So, I squeeze my eyes shut, pride crumbling at my feet. My face falls, my nose pressing into his chest as I say to the man. "Thank you for coming for me."

His arms wrap around me, and his face dips. His breath tickles my neck as he says, "You're welcome."

"What do we do now?" I ask, pulling back. Because if there's one thing I know about Atiene, it's that he always has a plan.

"We go back to Merincillo and work through a way to get you and your family out of here safely. And you learn how to conjure fire and control it."

Surprise rolls through me, but then I remember what he said about not knowing being more dangerous than knowing.

"Did you know about the fire-conjuring when we were at the baker's shop?" I ask.

He turns and leads me through the woods.

"I didn't know, but after that, I suspected. Fire shouldn't have caught like that." There's a softness in his voice. The way Atiene used to speak to me.

"So, when you were watching us, why didn't you come to me that first night?"

"You seemed happy with Surrilo."

I stop as a shudder works through me, and my nose wrinkles.

"You thought Surrilo and I were together?"

"Most of the audience seemed to think so too." He pauses next to me.

I'm not sure how to feel about that. We're family, but not *that* kind. I shake my head to dislodge the thought and keep walking. He falls into step with me.

"What have you been doing this whole time?" I ask.

"Oh...you know." He snaps a twig off a branch as he walks by. Placing the twig between his fingers, he slides it through, shredding the leaves off. "Trying to grow up. Make my father proud. And live up to the family name. Atiene was my grandfather's name. It was my duty to be like him. Carry on that legacy."

"Are you?"

He shakes his head, and he tosses the stick. "No."

"What was he like?"

He thinks for a moment, snapping another twig off a tree as we pass. "Firm might be the nice way to put it. Strong. Unyielding. Some might have said cold."

"Your father must have been furious that you ran off to live on the streets."

"Once he found me, he didn't let me forget it until he was on his deathbed and even then..." He bats at the bushes in our way as if chopping them with a sword.

"I'm sorry."

He shrugs. "His passing put me where I am." The tone is accepting. Not bitter.

I nod and fall silent. I can't quite grasp that this is real. Just a short time ago, I was running from him, fearing for my life and that of my family.

"What about you?" he asks.

"After I ran from the baker's shop, I hid in a trunk inside a wagon. That wagon belonged to the entertainers. They're used to taking in strays, so they just...kept me." I shrug.

"And you learned how to dance, sing, and play?"

"Not like Alessi, but yeah."

"That's why your act works. She's the bright bird that flits across the stage, but the eyes that burn in the night are a different sort of flair."

I glance at him to see if he means it. He does. I'm so used to comparing myself to her, I hadn't considered that I was her opposite in a good way.

"What does it feel like to control fire?" he asks.

"Strange...heady. And in a way, like coming home. Like it was meant to be with me."

"Hmm...For what it's worth, it looks that way."

And we walk quietly for a while. I don't know where the road is from here. Part of me hopes we won't get there quickly. Part of me hopes we do, so I can see my family. Or maybe I won't see them. The majority, that is. Alessi will be back at the castle by now. Hopefully bandaged up and taken care of. I guess we'll see what happened with the other carriage, too.

"Is there anything else I need to know before we get back?" I ask.

"Just don't speak of this to the others. Even your family. Spies are everywhere."

"You said the king was putting pressure on the Chelees to turn me over."

"Yes."

"What kind of pressure?" I ask.

"Bribery and threats."

"But the Chelees won't do it? You must have solid influence with him."

His eyes narrow as he glances at me, blinking in surprise. A small smile tugs at his lips.

"You don't know?" he asks.

"Know what?"

"You thought Ilano was the Chelees?" he asks with a laugh. "What do you think I am?"

I stop, turning to face him. "*You're* the Chelees? Merincillo is yours? The knights...Who's that other guy?"

"My half-brother."

"Oh..." He did say '*my* castle' before. I'd just skipped over it with everything else...

This explains a lot. And also means he has a lot to lose. Guilt spreads across my chest, like puff weeds when the wind carries their seeds across a meadow. "In my mind, you were a captain of the guards. So, when you're talking about the legacy of your grandfather and father, you mean nobles."

"Old names of wealth and power are dying out. New ones rise through treasonous games. It was the desire of both my grandfather and father that our name endure."

Then what are you doing, destroying that?

"What is the king threatening you with?" I ask, almost afraid to know, but I *have* to.

"We're getting close to the road," he deflects, flinging the stick away. "My men might still be out looking for your family."

I'm not comfortable leaving it like that, but I don't press because survival doesn't care about comfort. So, I take a deep breath and consider my role from here.

He pauses beside me. "You can leave right now if you want."

My brows crunch. "What do you mean?"

"If you want to, you can finish Surrilo's plan. Get on a ship and sail to the mainland."

I'm offended that he'd suggest it. "Not without my family."

"I figured you'd want to be the last one out, but I thought I should give you the choice. It only gets more dangerous from here."

"I know, but it's my fault. It's the least I can do."

"Stop blaming yourself for things that aren't your fault. Such a thing fails to acknowledge the underlying culprit."

My eyes narrow as I consider that he knows more about it than I do. "Fine."

And we fall silent as we continue. Despite the fear of returning, of not knowing what awaits, I feel oddly solid. So, I roll my shoulders back, raise my chin, and brace myself mentally to step back onto the stage.

CHAPTER 10

The gate is shut when we approach, but Atiene hails the guards on duty, and the heavy iron thing swings open for us. Braziers light the courtyard. Not knowing the usual routine around here...is that a good sign or a bad sign?

I have no trouble scowling at the knights.

"Where's Alessi?" I demand as soon as we're inside the courtyard, but the soldiers ignore me, which only inflames my annoyance.

"How many were recovered?" Atiene asks, his tone deep and commanding.

"Five."

"Which ones?"

"The old lady, the giant, the boy, and the two blonde ones."

"And the others?"

"We'll find them."

Atiene nods and then gestures to me. "Take this one to her room. Post a guard."

A knight reaches for my arm, and I jerk away.

"Don't touch me."

Another comes up on the other side, asserting control by grabbing my other arm. Not particularly gently. The first soldier succeeds in restraining me, too, so that I'm sandwiched between the two of them.

"Carefully," Atiene says. "We've no idea what will set her off."

His eyes seem hooded, tired, as he watches.

They drag me towards the servant's quarters. I don't fight them because I'm eager to see my family.

So...they recaptured Della, Big Henri, Little Benji, Alessi, and Surrilo. No doubt Surrilo was taken with Alessi when he went back for her. That means Haweth, Gribble, Braun, Ollio, Lalina, and Letta got away. Where are they now? If the king has spies here, then he'll learn about the disappearance of half my family and send people after them. I'm caught between worry and hope.

Were they able to find each other? To meet up wherever Surrilo planned?

So many questions. I'll have to wait for answers. It does no good to wring my hands and pace over their fate. Better to do what I can here.

Which brings me to the realization that I have very little knowledge about Atiene's plan. All I really know is that I'm to keep up appearances and learn to wield fire.

As the door to my room opens, Alessi shifts on the mattress, pulling herself upright.

"Whistle," she greets. The guards push me onto the mattress next to her, and her arms wrap around my neck in a protective sort of way. The knights turn to go, and the door closes firmly behind them. I push myself up and turn so I can sit against the wall with Alessi. Then I hug her back, because it really is good to see her.

"How bad is it?" I ask, gesturing to her ankle. She shifts her blue skirt with pink petticoats to show me a splint sticking out of her boot.

"I'll live. Not happily, but then again, a castle is a better prison than a wagon."

"They didn't hurt you?"

"No, but they beat Surrilo. He told them the escape was your idea."

"It was *his* idea."

"Yeah, but..." she says with a nod full of meaning. I get it. The fool told them it was *my* idea to keep *me* from being punished.

Would Atiene really have let that happen? And if he and Surrilo are working together, did he *allow* Surrilo to be beaten? Does Surrilo know who Atiene is? Did they make a deal? Either way, Surrilo is hurt.

"Is he okay?" My tone dips with anger.

She scoffs, flipping her skirt back down. "I haven't seen him."

I don't know how much she knows or what I should say. And how far the spies reach is. So, I won't share things that are sensitive. Just in case.

"Where is he?"

"Across the hall. They won't let you in, though. No one's allowed in there but the physician."

I curse in the 'low' language.

She laughs. "Yeah, that's accurate."

"What about Della, Big Henri, and Little Benji?"

"Sequestered to another room across the hall. Big Henri had some cuts on him. Della couldn't run, and he refused to leave her behind. She was cursing when they brought her in. Little Benji was too little to run, so he's with them."

I exhale loudly and lean my head back against the windowsill.

"And you?" she asks. "How did you get caught?"

"I tried to follow Surrilo back to you, got lost, and the Chelees found me."

She nods, waiting for more with a little smile on her face. "I knew you loved me."

I roll my eyes. "Shh..."

She just laughs and leans her head on my shoulder. "You're a fool for coming back, but I'm glad you did." She takes hold of my hand in a sisterly way and then pats it.

I let her, leaning my head on hers. "Me too."

Despite our late night, Alessi is up with the sun, fixing her flowers in her hair, humming, and smoothing down her dress. She moves the leg delicately, grimacing until she can get up with the use of a crutch. It seems a little long for her, jarring into her armpit. Still, it's something. Then she finds a mirror and echoes the sounds of the birds outside in little vocalizations.

If we were home in the wagon, I could sleep through it, but with consciousness comes the reminder of circumstances. So, I rub my eyes and push myself off the mattress until I'm sitting against the wall. I yawn loudly as Alessi fluffs her hair one last time and checks herself in the mirror from both sides. Deeming herself ready, she works her way slowly toward the door. Then she balances on her good foot and bonks the wood with the bottom of the crutch.

"We've learned our lesson. We'd like to come out now," she calls through the door.

With a sharp movement, the door opens a few inches. Then it opens more as she steps back to give more space. The man's expression is unamused, and he doesn't speak.

"I'm guessing you're my escort for today." She grins as if she wasn't running from him or his colleagues just a few hours ago. "Which way to breakfast?"

He stares a moment, his mouth pursing in barely muffled annoyance. Then he gestures for her to follow him. She does, leaning on the crutch. Her hand lands on another guard's arm to steady herself.

I yawn again, running a hand through my hair. Then I stand and stagger to the door. But before I can follow Alessi, the barrier of Surrilo's door catches my attention. I step towards it, and a knight puts his arm out to stop me.

"You don't have permission to enter," he says.

"He's my friend."

"Don't care. I have orders."

I glare, but pull back, letting my frustration be known in the draw of my eyebrows and the lift of my chin.

"Where are the others?" I demand.

"Down the corridor," he answers, not intimidated by me in the least. I whirl away and follow Alessi.

There's a sort of room built into the corridor, like an inlet with a small, round table and a few chairs. A window peeks into the courtyard, where we were all performing stiffly the night before. Now the only reminder is a black pile of ash. The instruments have been taken away. That's for the best.

Della sits at the table, massaging her elbow with her craggy, branch-like hands while Big Henri tracks the knights as they pass or get close. He sits between them and Della. Little Benji runs to hug Alessi's legs and then mine. He doesn't say a word and quickly returns to Della's side, where she absent-mindedly puts an arm around the boy.

"Caught you, did they?" she asks.

"It's good to see you, too," Alessi says, flopping into a chair and propping her splinted leg over the other like a display. She helps herself to the tea on the table, pulling a cup closer to her, and popping a biscuit into her mouth. She pours the tea and pops in a few sugar cubes like she does this every day.

I move around her, so my back is to the window, which makes me uncomfortable. I'd rather be able to see everything, but Della and Big Henri have the other side occupied.

Alessi stirs her tea, taps the little spoon twice, and sets it aside with a sigh. And with our settling, the silence stretches between us, growing stiffer and full of words left unsaid. Words that shouldn't be spoken in the presence of the knights anyway. How do we act now? How do we say we're glad the others got away without drawing suspicion that we'll try again?

Della's cup lands back in the saucer with a clink that echoes far too loudly.

No one knows how to break the silence or relieve ourselves of the things on our minds, so instead we avoid eye contact with each other. The silence rakes my skin like fingernails over and over until it's raw.

I rise abruptly.

"I didn't get to explore the castle yesterday," I say, scooting my way around the table, ignoring their curious gazes.

"Don't get into trouble," Alessi says sarcastically, before taking a sip. Her leg dances in faux nonchalance.

"Too late."

I peer down the corridor towards our rooms, checking that Surrilo's room is still under guard. It is. I'm certain the soldiers set over me wouldn't let me go in anyway.

Turning the other way, I stride down the hall as if I know where I'm going. I don't, but it hardly matters. The point of exploration is to *not* know.

The steady tromp of metallic boots follows me. The cadence carves up what ought to be the serenity of this place. In another time and place, it would be serving its function. But the soft effects of the light and warm tones fade under metallic glints and watching eyes.

The farther we get from the plain servants' quarters, the prettier it becomes. Plaster forms grapevines and leaves along the wall that demand to be touched. Which I know I shouldn't do...creating a tug of war inside my mind. One time won't hurt. I just want to feel it, and then I'll know what it's like and won't have to do it again. I run my fingers over the rounded bumps of grapes and the shape of the leaves that curl in a lifelike way, creating levels to the plaster. I flick my fingers over the edges. Then I stand back to take it in as a whole and follow the designs to the end of the corridor. It opens on a room with a large, dark red carpet. The walls are also red with gold accents. Two white pillars mark this space. It's not a large room but seems cozy for sitting with a fireplace and comfortable couches. I let my fingers drift over the velvety cushions, wondering what it would take to cast fire into the empty hearth.

I'd better not find out right now.

I move on, thinking of how strange it is that Atiene lives here, that he ran away from a place like this to live under a bridge in the muck and grit with several other kids, all dirty and somewhat feral. What was so bad here that he felt that a few crates, holey blankets, sparse food, and bugs that danced over the surface of the water were a better choice? What would have spurred me into making that choice?

I had no choice. He did.

And what has he been doing all this time? What is he really like now? I hate the thought of trusting a memory only to be wrong. But I can't deny what's been done. And yet, where does this leave us all? In the light of day, things appear differently.

Not that I don't trust him. I don't have a choice. But I don't know where all of this leads. Part of me wants to just follow his lead. Part of me wants to know *where* we're going first.

I don't want to think about what happens if the king gets his way. The thread holding me together right now is my family...and the rest of that thought doesn't require my attention...in fact, I'll just pack that away nice and neat.

I come upon the hall again, but now I have the opportunity to appreciate it. The ceiling is high with a beautiful chandelier that spreads out, dripping with gold and...diamonds? Crystals? Glass? I can't tell, but they're pretty.

The big thing hangs over a large, dark red rug in the middle of the room. Wood floor stretches from either side, polished and showing intriguing grains of red and dark wood. Several more couches scatter throughout the room, placed as if centered towards the instruments on stands near the wall.

Ohh...

Immediately changing direction, I go to the instruments, taking them in today with more focus than last night. I have time to study the little details like the swirls and curves. Delicate pieces of art in creation and in performance. One with a beautiful wooden case holding the strings catches my eye, and I pick it up and pluck a few strings just to hear the sounds. The sound reverberates richly, so I do it again, trying to pick up the pattern of notes and where each string jumps to.

Hearing one of my favorite songs in my head, I work the strings until I can match the notes correctly. With a little trial and error, I get five notes to line up, and then I master where the ending note dips into another. Hearing it work is satisfying. I could eventually get the whole song on this gorgeous instrument. But it's slow going, and not what I came for. So, I replace the thing on its holder and stroll through the room.

Once I filter out the sounds of the guards following me, it's actually quiet and calming. I test one of the couches, bouncing on the padding. Why do we have straw mattresses when these exist?

Realizing how tired I really am after everything, I lie down on the soft thing, staring out the window over the ocean. From here, I can't see the sandy beach or the wings of the castle spread on either side, but I can imagine them. And the cry of seagulls isn't far away either.

The tug of sleep settles over my mind for a moment, and I know I should get up.

But I'll just rest my eyes for a moment.

A door closing snaps me awake, and I flinch hard, looking around. There's no immediate danger. Just the two guards who stand off a bit, slouching as they wait. Awkward. At least they've given me some space.

The calming blue sea through the window greets me, and the sun hangs over as if teasing the water with how slowly it approaches.

I've slept all day. What did I miss?

I rub my eyes, sitting up, noting the blanket that slips from my shoulders. That wasn't there before...

Shivering at the implication, I push the thing off me and rise to get distance. I stretch and resolve to check on my family. Heading back the way I came, the tromp of boots follows me. And it occurs to me that this may be a new constant. Potentially to the end of my life.

A guard still stands at attention in front of Surrilo's door. Alessi isn't in our room. I should have guessed she'd have wandered off.

But before I have to wonder where she's gone, I hear clattering in the courtyard and see Big Henri dragging wood to the fire. Della sits in a fancy chair again. Little Benji jumps, clapping his hands and dancing in circles around Della and Big Henri. Alessi balances on her good leg, directing knights with her crutch to drop more wood on the fire. She flashes a dazzling grin as they comply. She thanks them by kissing her hands and fluttering waves.

A small smile pulls my mouth, and I head outside to meet them. A tug of guilt in my stomach as I pass Surrilo's room, almost makes me stop, but then my eyes flick to the knight. So, I just continue on.

Why won't they let me see him? It doesn't make sense.

But it's no use trying again, so I continue through the corridor to the stables and out into the courtyard.

Alessi claps her hands together to show her approval of the collection of firewood now. Then she sees me and reaches in gesture as if fluttering her hand at me will drag me closer.

"Oh, Whistle. Perfect. We're all here. I've asked for instruments to be brought, but I was curtly rebuffed." Her curls whip and settle as her head shakes. "Can't imagine why."

A knight brings a torch, and Alessi takes it from him, shoving the thing into the bottom of the pile so the blaze can rise through. And Little Benji cheers as the fire catches on. Then she pulls it back and holds it out to me.

"Want to dance?"

"Maybe later," I answer as she tosses the torch into the gravel to spit and sputter harmlessly until needed again.

The shadows lengthen around us. They seem to rise like mist permeating the air itself, swallowing the bits of day that remain.

Alessi sighs and tips her head back to stare at the stars beginning to peer at us as if waiting for a performance. *She* waits until there are 'enough' to adore her. Then she lets out a few light notes. Pausing abruptly, she says, "We should gather the servants and the other guards."

"They'll gather if they wanna hear you," Della says as Big Henri sits on an upturned log, watching the flames. Little Benji leans on Big Henri until the giant takes the little boy on his lap.

A terrible thought protrudes: what if this is what's left of my family? This and a torn-up Surrilo?

No, I can't believe that. So, I listen to Alessi as she launches back into her song, starting over to get the full effect of the rising notes. Della hums along as I take out my whistle.

A few harmonized notes feel somehow more tense than relaxing, and after a minute or two, I take the whistle from my lips, rubbing the carvings with my thumb. Della stops humming and leans back in her chair as if giving up. And Alessi strains alone through a line or two more of her song before it fades into the night, replaced by the sounds of fire munching wood with snaps and crackles, oblivious to our pain.

Alessi drops onto a log, her cheeks resting in her hands and her elbows on her knees. Her eyes droop as if tired. Tired of trying to hold us together and lift us with music. Trying in general. It's like her wings melt around her.

I stare at the flames pouncing and blending into one another. And closing my eyes, I can hear it still, seeing the faded, bobbing glow from the insides of my eyelids. Then that feeling of comfort sinks onto my skin, and a flowing pattern of settling, soothing snaps seems to emerge. It is music in and of itself. Singing at times in the hissing of wood, but most often giving that underlying whoosh and putter of air like breath, along with the little tinkling taps.

"Sing the one about the stargazer," I say. Alessi's head raises, her brows furrowing, as her hands rub her arms.

"That's a sad song," she answers. "The character dies."

"Don't we all," I reply.

"Alright," she sighs as she rises from her seat, and her clear, melancholic notes waft over the fire with a soft vibration, giving us a direction or a 'stage' to round out with our varied talents. I raise the whistle to my lips and add the deeper notes in a different sort of pattern that echoes the fire. One of the lower stringed instruments would help right now, but Big Henri's 'hmm' blends into a bass for us. It fills the piece in a darker sort of way.

Little Benji tries to match Alessi, and Della just sighs, curling up in the chair.

And the character undergoes his passage from a farm boy to a man in love with a merchant's daughter. Gazing at her window each night before the candlelight blinks out is like gazing at the stars. As the days wear on, she marries someone else, leaving him gazing at the stars, longing to join them. "If my wish to be with you cannot be granted, let me live among the stars, and that will be second best."

Della sniffs and wipes at her face.

Finally, the character's wish is granted, and he goes to live among the heavenly things as one of them, shining on other hopefuls below.

I drop the notes a few bars before the end, and so does Big Henri. All that's left is Alessi's haunting tones that linger over the crackling fire. We sit in it until the fading song echoes only in our hearts. Only alive within us.

Then, with a small smile, Alessi looks at me and cues me up for another with slightly more bounce, but along the same line. Big Henri taps his heel to add a beat to this one, and Della adds a light vocalization to offset Alessi's voice.

I sway with the music now, letting the whistle dance over the notes with a quick softness like rain. I open my mind and heart to the fire, letting the warmth sweep through my chest. And as I continue to sway, I hear Alessi say, "Whistle, look."

I *do* look at the fire where she's pointing. It's calm and settled like the music I play, burning low, but little streams of it reach out for me.

My first instinct is to pull back, but I keep playing just to see what happens, still feeling the influence settling over me like waking up in the wagons in a new place or dancing on the stage while Surrilo plays.

Or when Atiene gave me the whistle.

The fire leaps at me then, wreathing itself in a warm glow before my eyes and around my body.

Alessi steps toward me, but Big Henri holds her back.

I'd be afraid, but I don't feel the burn. Only comfortably warm, so I stop playing. Entranced by the movement of the fire. I reach out with my hand.

"Stop," one of the knights commands.

"She's not hurting anyone," Alessi says.

But he's right. So, I pull back, and the fire dies, having been cut off from its source.

"If she's going to wield magic, we can't have her around fire," one of the knights says as much to my family as to me. I turn to him and nod as if I understand. But I'm not happy about it.

Being cut off from it leaves me quaking lightly, and my hands tingle as if I were so close to something. To what exactly? To understanding it? To feeling it?

I sit down, whistle still clasped in my hands.

It's there at the tips of my fingers or perhaps from within my chest. But there is something to go off of. It responds when I open up inside. When I welcome it. Does all magic work that way? Or just fire?

Music entices those deeper parts of me. Dance also. The fire merely wants to be a part of that. I don't think the connection would be so bad.

I'm not a monster. A potential dragon, but not a monster. There's a difference.

Silence is punctuated by the crackle and pop as the guards, wary now, keep an eye on me. I simply put my whistle away and enjoy the warmth of the fire.

But I can't help feeling a little smug for what I did get away with.

CHAPTER 11

I wake before Alessi because my stomach hurts. I can't remember the last time I ate.

Rising, I stagger to the door and throw it open. Two knights jerk to attention, their spears pointing at my chest until they recognize I'm not a threat.

"Where can I find something to eat?" I ask.

"Someone will bring a plate," one knight says, and then stands still against the wall as if waiting for me to retreat. So, I do, putting a hand on my stomach and collapsing into the chair inside our little room.

Through the window in the graying morning, night retreats as day bites back. The pile of ash from last night reminds me of what I did. What I could do.

A servant knocks on the wall and then enters the room, placing a cup of water and a plate of cold meat, cheese, and a hunk of bread in front of me. I dive in.

Alessi yawns, turning over. Her thin arms reach toward the window as she stretches. Then she plumps her hair around her head.

"Breakfast?" she asks.

I flourish at the plate like Ollio when he makes things appear out of nowhere. She rises and breaks a piece of the cheese off. She nibbles it as she turns back to the window.

"What mischief shall we get into today?" she asks.

"Whistle?" a knight calls through the door.

"What?" I respond through a mouthful of food.

"You're to see the Chelees as soon as possible," he replies.

Alessi's eyebrows rise as she takes a bite of her cheese.

"Is this about last night?" she asks for me while I chew, staring down the guard as if he can wait.

"Not my business. I'm just to escort you."

Alessi makes a face and saunters back toward the plate of food. We both pick bits of meat and bread, moving around each other, offering and accepting by turns with noises and gestures. She knows I like the crusts, and I know she doesn't, so we carve the 'innards' out of the crust, each taking the part we like best.

Then, when I've had my fill, I stand, gulping down water. I wipe my chin, run a hand through my hair, and brush crumbs from my clothes.

"Wait," Alessi says, stuffing her piece of bread in her mouth while she fixes one of the clips in my hair. A bit of bread hangs out of her mouth while she works. Then she indicates that I'm acceptable with a dismissive wave. She removes the bread from her mouth and turns back to the plate.

My tummy gurgles as I follow the guard. Happy to have been fed. Not happy to have had so much stuffed down at once. That's fair.

When we reach Atiene's office, he's standing at the desk with letters in his hand. His eyes flick from me to the guards.

"Leave us. Under no circumstances am I to be disturbed," he orders. They back out of the room, closing the door.

"That's nice," I decide. He smiles, sifting through the letters without answering. I'm not sure what I'm here for, so I step to the window to soak up the view while I can. I sit on the large window seat with one knee pulled up in front of me, so I can see him and the sea.

"The king is on his way," he announces.

My skin sizzles with this information, and my face falls. His gaze meets mine.

"He's angry that I won't make a deal. Hopes his presence will force my hand."

I blink and look away, contemplating. Then I nod as my eyes narrow.

"He's traveling by ship. He'll arrive in four to six days."

"And what do you intend to do?" I ask, brushing at my skirt to make it fall over the trouser portion of the costume. I don't dare look him in the eye now. Just in case betrayal is on the horizon.

He shifts, and my eyes flick to him to watch what he does. He glances at the door and then goes to the bookshelf behind his desk. He lifts a book and flicks something on the shelf, and the whole shelf springs open a few inches. Turning to me, he motions that I should follow.

Curiosity burning inside, I rise from the seat but hesitate. He holds out his hand, waiting, watching. My ears burn, but I slowly step forward to take his hand. And he leads me through the opening and into the dark.

Once I'm inside, he latches the door. Darkness envelopes us, but I hear him shift, looking for something. Then a flash of sparks accompanies a rough scraping sound. It happens again. And one more time. Then the spark catches. A small flame buzzes like a bee waking. The flame bobs and touches a candle wick, and once it's caught, he closes the lantern. In the dim light, I see a framework made of wood, like a tiny room around us. A little shelf protrudes for lighting materials, on which he replaces the flint and steel.

Ahead of us, the framework holds up what appears to be a channel cut from stone that leads down. Stairs carved from rock, and he takes my hand again, telling me to watch my step as he descends.

"What is this place?" I whisper.

"This leads to the grottos under the cliffs."

I pull my hand away.

"I already told you I'm not leaving without my family."

"We're not leaving your family behind. You need somewhere to practice where no one can see."

"And once I practice, what then? What happens when I learn to control it? Or in three weeks when the king comes?"

"We're still working on that," he admits. "He was never going to hold out forever. It was only a matter of time."

"What if I can't control the fire by then? And who's we?"

"Whistle," his voice dips with softness, and he sets the lantern aside. I cross my arms as he turns to face me. He's two steps lower, but tall enough that we're eye level. His gaze bounces between my eyes.

"Come here," he says, stepping up and wrapping his arms around me for a moment. His chin rests on my shoulder. I let him, but I pin my lips together and stare over his shoulder at the flickering orange glow. A living thing in this barren place. After a moment, I breathe out heavily and relax into him. Uncrossing my arms, I wrap them around his back and rest my face against him.

"Surrilo was hurt," I say, as if that explains everything. The knights that watch us constantly. The fear that my family is irreparably damaged, and that the others who are free are being hunted and might be dead. The fear that the rest of them might not make it. Della withering in captivity. Alessi is strong, but wilting. Big Henri holds it together for his adopted mother and Little Benji...a child shouldn't have to contend with these hard things. And what Surrilo suffered, I don't even know because they won't let me see him. Isolation will kill him if the wounds don't.

"I know," Atiene whispers. "We're going to find a way to make sure you and your family are safe."

"How?"

He pulls back, looking at me with sadness in his eyes. "I don't know yet."

"Whatever happens, promise me that they'll be okay. Get them out even if the king gets ahold of me. Make a deal for them at least."

"Okay," he says as his eyes fall. But whether in thought or genuine acquiescence, I don't know. Or he's not sure.

"And you too," I add. "Don't let the king destroy you for my sake."

His eyes flick back to mine, and though I only meant he shouldn't sacrifice everything for me, I see it has a different sort of weight.

Like I finally get to go back to the baker's shop for him. But more than that, somehow, and that catches me off guard.

We both pause because there seems to be something different in the air. Something I can't quite grasp or name, but it tickles my chest and perches on the edge of each breath.

He seems to want to say something. But I breathe once...twice...three times, and he doesn't speak.

"Please," I whisper, because I can't stand the thought of what the king can do to him if he keeps holding out. He doesn't deserve that.

He raises a hand to my face, but before he can lay his fingers along my cheek, the fire sputters wildly in direct response to my heart, echoing the shiver that works through me.

A smile pulls at his mouth as he recognizes the reaction of the fire.

"You still need practice," he says, taking his hand away slowly and then reaching down to grab the lantern.

Curses.

But he reaches back to take my hand, and that's some small consolation.

We're silent as we get to the bottom of the stairs, and he lifts the lantern so I can see the arches of the cave overhead. Craggy white rocks glitter. Stalactites reach down while stalagmites reach up, trying to grasp hands. The light reflects off several pools, one of which is luminous with blue light. Waves of sunlight dance through the water. And I think I can hear the lap of waves against the shore somewhere nearby.

"That way leads to the little shore outside," he says, gesturing with the lantern. "Ilano and I used to swim through the tunnels to the beach and back. Almost drowned a time or two."

"Almost drowning, running away to live on the streets...what did your father do with you?" I ask, shaking my head.

He just grins and sets the lantern on the ground. Then he finds several sticks on the cave floor, perhaps washed in by the current. Perhaps brought in by curious boys. He pokes one into the tiny flame of the lantern, waiting for it to catch. Then he hands it to me.

"See what you can do with this," he says.

I shake my hands out. Taking the stick, I latch onto the flame with my gaze. Inspecting the tiny bouncing baby of a light, I can already feel the connection. It's surprisingly close, but given the encounter I just had...

Stop it.

The flame sputters as I feel it taking hold of the opening in my chest.

Life...it feeds on life. It feeds on *my* life. That's why it doesn't require an anchor or base in a physical element to devour. I'm the element...and it *does* transform to something ethereal. I can feel the change from seemingly alive to fully blooming. It pours off the end of the stick, reaching around me, lapping at my arm and chest, snuggling closer.

The thickening of the flame grasps onto me like a thirsting creature, and I breathe it into my lungs. But it doesn't choke or burn.

It is a little suffocating, though.

Don't panic. Don't panic. Don't panic.

Coughing, I force myself to think about it, wondering if I can 'ask' the fire to step back and not consume me like this. Melding the feeling in my chest to the fire, I seek its core, or the source of its will.

Move, I think to it. But that doesn't work. It's a little overpowering in the sense that I've opened myself a lot but can't seem to breathe without the warmth coating my throat and barreling into my lungs.

I cough again, trying to force it out of my airways and away from me.

"Whistle," Atiene's voice breaks through the crackle of the fire, and I drop the stick, fear beginning to close me off. His hands are on my arms, but he doesn't know what to do. I bury my face into the crook of my arm to cough out the remnants that feel a little like ash in my throat. It makes my eyes water.

"Are you okay?" he asks, but it takes me a minute to respond.

"Yeah," my voice comes out craggy. My throat is dry, and I need some water. "I'm fine. It was just a bit much, is all."

"How do you slow it down?"

"I don't know," I answer honestly. "I tried."

So, connecting is the easy part. The hard part is opening and closing like a water duct. Enough to control and not be overwhelmed. Balance is needed.

I guess I should have known. Fire is eager.

Luckily, it doesn't burn me, or I'd have been toasted.

I should try again.

"Where's the stick?" I ask, looking around.

"Are you sure?" he asks.

"The feeling is still fresh," I answer, bending down as he lets go and stands back. "If I can get the balance right, I'll know how to do it."

The makeshift torch has a tiny ember on the end, still glowing. Eventually, I'd like to get good enough to start fires, but that's something to build towards. One thing at a time. I bend to put the stick back into the lantern's flame until it starts again. The tiny ember reignites. The fire dips as if trying to slide down the wood.

I watch the smoke curling off the end almost imperceptibly. Breathing out through my mouth, I shake my head and roll my shoulders back.

Okay, just a little bit.

But even as I work to open myself to it, there's something keeping that door closed inside my chest. I stare at the fire, wondering what happened. It feels dead to me now, unreachable.

Narrowing my eyes as if it's the culprit, I will it to come to me. It doesn't.

"What's wrong?" Atiene asks.

"I'm not sure," I respond. "I'm trying, but it's not responding."

"Walk me through it."

"I have to open myself up to it. Like in my chest, I feel it sometimes, but it's like I can't right now."

"Ah!" he says and steps closer. Immediately, the fire sputters. He laughs as he steps away. "You'd better get that under control. That could become dangerous in a hurry."

Traitor fire.

But it worked. That feeling is back, and the fear has ebbed.

We can do this. No problem.

So, I reach my hand out to the flame, running my fingers over the tiny orange blaze that bobs in response, grazing and grasping lightly. Gently, it lifts from the source, curling around my hand. And I hold it at bay, fascinated by the way it hugs and skitters over my hand. It works down my wrist, and when it gets far enough, I close that part of my chest, so it doesn't take over. And the fire dies.

Progress!

Like playing an instrument, finding the right notes by ear will take some time, but it's doable. I can learn to control fire.

"It's incredible," Atiene says. I nod, speechless and overcome because power like this means I'm not entirely helpless in the face of the king and his men. I can bargain, and I have a last resort. Atiene doesn't have to stand alone between us and annihilation.

"We should get back," Atiene says. "But you're welcome to come down here during the day and practice. I'll bring a bucket next time."

I douse the tiny flame in one of the pools and toss the stick aside. Atiene grabs the lantern and then reaches for my hand.

"Wait...is this a good idea while I'm holding the lantern?" he teases.

I roll my eyes, but the tiny blaze does flutter.

"See? Gotta stay safe," he says, shrugging.

"I'll tell it not to hurt you," I reply, and he laughs and takes my hand. We go up the stairs, and he shows me the latch from this side, so I know what to do if I come by myself. Then shows me the fire-steel and lantern before he puts out the little flame. I feel it sigh as it dissipates.

Then light floods the little room as the door clicks open. It takes a moment for my eyes to adjust to the sunlight pouring through the window. There's no need for lanterns here. In fact, the whole castle has no need for firelight during the day with such big windows.

He makes sure the bookshelf closes properly and then shows me the mechanism from this side.

"You're welcome to stay," he says, gesturing to the window and the view. "Are you hungry? I'll send for something to eat."

"No, but I'm suddenly tired," I respond, a little surprised at that. Does the fire feed off energy, too? Extreme emotions tend to make me tired. Perhaps it's linked to that.

I plop down on the window seat and maneuver around until I'm cross-legged, staring over the sea.

What's on the other side of that sparkling blue? Where does the sea end?

And the thought sends thrills through my chest. What would it be like to find out? To chase the sun and learn where it rests at night. Or perhaps *not* find out which would be just as fun.

Lying down on the comfy seat, I curl up like a cat. Why can't we get a passage across the sea? What would that cost? For all of my family? If I could find all my family. I'm still left to puzzle over Riccard and Theliane's disappearance when we were captured. Where did they go?

My family might be scattered from one end of this island to the other for all I know. I can't exactly put out word for them to come to me. They're just as likely to get caught by the king's men that way.

And the dam of thought I've been holding back breaks.

It's no secret what the king intends to do with me. He'll do exactly what's been done with others. I'll be disabled in some way from using my gift, and then he'll either hunt me or kill me outright. Wind sorcerers get weighed down until they can't move. Sun sorcerers are kept in the dark so they can't get away.

But fire sorcerers are the real prize. Not just because of their rarity, but because of the tales that accompany the forging of our very nation. This kingdom was built on their bones. Exiles from the mainland.

We've all heard stories. Stories and legends are entertainment gold. We thrive on them. So, around the campfire, we've told and retold tales of fire sorcerers being drugged so they can't conjure. Then they're turned loose, being given a head start into the forest before being run down and killed.

There hasn't been any type of magic known on this island for years. I really did think it was extinct.

Which makes me wonder where *I* got it.

I never met my parents. The farthest back I can remember is being on the street, begging for food. One or both of them must have had magic, though. I don't know much about it, but I do know it's passed down from parent to child.

I've often speculated about what happened to them, but I have no way to be certain. They may have died. And if so, how? If not, how did we get separated?

It occurs to me now that they may have died the way other sorcerers have. Then again...they may not have if they were never known.

Feeling drowsy, I decide to go back to my room before I fall asleep on the window seat. So, I rise, rubbing my eyes and yawning. I make my intentions known to Atiene. He sends for guards to collect me for appearance's sake. I make it to the little room, find it empty, and briefly wonder what mischief Alessi got up to before I sink onto the mattress. Lying on my stomach, I prop my arm under my head for a pillow.

Snipping of scissors and humming break through the wall of black over my mind. Groaning, I shift, and my eyes slide open slowly.

Alessi nests in an explosion of material. It spreads all around her while she sits on the mattress with her good leg curled up. The other is stretched out. Pins in her mouth, she takes two pieces of cloth and holds them together, eyeing the sides to make sure they line up. Then she sets them back on her mattress and starts pulling pins from her mouth. Stabbing the pieces, so the hold, she shows me her treasures.

"Found these."

"No one was using those, right?"

She shrugs. "How am I to know that?"

"Okay," I answer with a nod, rising so I can get a better view. It's red cloth. "You don't wear red. You don't wear anything that's in fashion."

"I *am* fashion," she responds, but doesn't explain further.

I just leave it at that.

"Those are for us," she says, gesturing to a pile of dresses laid across the chair and table. "I'll have to do them up before they can be worn. Horrendous. But it's not totally hopeless. Some of them will make nice bows or accents for the others."

"Did you steal these, too?" I ask. She scoffs as if offended.

"They were a *gift*," she says.

"From whom?"

"Who do you think?" she asks with an eyebrow lifted as if that's a stupid question.

So, they really *were* a gift. Which means they came from Atiene. I look down at my costume. It would be nice to change. I scoop up the whole pile and plop it on the bed to sift through.

She gives me a knowing smile and then refocuses on the sleeve that's beginning to come together. She seems settled into her task, flipping the cloth and pinning some more, so I let her alone with it. She's creating. She likes her space when she's working, so she can 'see' what it will be.

I hold up a satiny golden dress meant to have an underdress, and there is a cream one that appears to go with it, but there are frills on the bottom. It screams 'court.' That's just not me.

Laying the dress aside, I hold up the next one. It's a simple red underdress with a square neck and very short sleeves that aren't meant to be seen. Then there's a cream overdress for that one with embroidered flowers and embellishments to match. It cinches at the waist with a wide, red satin band. The underdress isn't bad, but the top is overdone.

I wrinkle my nose and lay it on top of the gold one. I may be too picky about this. It's a nice thought. But...

The next is black with red designs woven into it. It appears to be a mourning dress with simple lines and a skirt that doesn't flare as much as the others. I can see why Atiene would have added this to the collection. It more closely resembles my orange costume, with the 'V' neck and the design down the front and over the stomach. My mouth squishes as I contemplate how to salvage that one, though. I'm not one for sewing.

"I can fix that one," Alessi says as if in answer to my thoughts as she threads a needle.

Then I hold up the cap. It's golden and puffed with a string of pearls hanging off.

We giggle over it as I put it away. Nice thought. Terrible selection. But I won't tell him that. Alessi is right, though. How can we possibly wear these?

No...I'll wear one or two because it's the gratitude that counts. I'll just pretend I'm in a play.

The last one is closer to what peasants wear with the looser sleeves and the tight stomacher.

This just isn't my thing. I drop it onto the poofy pile and plop my hands in my lap.

"I wonder what new clothes Della and the boys will be wearing," I say. She scoffs, pulling the needle through the sleeve.

Choosing the mourning dress, I change. The sleeves aren't as loose as I'm used to. In fact, the whole dress fits close to my figure, feeling a little more like a trap. I slip some of the lock picks where they'll be hidden. Who knows? I may need them. And then the whistle and leather holder get buckled around my waist because I refuse to go anywhere without it.

Alessi laughs at the face I make, looking into the mirror and keeps working.

"Tell your admirer 'thank you' for me," she says, pulling the threat tight, and swooping in for another pass with the needle.

"My...what?" I bluster, but she raises a brow at me. She sticks her tongue out and blows air, so it makes a 'bpp' sound.

"Please. He watches you dance. He calls for you. He doesn't treat any of us like we're really prisoners. He dresses you like this," she says, sweeping her hand over the nice dresses. Then she shakes out the sleeve with a snap. "Don't get me started on you. You went from firing crossbows with your eyes to a tamed kitten. Tell me honestly, what happened in the forest?"

I stand for a moment, contemplating. If she knows what's going on, does anyone else? What does this look like to them? Is this something that should be hidden? He said to make it look like I hate him, but...that doesn't seem to be coming across.

I exhale slowly and move to sit by her, not liking how the dress pulls and how tight the sleeves are on my wrists. I pull at them, but there's only so much freedom to gain from them, so I give up and let my hands flop into my lap while she waits.

"He's the boy from the streets," I answer because she knows about Atiene.

Her mouth drops, and then her shock turns into a grin. "No."

I nod.

"*The* boy? And you learned that in the forest?" Her sewing sits unheeded in her lap now as she stares at me.

I nod again.

"All this time? And he was *looking* for you," she says, putting the bits together. She makes an 'ooo' sound and pokes my arm. "This explains so much. How did he tell you? It's been so long since you last saw each other. And you *hated* him when you saw him again after all that time, not knowing who he was. But he is handsome. And how *romantic*. Tell me!"

My cheeks heat, and I fiddle with the tight sleeves, trying to pull them over my hands. But I do tell her about the whistle and the little details. About his scars. I watch her face as she waits eagerly for each word. And then I say as much as I'm comfortable with, she leans back against the wall as if letting it settle over us both.

"You *like* him," she teases.

"Shush. I..." But I don't know what to say.

She squeals, giggles, and wrinkles her nose at me. Then she says, "Well, you've nothing to worry about. Look what he's done."

Yeah, I mean he has-

Wait...Something about the way she says it tickles my mind in a suspicious way. Why is she not asking the obvious questions? I pin her with my gaze the way she pins the cloth.

"What do you know?" I whisper.

"Nothing," she answers quietly.

"Alessi..."

"Nothing," she asserts, her gaze darting to the door and then back. Then she waits for me to acknowledge.

What does she know? *How* does she know? Did Surrilo say something? How and when would he have conveyed that? What does this mean? And why didn't they tell me?

Hurt spreads through me like a wave dousing my fire and settling in my toes and fingertips.

"Love is hard in general," she says, going back to her project. "After so much time, it's hard to know if it's real, or if you're just trying to get something back that may not be there anymore. Neither of you is the same. But give it time. You'll know."

That doesn't make me feel better. Instead, it gives me one more cause to worry. I resist the urge to get up and pace the corridors.

"What of you?" I ask instead. "Are you ever going to pick from among your many admirers?"

Her head tips back as she thinks for a moment. Then she shakes her head. "Most young stags are only interested in the beautiful or the interesting for as long as it's new or exciting. The real test is whether they're in it for when life gets tough. But you'll never know until you get there, so you're taking a chance no matter what. I'm not sure I've met many with that determination to stay through those times and not just bemoan their circumstances, you know? What's a pretty wife when the crops fail and the roof springs a leak?"

"Most people might take comfort in a companion then."

"Some would. Some would be too annoyed. Life is ups and downs, but for some people, it's like there's almost no middle."

I recall the details of her personal history. Ran away from home when she was nearly ten years of age. Difficult family life. Not a whole lot of information about how or why it was so hard. And perhaps as a child, she didn't understand all that was going on. She knew enough to know it wasn't what she wanted, though.

"I'm not an object to be cherished only at a whim," she concludes. "The young stags are nice, but if I chose a town and settled there, how long would they *really* be interested?"

Oh.

"So, you're *afraid* of settling down. You're afraid they won't really love *you*."

"I'm adored for a day or two. Especially when I step out onto that stage and hear the applause and hear the coins ring," she pauses as her head sinks back and her eyes close. It's as if she's there for a moment. "Then I go back to the ones who love me for me and expect nothing more of me than to be myself."

I let that simmer. I didn't realize she felt that way.

I put my arms around her neck and lean my head on hers.

"I'll always love you," I say.

She pats my arm. "I know."

CHAPTER 12

Morning hardly dawns before I'm awake, pushing scraps of fabric off my body because somehow I became a holder for Alessi's work while I slept. She's curled up with the red sleeve still clutched in her hand. Luckily, the pins are all put away where she won't prick herself.

I ask the guard on duty for food, and he answers that the servants will bring it.

Surrilo's door is still inscrutably blank to me. Inside has been incredibly quiet. Are they sure he's not dead? But my face conveys something the knights don't like because one of them shifts as if waiting for me to pounce at the door.

I narrow my eyes but let it go. I hate that my every move is watched.

And the servant sets food and water on the table. I eat about half of it, leaving the rest for Alessi. Then I stride down the hall towards the study. When I arrive, the knight holds up his hand for me to stop before knocking at the door, and I can't help but wonder what they think now. Do they see what Alessi sees? They must see it, right?

The door opens, and Atiene's eyes land on me in the black dress.

"Come in," he says, pushing the door open further. As he closes us off from his knights, he smiles and says, "I thought you'd pick that one. It suits you."

"Mourning suits me? That sounds like a curse from a fortune teller."

"Luckily for you, fortune tellers are notorious for being wrong."

I just smile as he gestures toward the secret door.

"Shall we?"

He lets me work the mechanism, so I'm familiar with it. Moving the book and working the hidden switch that's painted to look like the bookshelf. The door springs open, allowing access. So, we go down the stone staircase.

The lantern casts firelight around the cavern. As soon as he sets the thing down, I ask what Alessi knows.

He looks surprised for a moment as he bends down to fetch a stick for me to practice with. "What did she say?"

"She *wouldn't* say. But she knows something."

"Surrilo said she could be trusted. I trust his judgment when it comes to your family." He pulls some seagrass from the stick and tosses it away.

"Why not tell me?" I ask.

His eyes seem to crinkle as if he doesn't want to tell me a difficult thing.

"Acting."

There it is. One word. And it's true but still stings. The reason I only got to play a peasant in the play about the dragons. A small part with only a few lines here and there. Never the big parts.

"We didn't have the time to go over everything with you before it happened," he continues. "No time to rehearse."

Surrilo is the other half of who 'we' is then. He'd have been the one to stress my inability to pivot like he can.

"How did you get Surrilo to help you?"

"The same way I got you to cooperate before you knew who I was. The family was in danger."

"Why can't I see him?"

He studies the ring of light as it bounces on the floor. "We'll tell you everything when the time is right. Can you trust me right now?"

I consider what he's asking me, hating that I'm backed into a corner. It's not the worst corner to be backed into, but it's still a corner.

I reach for the stick because I *do* trust him. He hands it to me, and the thing pats into my palm like a bargain being struck.

Poking the tip of it into the lantern, I wait until the fire tests this new source, grazing like a herd animal. It transfers slowly, and I remove it from the lantern, holding it in front of my face now. I breathe in slowly and then exhale through my mouth.

Let's not repeat what happened last time. Focus. Feel the door inside. How much to open, how much to keep it closed?

We can do this.

Enough connection to keep the fire alive without its natural source, but not enough to suffocate me.

Atiene waits nearby with a bucket of water on hand. Huh...he must have brought that down earlier. I'm pretty sure it's for drenching me should the fire get out of hand again, but I don't want to find out.

I close my eyes, trying to see it the way I saw it that night when I was on stage. And trying to imagine the door inside and how the mechanism works that lets the fire live through me. If I can pull those things together, maybe that's a way to control it.

As long as it doesn't consume me, this should be fine.

When I'm ready, I set my hand over the flame, feeling the warmth without the burn, inviting just a little with the opening of the door. And it spills over my skin, and even as it cascades, I see it in my mind, building from a spark as soon as it connects. It's like the rest of the world is black, but the fire is golden where it feeds off me, surrounded by a haze of orange. The further away from me it gets, the more it dies. And to test that theory, I pull back. The color dulls as I suspected, fading to black.

We can work with that. So, I pull a little more fire.

Its personality shines as it flicks this way and that, as if waiting to dive towards something to explore.

Ah! That's something.

Fear cuts it off. Excitement, exploration, music, dance, emotion, as Atiene said. These things maintain it. Excitement for what?

I have an idea.

I release the fire and take out my whistle.

"Play something," I say, surrendering the instrument to his care. He holds it carefully, noting the age and the wear. A little smile wafts over his mouth as his thumb rubs over the old carvings. Then he tilts the whistle, so he can see in the very end, at the little 'A.' Then his gaze meets mine.

"Just had to check," he explains. He places his fingers carefully over the holes, presses the mouthpiece to his lips, and tests the sounds of cascading notes. Then a short, trilling tune spills from the opening playfully.

His eyes seem alive as he looks at me to confirm that I'm ready. Then he begins a version of a song he taught me a long time ago.

It is a little strange for me to see him playing it again. He was so little then, but now the whistle seems tiny. Very much like a toy in comparison to him.

I cut my eyes back to the fire to refocus. And as I let the notes float in and around with everything they've meant to me...Renditions of that song I've done myself. Renditions with my family, where they added their own flair to the music. And I use that feeling to open the door just a little, keeping the notes floating around my head while the fire pursues the opening in my chest, flashing out from the makeshift torch, trying to collide with me.

But the feelings I have with the music, the knowledge I have of the notes and where they go, what comes next, intrigues the flame. And it burns as if curious. And the curiosity keeps it from trying to pour down my throat again.

It's as if we're in a negotiation where I can finally establish a sort of rule of conduct with it. And fascinated as it seems to be with the music pouring through my mind and memories that surface, it does appear to listen, hanging in the air before me like a ball, coursing around itself with flares and dips.

Elated with the progress, I reach out to it, expecting that it will clamp down on my skin, but it reaches softly now, wreathing around my wrist.

Let's dance.

The fire needs something to do.

Tapping my foot, I sway from side to side. Immediately, the blaze anchors to my wrist, swirling around in a fury of orange and yellow. Tamed, but not connected to me. Mysterious and inscrutable, with a vague sense of acknowledgement of me without a tether to my will.

How do I coax it to do what I'd like? How do I ask or tell? Thoughts don't work. I tried that last time.

Or…

An inkling only half-formed presents itself to my mind. One that makes me wrinkle my nose and want to pull away from the fire.

There may be a reason it doesn't respond to me. And it may have something to do with why it tries so hard to attach itself to me like a clingy pet. We're not one entity. We're two separate entities trying to work together. Or at least I'm trying to work together, but it's not because that's not what fire does. It consumes.

What if that's the answer? What if it *is* suffocation?

No, that's crazy. Dying is not the way to learn control. That's just…death.

But as the fire continues to chase its tail around my arm, I can't help but think it's not getting everything it needs. And neither am I, to be honest.

I could try…

Atiene won't like this. Better do it before he figures out what I'm thinking.

Relaxing my shoulders, I imagine the door inside. Then I imagine myself reaching for the door with an ethereal hand, and with a quick shove, I throw it open all the way.

The flames respond like a wave. Not just the one on the stick, but the lantern too. Both leap at me, and I shove the fear down into the pit of my stomach, watching the glow closing in. Waiting for the inevitable.

Taking one big inhale and holding it as if plunging into water, I let it sink into me. It heats my throat, coats my tongue, and crowds my lungs, settling into my stomach and burning through my limbs and in my veins until it reaches the ends of my fingers and toes, then rebounds, curling on itself and coursing back through. Zipping through my body as if exploring this living thing, I feel its eagerness eating through me, as it studies this new 'toy.'

But as soon as it familiarizes itself with me, it crackles with delight and dies like an ember, leaving only a warmth behind.

With the fire of the stick and the lantern gone, the cavern whooshes into darkness, and the song has stopped.

"Whistle, are you alright?" Atiene calls out, and I hear shuffling. The wood of the bucket scrapes, and then water splashes over the rocks as if the bucket has turned over. "Curse."

"I'm here. I'm okay," I say, a little confounded by the fire. Why settle inside me only to disappear? Is that what it feels like for other fire-conjurers? What did that do? What was it *supposed* to do?

Is that it?

And here we are in the pitch dark...I'm sure Atiene can find his way back up the stairs, familiar as he is with this place. And there is the luminous pool, and I can see the shapes of rocks as my eyes adjust to the tiniest amount of light coming through. But I don't dare move in case I step into one of the dark pools and get lost.

Atiene's boots scrape over the rocks.

"Keep talking," he says.

"I'm here," I reply. Stones crunch underfoot as he moves closer.

"What happened?"

"I thought that if I let the fire do what it keeps *trying* to do, we might figure out how to communicate." More scuffling sounds.

"It communicates with you?"

"No, but it wants to."

And something inside where the door used to be snaps into place. Like a hum or vibration of something extra, something more. Something definitely not me. But part of me now. Buzzing under my skin.

A shudder works through me, and I feel a tingle in my arm. It's still here. Somehow...doing what exactly? Can I use it?

Come through, I call to it. *Ignite the stick*.

And the faintest buzz and sense of warmth coalesce in my hand, but externally, nothing happens. Can I not conjure?

Does it need more energy...or something else?

I blow out my cheeks in a frustrated sigh, and I feel the shift of it in my chest. It does respond. But not enough to come *out* of me.

Atiene's searching hand finds my shoulder.

"There you are," he says, settling beside me. "We'll have to get the fire-starters from upstairs to light the candle again. I should have brought them with us."

"Sorry about that. I didn't know both of them would attack me."

"It's okay. We just pivot. Let me move around you, and I'll find the way back."

"Here. Take the stick," I say.

"Hold onto my shirt and walk behind me." I feel his hand close around mine as he takes the stick. Then I hear his boots over the rocks. He keeps hold of my hand until he's in front of me and feels my grip on his shirt.

Taps of the stick on the stone tell me he's testing the ground in front of him. And then he moves, I step with him. We work our way slowly to the stairs, and at that point, he reaches back and takes my hand. And I can tell he ascends, so I reach out with my foot to touch the bottom steps. Once I find it, the rest of our travel becomes smoother.

I hear the brush of his hand over the walls, and eventually, we reach the top. Then the door clicks open, and the space is flooded with blinding light.

Squinching my eyes shut, I hide my face.

After a moment, he says, "Got it." The metal from the second lantern squeaks, and the flint rasps against steel. I *feel* the sparks as they sputter, and the flame inside longs to connect. Almost like it lunges.

"Let me," I say, reaching out quickly to take control of the materials. I don't want him to get hurt if I can't command it.

He steps back, and I place my body in front of the fire-steel and candle like a barrier. Working the pieces together, the flame inside seems to watch and wait with bated breath. And when the sparks fly, the flame seems giddy. The second time, the candle catches, and the flame immediately jumps into a healthy tapered glow, bouncing happily. And the fire inside responds in an elated way as if calling to a piece of itself. It's like it wants to leap through my skin and join the tiny thing.

I'm going to need to keep fire-steel on my person from now on, everywhere I go.

Why did it take me so long to think of that?

I close the glass on the lantern and hand it to Atiene. He reaches around me to close the door since we no longer need the light. Then he takes the fire-starters from me and stows them in his pocket.

Then we descend the staircase to try again. He lights the other lantern, so we have more light, and then gives me back the stick.

As soon as the stick catches fire, I feel the vibration of the flame inside, desiring to unite, and the little flame responds, building and building until it burns brightly. Too brightly, and I try quelling it by trying to shut the door like I used to, but there *is* no door anymore. There's just a constant, vivid sense of the flame and its will.

This may have been a mistake.

I drop the stick into one of the pools, hearing the hiss and sizzle of it as it touches the water. And it blinks out immediately. The fire inside retreats, but I still feel the tug of it towards the two tiny flames still casting light around the cavern. It's all too easy to connect with the devouring thing. That's not the part that scares me. It's what happens if I can't stop it from getting bigger and bigger.

I stare at the ceiling in defeat, hearing the lapping sounds of water as if it could put me out, too.

What if I can't control this? Am I going to have to carry water for the rest of my life just in case things get out of hand? What have I *done* to myself?

I place the sides of my hands against my forehead, now retreating into myself as well.

If I can't do this, I can't help them. And the king may as well hunt me to extinguish this uncontrollable flame I've just joined myself to.

"Do you need some time alone?" Atiene's voice reaches across the void in my soul now. I nod.

I need some time to mourn. Something I've been avoiding.

No. Mourning is an admission of defeat. I refuse to be defeated.

But I am losing time.

He takes one of the lanterns, and as he passes, he pauses, reaches out, and puts his hand on my arm.

"You'll get it," he says, and then he hands me the fire-steel and the whistle.

He drifts away. I hear him going up the stairs. I see the ring of light bobbing in my peripheral vision until it disappears, and so does he. The sounds of the hidden door let me know I'm completely alone now. I sink to the ground, hugging myself and staring at the tiny flame separated from me by the glass.

Sitting cross-legged, I plant my elbows on my legs, clasping my hands in front of my mouth.

How do I control you? I ask the tiny candle as I drag the lantern closer and open the little glass door to remove the barrier.

It's not fire that's controlled, but the circumstances. Fire does what it does as a result.

So how do I control the circumstances where it's inside me, feeding off of me? Use some sort of ethereal bellows to inflame it and metaphorical water to quench it? It would be easier if someone could just teach me how to do this. Or tell me where to start.

Think, Whistle. You have to figure this out. Start with what we know...what does it feed on?

That's not the problem. It's what squelches it.

So...the opposite?

The opposite of emotion is apathy. The opposite of life is death.

...start with apathy?

I *do* sort of feel out of control. With everything going on.

I thought we were gonna try-

It doesn't make sense. And what are they planning? And is Surrilo okay? And why should I have to die in order to satiate a king? I didn't even do anything dangerous or wrong.

And there's nothing I can do about it.

I sigh, closing my eyes to see the little source of light inside. Reaching out my hand, I pet the flame, watching it bob between my fingers, always reaching upward.

Then I cup it like a little bug, pulling it closer while still leaving some to devour the candle still and cast the needed light around the cavern.

The tug in my chest grows, but I'm not afraid now. *I* won't burn. And there's nothing down here that'll be hurt by it. It can't burn stone or water. And if the lantern goes out, I'll just light it again. No problem.

Opening my eyes, I see the tiny blaze inside my hands. Immediately, fear tickles my temples and cheeks.

No...this isn't scary. This is fine. Remember? Nothing can be hurt.

And it just flickers in reply as if blinking lazily.

I poke it with my finger just to see what happens. It wraps slowly, carefully around my hand, and I move my fingers to allow it to twist and slip around them.

Acceptance. Not apathy. Patience. Not the diving, devouring curiosity. I'm not meant to be *fire*. It is what it is without me, so it doesn't need me to feed that side of it. I'm meant to be its counterbalance.

I toss it in the air, not demanding, not expressly stating through thought what I expect of it. I simply act as if it already knows. And it hangs there where I placed it, rolling around itself. Remaining the same.

Calm. Controlled, I blink at it to put it out, and the light winks out as if it never existed.

Relief and excitement flood my body now, and the fire awakens inside, making the candle's flame burn hotter and brighter. It rises.

So, I breathe and cool my emotions like dousing myself.

Find a center. An anchor. Something to cling to.

Dance is a form of acceptance. And music. Maybe that's why they're so appealing to fire?

I rise now, seeing the fire again in my mind and scooping a little bit to hold in my hand. I swirl my hands, giving it motion, direction, and it does move with me. Dipping and diving, twirling, and wrapping around again. I let the flame grow, and now it's as if I'm working with a more sophisticated door. One that requires a specific, measured touch.

Livened by the extra, it grows brighter, warmer, into a thick wreath that waits. And I dance with the ethereal thing as if I can hear music. Making it act as the torches at first because I'm familiar with that, but there's a whole world of movement opened up here. I can literally have the fire act independently of physical elements.

And after a few minutes, I note how drained my body feels. Not from dancing, but from monitoring the fire and controlling myself to control it.

I'm done with this last test, so I let it hang in the air for a moment. And then I blink it away just like the first.

Balance. We are one entity. We can work together. It *can* be done. But while it feeds off of me, it needs to be harnessed in a very specific way.

I can't help the flame in my cheeks now as I take the lantern and head towards the stairs. I've found something, and that's worth celebrating.

Turns out true control is about letting go.

CHAPTER 13

Atiene isn't in the study when I come through the bookcase. I *did* set the lantern and lighting materials back on the shelf for next time and closed myself off from the secrets the grotto keeps.

My news will have to wait.

I go to the window, stretching out my hands to echo the wings of the castle spreading out on either side. From here, I feel like I'm on top of the world, staring over the ocean to where it kisses the sky. Do ships ever come by? I haven't seen any yet, but that doesn't mean that they don't come this way. There's a port in the city. Ships go both directions from there to other port towns along the coast and to the other islands.

Shipping is the fastest mode of transportation and is how most goods get transported. Except for those that are more inland. Shipping is a lucrative business.

Will I see the king's ship pass by before it docks in the port?

I let my hands drop. And then I sit on the window seat. The repetition of the sea makes me drowsy, so I lie down on the window seat with my head propped on my hand. And then slowly, I melt until I fall asleep.

I wake when the sun turns the water golden. The sinking orb taps the sea and begins to melt into it.

I could get used to waking up to a sight like this. Stretching, I notice Atiene's coat over me like a blanket. He's sitting at the desk now, poring over papers with his finger holding up his temple and a pen in the other hand, drifting over the papers, and dipping at turns to make a mark.

Sitting up, I wrap the coat around my shoulders. He glances up with a smile, then sits a little straighter in his chair like he wants to ask how it went in the grotto.

I don't answer right away. Instead, I rise, saunter over to the table, and lean against it, half-turned so I can see the documents. A ledger, some letters, official-looking documents with flowy script.

"What are these?" I ask, pulling one closer, so I can read it. 'Sea Sprite' is scrawled across the top.

"Shipping manifest for one of the boats." He drops the pen into the ink.

"You have boats?" My eyes graze over the list quickly. Crates and barrels of food, dye, straw, cloth, etc.

"You say that like it's a surprise." He leans back in the chair with his hands clasped over his stomach.

"There's a lot I still don't know about you."

"What do you want to know?"

Not entirely sure what to ask, I lift myself onto the table and adjust the coat around me.

"Everything," I answer. "What was your father like? What is your brother like? What was it like growing up with a view like that?" I point to the window now where the golden glow darkens.

"I'm sure as a traveler you could have had any view you wanted," he says, but I think he likes that I appreciate his view.

I shrug. "What views we had...that wasn't up to me."

He nods, leaning his face on his hand. "My father was a lot like my grandfather. They had the same streak. Like father, like son."

"Not for you, though."

"I have too much 'mainland' blood, I guess."

"Your mother was from the mainland?" I raise my eyebrows. "I'm surprised a Chelees would have married outside the islands."

"New blood. New money. A potential alliance with wealthy mainland merchants and nobles. Seemed like a good idea."

"What happened to her?"

"She passed away when I was young. My father remarried, and Ilano came along."

"Is he like your father and grandfather?"

"Moreso than me. My father approved of that. Wished Ilano had been born first."

"Is that why you ran away?"

"Yes. I thought I'd oblige him," he answers, but the memories don't seem to cause him pain. Instead, he's merely thoughtful. "If I disappeared, Ilano would inherit, and my father would approve."

"Did that create competition between you and Ilano?"

"At first perhaps, but we're long since passed that. He helps me run the estates. We prefer the different aspects, so I handle the paperwork, and he handles the business or the deals with other Chelees."

"He has that look," I reply.

"What look?"

"The look of the nobles."

"I don't?" he scoffs.

I shake my head, tapping a few papers, so they're aligned.

"That's why you thought Ilano was the Chelees," he reasons.

I give a half shrug.

"Perhaps you'd fit in on the mainland?" I suggest.

"Perhaps," he says thoughtfully. And we get caught in the silence like flies in its web. It's thick and encompassing. Reflecting all that needs to be said and done, but with care.

"So, if your father and grandfather are...like them," I gesture, hopping off the table and turning around, leaning against the wall. "What makes you like you?"

"Mainland blood," he answers, "As any Chelees will tell you."

"Is that true?"

He shrugs. "Seems as likely as anything else."

"If they like to point out the softness of mainland blood, I might wonder how it so easily overtook island blood in you." I shrug as if it's something to consider. Any islander will laud our home over the mainland, but I wonder how much of the hate is based on logic. Or if it's just blind. We were *all* mainlanders at one point in history. The current attitude is really just prideful, extreme self-sufficiency.

And again, the silent spider wraps us in its threads. So, to push back, I slide my arms through the armholes, pulling the long sleeves over my hands.

"A bonfire is being built in the courtyard. Alessi has my knights at her disposal," he jokes.

"Knowing her, it was bound to happen." I cock my head at him. "Is that your way of dismissing me?"

"Giving you the option."

I drop my gaze now, playing with the large buttons on his coat.

"I'm not entirely sure I should be around fire at the moment," I answer, matching one of the buttons with the leather strip on the other side. Simple, yet fancy. I believe that's what Alessi might call an 'embellishment.'

"Did something happen?" he asks quietly as I turn my attention to the cuffs of the coat, playing with the button on the right one.

"Maybe..." I answer, flicking my gaze up to meet his with a smile.

"You found something."

I shrug, but I can't stop smiling.

He leans forward like he might rise, and his voice stays low as he says, "I knew you could do it. How? What did it?"

"I'm not sure how to explain it," I answer, but I launch into a brief explanation of what I tested and the results.

He listens eagerly, and at the end of it, he says, "That's great. I was just in your way then."

"You weren't in my way. You were..." I can't really think of how to end that sentence. He waits, though with his brows raised.

"...In your way," he reiterates.

"A pleasant distraction?" I soften.

"Flattering."

"I try."

A knock sounds at the door.

"Chelees?" a knight calls through the door.

"Enter," Atiene commands, and a guard does, his gaze bouncing from his Chelees to me and back.

"The old lady wants to know when this one will be sent back to the family," the knight says.

"I was just about to dismiss her," Atiene answers. "Wait outside."

As the door closes, I remove the coat and lay it over the back of his chair.

"It's hard to know who the Chelees is around here," I tease.

"Knowing her, it was bound to happen," he echoes.

"Or is it because of the 'mainland blood?'"

"We'll call it both."

I grin and head to the door. Accepting the guards who fall in behind me as I go to the courtyard.

I can't stop smiling. Alessi is right. They're *all* right. I'm really bad at acting...

We sing and play with gusto. Or at least Alessi does, dancing with her arm hooked around Little Benji's. He grins as if there's nothing to worry about. And I'm grateful for that at least.

Even Della and Big Henri enjoy themselves again. Della even claps to the beat.

Do they know our lives will be turned upside down in a matter of days? Or are they just relieved that the waiting will be over? Which is also fair. The suspense has been torture.

I keep an eye on the fire, making sure it doesn't betray me. And I feel the tug inside, having to settle myself and breathe. It's difficult to do, and I end up going to bed early.

CHAPTER 14

Day dawns, and I lie in bed for a moment with my hands under my head, feeling bubbles of anxiety pop in my chest, releasing the noxious stuff into my lungs, so that it's in every breath.

Luckily, I'm used to tamping feelings down. So, I take a long inhale of fresh air, steel myself, and push the anxiety into the pit of my stomach where I will deal with it (or not) later.

What is Atiene planning? All thoughts connected to it ultimately smack their heads into the impenetrable wall of the simple fact that I don't know. And I won't know until he tells me or it happens.

I know *my* plan: I bargain for my family's release and for leniency for Atiene. I'll go with the king without a fight if he gives me those things. Despite what Atiene has planned, that's the bottom of the barrel. The worst-case scenario.

And if the king doesn't take that bargain?

I turn over, uncomfortable with the answer. And then immediately shove the blankets off of me and rise. I have to practice.

The morning routine is the same. Breakfast, then the study.

Atiene dismisses the guards and accompanies me to the grotto, but as we close the bookcase, I note the glow of another lantern casting orange light at the bottom of the steps. Atiene doesn't seem surprised, though, so I assume he must have prepared.

But as we descend, a figure sits behind the lantern with his arms hanging over his knees. He rises casually as we enter. Hands tucked into his belt. Blonde hair. Unruly, proud grin.

Surrilo.

Is he really just standing there as if he's completely fine? Why does he look so cocky?

I rush to hug my partner.

"Are you alright? I heard you were beaten. They wouldn't let me see you," I ramble, pulling back to look him over. He appears completely fine, but bruises or cuts could be hidden.

"I'm okay. The beating was just a ruse," he answers.

So...there are no cuts or bruises.

"You let me worry? On purpose? Why didn't you tell me?" I ball my hand and punch him in the arm.

"Ow! What was that for?"

"It was part of the plan," Atiene says, setting the other lantern down.

"What plan?" I ask, stepping back, hands on my hips now as my glare bounces from one to the other.

"Someone had to be punished for the escape. Surrilo took the fall. He was never hurt. We perpetrated the lie so he could sneak out of the castle and put pieces in place for your family's escape. I placed a guard on his door and only let the physician in and out. The physician can be trusted. No one knows Surrilo hasn't been in there this whole time."

"You both lied to me," I say with an accusatory finger. "Again."

"If we're to pull this off, I'm going to keep hiding things from you. It's like on stage," Surrilo answers. "The audience matters. And we're working to pull something off. Something *big*." His eyes widen with excitement.

My eyes narrow. I take the hug back mentally.

Atiene's approach is more diplomatic, as he says, "I'm sorry I lied again. The fewer people who know, the less likely it'll get out. Even now, we have to sneak him back to the servant's quarters without being seen."

I cross my arms and pin Surrilo with a glare. "So, what did you do while the family was fretting over you?"

"*Part* of the family," he corrects. "Mostly just you, since the others knew."

I'm about to protest when Atiene breaks in.

"He met with Ilano in town, oversaw preparations, and helped Haweth line out transport. Braun, Letta, and Lalina are on a ship headed for the mainland. Haweth gave them papers of introduction to some old associates of his, so they'll be taken care of until we can meet up with them."

My mind pauses over the word 'we.'

I stare for a moment. "You...you're coming with?"

"Yes," he answers with a nod, and the air is still and silent while he waits. A slow smile spreads over my face, but before I can fully unpack that thought, I think of everything he's offering to leave behind.

"But...all of this?"

"It's not a hard choice," he answers quickly. "I'm settling my affairs on the island and turning over the estates to Ilano."

Guilt for feeling angry washes away the remnants of haughty peevishness. It's replaced now by gratitude that he thought of all this and the embarrassment of not knowing what to say. I duck my head now, noting how the candles seem to do the same.

"When did you decide that?" I ask, fiddling with my fingers.

"Okay, first, I don't want to be here for this," Surrilo breaks in. "Second, we have a ton of work to do before the king gets here. To make the most of this, we're going to throw a party celebrating his arrival. It's going to be a spectacle, so we can't screw this up. But I guarantee if you stick to the routine, this show will be talked of for years."

I shoot him a withering look, but I don't press anything. Atiene just hides a smile.

"Guess I'd better leave you to it," the Chelees says. "Good luck."

Awkward silence ensues while he takes the other lantern back up the stairs.

"Atiene said you figured out how to use your skill," Surrilo says. "Show me what you can do."

"'It's nice to see you, Whistle. I'm glad you're okay.' Oh, thanks, Surrilo! I'm glad you're okay, too. 'It's impressive that you can wield fire. That must have been so hard to figure that out.' It *was*. Thanks for mentioning that. But now that I know a little bit, I feel much better about the whole thing and somewhat confident that this newfound skill won't end up hurting people accidentally, even while I sleep," I answer, deepening my voice for his parts and accentuating my point with a look.

He rolls his eyes.

"Okay...I get it."

Skepticism lifts my brow.

"I knew you and the others would be fine. That's why Atiene had them stay here. It's comfortable. There's food. And Alessi could rest and heal and be catered to by knights. Tell me she didn't enjoy that over hiding and sleeping in a pig's hovel at night."

"What preparations did you make?" I ask.

"Do you really want to get into all of that now?"

"Do you really want to see what I can do, so you can fold it into your *grand* routine to impress the king or whatever it is you intend to do?"

He doesn't answer...He waits, watching for a break in my resolve. Arms crossing like mine as he pops a leg out. We stand that way, staring, silent, waiting.

"It's really better if you *don't* know right now. You're terrible at keeping secrets," he answers finally. "If anyone outside of the family gets a whiff of what we're trying to do..."

"There's only so much hiding you can do if you're planning a sea voyage. That kind of thing isn't small."

"No, it isn't. That's why we are being careful and only letting certain people in on it."

"I don't like being used or played," I reply. And that's what this ultimately comes down to: the fact that my emotions are being toyed with to keep their plans hidden.

"I know. But we don't really have a choice if we want to get *everyone* out. We could have left. But we didn't because home isn't a place. It's all of our family. So, stop being stubborn and pouty. Show me what you can do, so I can create a routine that arrests attention."

Eyeing him for a moment, I bend down and open the door on the lantern and scoop up fire like a little pet. It flits around my fingers as I say, "Stand back."

Once he gives me space, I allow the flame to grow, and then I toss it into the air, making it fall gently like rain, and then gathering it back into a mass, stretching it like a snake, and twirling it around my arms and torso. I fling it out to my side like a whip and then bring it back into my hands. Then, I swish my hands like Ollio might, killing the blaze in an instant.

But unlike Ollio's tricks, the flame doesn't reappear.

His hand is on his chin. "You can't conjure it yourself? You have to borrow what's already burning?"

"I haven't had a whole lot of time to work with it," I defend.

"You'll need to conjure it from nothing. I doubt they'll want you near fire."

"What about Ollio's flash powder?"

"Still needs a spark."

"He uses fire-starters."

"Those are obvious and unreliable. You need to be able to conjure fire consistently."

"What exactly is your vision for this whole thing?"

"Why do the nobles always kill the sorcerers?"

"Prestige. Power. Domination."

"Exactly. The king wants to slay a dragon. I say, we give him one."

"Without the slaying part, right?"

"Well...He can slay whatever he wants after we're gone."

"How do you intend to get us out?"

He smiles as if to say, 'Nice try,' and then claps his hands.

"Okay, focus. How do you do this? What will it take to conjure?"

"If I knew that, I'd have done it."

"You know what I mean."

"For me to figure it out, you're going to need to leave," I answer. "I can't do it when I'm too focused on *not* hurting whoever's near."

"That's not the best use of our time, then, is it? New plan. We work on a routine, then you learn to conjure on your own. I still have a lot to do, and I still need to make an appearance in the servants' quarters."

"Fine. What do you have in mind?"

He takes charge of the whistle to provide music. He plays a few notes, and I see his retreat into his mind as his eyes take on a faraway look.

Abruptly, he stops and says, "We need to combine the beginning of 'Lambs in Pastures' with 'Jig of the Sea.'"

Holding both in my mind, I ask for the transition point.

"It's not that simple. Not from one to the other. It's more like this," he says, pooling moves from both dances, pausing to show me where he'd like me to present the fire and how it should act.

Doing away with the stiffness of the torches lends a fluidity to the movement, a sense of mystery, and freedom. He leans into that, playing with the shapes and way the blaze moves. And when I recreate the moves he showed me, getting the shift of the fire down precisely, which is not easy considering the emotional and mental work going on inside to get the concentration of flame just right.

"Creating a story," he speaks more to himself than to me. "And then we lead to the climax where poof! Dragon."

"You're going to turn me into a winged beast with sharp claws and teeth?"

"Something like that."

"And the king could slay that creature?"

"Interactive elements of entertainment. The audience loves to participate," he says. "But...We'll have to see how this goes. However, if you're dead, he has no more reason to look for you."

"Wait...are you going to fake my death?"

"Maybe. It's a potential scenario. Definitely under consideration, but nothing's decided for sure. We don't know how the king will actually conduct himself or what he'll demand. We'll have to pivot. Improvise. Another reason it would be helpful if you could conjure.

Let's go over the routine again. Remember, this takes place in the hall directly underneath the chandelier."

I practice the moves until the fire moves fluidly enough for him, but it takes a lot out of me. And I can tell by the flutter and growth of the flames that I'm losing the battle with fear. Wearing down under pressure.

I need a break.

Surrilo notices too, calling a halt.

"It's a start. Will you be able to figure out how to conjure in this state?" he asks.

I shake my head.

"Rest now. Try later."

"Thanks. That never occurred to me," I say with a smirk.

"I didn't think it had, so I thought I'd better bring it up," he retorts, grabbing the lantern and closing the little door. "Shall we?" He gestures to the stairs.

"You're not going through the study, are you? Won't it look suspicious if you're suddenly there? Also, won't it look suspicious that you don't have any wounds?"

"Oh, I'm not going out that way. I just need Atiene's help with something. And I can *act* being hurt. It was never specified *where* I took a beating. The most likely scenario would have been stripes across my back."

I don't ask anything else. I'm tired of asking and not getting answers. I'm also tired of not knowing...but the battle isn't worth the effort.

We traverse the stairs, and he kills the tiny blaze before I open the door. Atiene stands as we enter. No words are exchanged between the two men. Just looks. And then Atiene follows Surrilo back through the door.

Curiosity gnaws at my insides.

Before Atiene pulls the bookcase closed behind him, he removes his coat and hands it to me with a smile and a wink.

I take the coat, holding it around my shoulders as their deeds are cut off from me. Then go to the window seat. I stand, leaning against it. My eyes are drawn to the sandy beach below. It looks peaceful. Like a lovely spot to just sit and watch the ocean in its constant pattern.

As much as my heart flutters to contemplate the sea and the sense of adventure rises in my chest, I'm not sure I'd really love it. The constancy of movement, sight, and sound would grate on me after a while. And I can't make any of those stop. No one can hold back the sea.

Make it a sea of glass. That would be stunning to see.

The truth of the matter is that I'm not comfortable with things I can't control. Like the rattle of the wagons that brought us here.

Will their plan work? That's what matters. It's not about what I know or don't know. And I just have to sit back and let it happen.

Suddenly, I'm torn from the view by the sound of footsteps from outside the room. A decided and quick stride. No metallic tap of armor...Still, it's unsettling, and by the rise of the sound, they're coming this way. A servant, perhaps?

"Atiene?" a voice calls through the door, as the knob turns.

My heart leaps into my throat. This is where he's supposed to be. What will they do when they find out he's not here? And I shouldn't be here when he's not. What will they do with me?

It's too late for me to hide.

The door flies open, and a tall, lanky figure in black walks in.

Ilano. Atiene's brother. His shocking blue eyes flick over me, then to the table and back as he closes the door.

"Is he...?" Ilano whispers, pointing to the bookcase.

I nod, relaxing only slightly. It's strange to come face-to-face with him. The last time I saw him was when my family was being arrested. And despite the ruse, he seemed uninterested. I'm not sure how to take him.

"You're Whistle," he says, sticking out his hand for me to shake. I take it, and he sort of clasps our hands together as one might do with a colleague. "Great to meet you."

He flings his coat out behind him as he seats himself in the chair, kicking his feet up onto the window seat. His hands hang to the sides.

"So...you're the one causing all the trouble," he says, but there's a teasing crinkle in his eye. "Here I was living a perfectly normal life, and now it's upended."

I don't think I'm meant to answer that, so I don't. Instead, I study him as I sit down carefully.

"Atiene says you're adept with business," I redirect. His eyes are hooded, but he smiles.

"What else has he told you about me?" His hands land over his stomach, clasping the way Atiene's do sometimes.

"All embarrassing stuff, I'm afraid," I answer as if sorry. If he can tease, so can I.

His brows shoot up, and he pins me with a gaze as if trying to read me now. "You know, he told me about you, too."

"Oh?" I say, pretending to be interested.

"Yeah," he insists, taking his long legs off the window seat and leaning forward. The short chair makes it difficult for him to get comfortable, and his knees jut upward awkwardly. "And I can tell you all about it."

Time to flip the conversation.

"I already know about myself. I'm more interested in what you can tell me about him," I reply.

"Ha! Well, I have an opportunity to return the favor then," he counters, eyes sparking with mischief, "A lifetime of brotherhood offers a veritable treasure of high-quality uncomfortable moments. Prepare yourself."

"I'm ready." I lean forward too, planting my elbow on my knee and my chin on my fist.

"Well, before he ran away to live on the streets-"

The bookshelf clicks then and swings open. As Atiene enters, his gaze bounces from me to Ilano and back, curiosity in his brow. Ilano shoots a knowing look at me and a mischievous grin as he leans back in his chair. He allows the suspense to hang on purpose.

Would he really be a brother if he didn't make this awkward for Atiene? Far be it from me to get in the middle of it, so I just sit back and watch it unfold.

Atiene secures the bookshelf, shooting a questioning look at his brother.

"You're back earlier than I expected," Atiene says.

"Finished early. Thought I'd come see that the preparations are underway for the king's arrival." Then he turns to me. "We're throwing him an extravagant party. Did you know?"

I gasp as if surprised. "The king is coming? I can't imagine what for. What an honor."

"Well, you see, he's *particularly* fond of Atiene." His eyebrows lift as if in earnest.

Atiene snorts, shifting papers on the table.

"So, what will this lavish party look like?" I ask.

"That, my dear, is a surprise," Ilano says with a wink. "But I shall relish the look on your face when it's unveiled. You'll come, of course?"

"How could I pass up a chance to see the king?" I ask as if helpless in this situation. "Seems like an opportunity to die for."

Ilano smiles as he drops the sarcasm. It melts from his face as he shifts his hair away from his eyes with a hand and stands. He turns to his brother.

"You're sure you must leave? It's not too late to turn back."

Atiene nods.

"Very well then. Captain Haweth has everything in hand. I'll oversee the preparations from here, and we'll get this settled."

"Do we have word on how far out the king is?"

"With the winds in his favor, he's set to arrive tomorrow at noon, but likely it'll be more toward evening."

Hearing it is like a hammer beating against my ribs. Like being clamped between two large pieces of wood while a large ethereal hand twists the screw mechanism, pressing the pieces closer and closer, slowly squishing me to death.

It's too late to get free now.

Atiene nods. The two exchange a look, though I can't see Ilano's face, I see Atiene giving and then receiving information.

"Well, I suppose you can handle things from here," Ilano says, turning as if unaffected by all of this.

This is what I expected from a Chelees. The flair, the commanding presence, the bold way of conversing that lacks restraint. Not the quiet, calm that Atiene exudes. I'm not embarrassed by assuming Ilano and not Atiene was the commanding noble that night in the square. It was an honest mistake. Even seeing them together now, it's not clear which one wields the power. Perhaps that's just their dynamic, though. Brothers first. Nobles second.

"You'll keep him out of trouble, won't you?" Ilano says to me. "He needs that voice of reason, and without me, I shudder to think what will become of him."

"Oh, I'm an expert at getting out of trouble and perfectly reasonable at all times." I flick my eyebrows at him.

With a smile, he leaves the room, closing the door behind him.

I wonder if Alessi has met him yet. They'd get along. It's too bad she can't stay.

How can Atiene *leave*?

I hate that choices require sacrifice on one hand or the other. I hate that he has to abandon everything he knows. And for what? Has he really thought all this through? Has he thought about what happens if he goes to the mainland with my family and me, and decides that a new life there isn't what he wants after all? What if he decides that building a relational 'we' isn't worth what he's given up here? Would he grow to resent me? Somehow that doesn't seem like his character, and yet, I'm no expert. Who knows what he'll feel when the waves and wind carry us away?

He can come back. But not if he burns bridges. And I get the feeling that what he intends to do is irreparable.

"You should rest while you can," he says as he sits in the chair and rearranges the papers.

There's nothing to argue in that, so I sit back down on the window, but it doesn't seem quite where I should be right now. I need a little more space. A little more privacy. To sort through some things. But if I go back to the servants' quarters, Alessi might be in our room, and I just want to be alone.

I do need rest, though.

My consciousness lands back in the present as I lift my eyes to the window. How much longer will I have to enjoy this view? Whether things go right or wrong, I'll likely never see this again after tomorrow. I want it etched into memory so I can come back as often as I want.

I put my arms through the coat and lay down.

This view is a representation of everything he's leaving behind. Everything that I've ruined for him and for my family. Do I really deserve this view?

How do I conjure?

What are their plans, and will they work?

What will the king do to us?

Why is Atiene so kind to a girl he met on the streets so long ago?

How do I conjure?

How do I make his sacrifice worth it? Or how do I make everything my family is going through worth all this?

How do I make sure they all get away safely? To live freely?

How do I conjure?

How do I conjure?

How do I conjure...

I push myself off the window seat because this is no use.

"I'm going back down," I say, and Atiene reads my face for a moment and then nods. Not as if giving permission, but in understanding.

I shouldn't be doing this. But I open the bookcase, light the lantern, and descend into the dark by myself. And when I've gone into the cavern far enough that I won't be able to find my way back, I blow out the candle.

Immediately, the space is plunged into suffocating darkness. Between me and the fire-starters are craggy rocks and dark pools. If I trip and fall, I may hit my head or plunge into the water. If I go under, I may not find the surface again.

Either I'll conjure or die here.

Or Atiene will come looking for me later if I fail or cower until that point. I don't consider that an option.

Weariness tugs at my mind and eyes. Fear melts my shoulders, but I roll them back anyway, stretching my neck. I shake out my hands and force out a sharp exhale.

I can do this. Others did it before me. So, it *can* be done. There is a way. I just have to figure it out.

Stirring up the fire in my chest, I coax it into my hands, feeling the tingle in my blood. Warmth pools in my palm and in my hands.

Come out, I think. I'm hardly surprised when it doesn't, but I am a little disappointed because I don't have many ideas for how I can take what's inside of me and make it physically manifest on the outside. It's like taking a feeling and giving it a physical shape and presence in the real world. How could that possibly be done?

Yet...I can manipulate it with emotion when fire already exists. How does that work, and can it give me an idea about how to conjure?

Even thinking about this is exhausting.

Rubbing my eyes, I heave a sigh and try to focus, but when I open my eyes, the luminous pool casts the barest blue haze onto the rocks nearest it. And it's soothing. A solitary light in this place. An opposite kind of light. Well...not really. It just sort of seems that way because of the way the sunlight filters through the water.

What must have it been like for Atiene and Ilano as children, coming down here to explore and swim through the tunnels into the sea? And to find the entrance from the outside to swim back inside must have been exhilarating. A victory.

I'd have tried swimming out of it, too. Learning. Expanding in skill and capacity until I found the ideal way. Despite how foreign to me the water tunnel is and how familiar I am with fire, it seems almost easier to swim out of the tunnel without drowning than to conjure.

But now is not the time for breaking or feeling sorry for myself.

Carefully, I sit down on the rocks, letting out a soft 'ow' when they poke into me. I shift to get more comfortable, staring into the blue water as if it could sweep me out of here and away from my troubles. But even if it did, I wouldn't go. For the same reason, Surrilo and the others didn't just leave the rest of us. Home isn't home without them.

Maybe it would be better if I just negotiate with the king. At least my family would be whole. And Atiene too.

No, I can do this.

What if I can't?

The quietude of this place echoes the silence in my head. Somewhere in the cave, a droplet hits the surface of a pool with a wet 'plink.'

Nothing? Not a thing in my mind or in the world around me to help? Fine. I can work with nothing. I've worked with nothing before.

I shift my seat to get more comfortable.

Start with what I know. I can get it to pool in my hand-No. No, it doesn't come from there. It's not an appendage that it shoots from. That wouldn't make sense. If it's an emotion coming out in physical form, it's not the emotion itself. It's the effects of it. Besides that, it never sinks into my skin when it's outside. When it did merge, it dove down my throat.

Do I breathe it? Literally? Like a dragon?

Surrilo would love that. It would add to his theatrical masterpiece.

However, I've breathed many times, and it hasn't come. Besides that, it doesn't feel like it's in my lungs. Or throat. Not that I know how dragons breathe fire.

How do I get this outside of me?

How is fire generated? Sparks, heat, friction...Striking the flint, rubbing sticks, concentrated light from the sun. And that's *real* fire. How is *ethereal* fire created? Heat? Sparks?

If it's inside me, free to roam throughout my body, attuned to my feelings...if control is instinctual and immediate...

I can tell that it wants to be loose. Sensing my desire, it roils inside like whipped-up wind. Frothing, squirming, seeking an exit. My cheeks heat with it, and I sense it moving through my body once again. So easily guided. Not so easily created.

Instinctual and immediate...

Heat and light...

Sparks...

Then it hits me...a thought half-formed. If managing my emotions directly influences the fire...overseeing the conditions in which it burns...but that's *control*. That's not spark. Sparks aren't dominated or directed. They snap and bite, jumping at random until they can cling to fuel. And friction and heat aren't things we necessarily control. We don't have the capability of perfectly regulating those things, just the capability to create the circumstances that make them happen. Then suddenly there's a burst of light and heat, and the flame lives.

Perhaps conjuring calls for a *lack* of control.

It's worth a try.

With a slow exhale, I release the terror I've been pushing down, the pain of what I've caused, the regrets I have about exposing this gift, the what-ifs, and the 'I take it backs.' The threats and the possibility of being hunted and killed. The fact that I may have such limited time left in this world, despite not feeling like I've gotten a fair chance. I've only just begun to live. There's so much I want to do...Things I missed out on. Things I *will* miss out on.

Oh curses. What if this plan *does* fail?

Who knows what happens to my family?

Oh curses...They don't deserve this.

My hands clamp in my hair as a shudder wracks my body. I let it wash over me like the luminous pool. The terror and pain bite my nerves and cling like claws in my ribs. I pull my knees into my chest, hiding my face in my quaking hands, hating that tears have pricked my eyes and rolled down my cheeks without permission.

The agony of the wagon resurfaces, like a tomb I'd been buried alive in. The immense weight of responsibility and all I'd done to my family. What if that's only a precursor to what comes? What if we were all buried then?

What have I done?

To Atiene. To Surrilo and Alessi.

Della drooping by the fire. Surrilo trying desperately to save us and keep us all together. Alessi's wings...

And I lie awkwardly on the rocks now, not caring that they poke into my sides.

Closing my eyes, I cut myself off from the world and sink into the waves of despair, hauntedness, and fear for the future.

I've failed them. A sob breaks loose, and my body shakes with unfelt feelings and unspent tears. And it's like my emotions burst out of my chest because I can no longer contain them. Shame rips at my insides. I want to dissolve into the rocks and become one of them.

I cry until my emotions recede. Then I take my hands from my face and wipe my cheeks.

An orange glow lands softly on my eyelids as I sniff.

My breath catches in my throat as I open my eyes. There in the air, no less real than if it had been started with flint and steel, bobs a little flame, searching and exploring its bounds. Bounds placed by the numbness of my soul now.

Staring, I sit up. And it grows along with my hope. Warmth spreads in my chest as I watch the thing spring just a little higher.

Somehow, it happened. Somehow, I did it.

Afraid I won't get it next time, I hurriedly send flame into the lantern to light the wick.

I don't need it though...

I might. I'll be even more exhausted if I don't. And I already feel the weight of the emotion and what it took to start this. And I need to practice. I need to do it again. I need to make sure it can be called upon when needed.

So, I crush the fire in the air into oblivion as if snuffing it with my hand.

Feeling the emotion again like a slicing cry through my soul, I wave my shaky hand, and a flame appears between my fingers, nestling and then reaching out into the world.

I shake it away.

Another heart and gut-wrenching release of emotion and a swish of my hand. Again, the dazzling glow bursts into life.

A relieved collapse of the soul rakes through my entire body.

I'm doing it!

And with that realization, exhilaration breaks through my chest, putting off exhaustion just a bit, and the fire whooshes brightly, freed from its prison and enflamed by my emotions. Folding in on itself, arching, and stretching as if wanting to engulf the entire cavern.

And it could. There's nothing to hurt here.

Elated to the point that I could cry all over again, I watch the fire grow and fill the space, but the sputter and power of it knock over the lantern, shattering the glass.

Oops.

I scoop up the candle, reining in my emotions, and let the flame ride my shoulders like a bird as I move back to the stairs, careful to avoid the rocks and seemingly endless pools.

And exhaustion hits. Like I've run into a wall. But I have to make it up the stairs. Releasing the fire to conserve energy, I use the candle to light my way. One step. Another step.

Just make it to the top. We can do that.

And finally, I do, resting against the wall for a moment. Watching the candle and the fire whoosh happily as I recall what I've just done.

It may not be enough. But it's something. It's something. And I can live with that.

Staring at the candle, I sit in the ring of quivering light for a moment. The image of light sears into my eyelids before I blow it out, and it fades entirely into nothingness. I still see it when I blink, and it takes a moment for that to fade before I can set the wax onto the shelf.

I lean my elbows on my legs now. I'll just rest a moment before I go in...

Does all magic act like this? Does it require so high a price regardless of the kind? Or is it just fire?

Burning energy is costly.

Instead of opening the bookcase, I knock lightly. I hear the mechanism release, and white daylight pours into the space, outlining a dark figure. A familiar figure.

What a good sight.

He's quiet, calm. Doesn't ask. He just steps to my side and leans down to pick me up. I wrap my arms around his neck, nestling my face into his chest. And my heart gives a little burst, so much so I'd check for flames if I wasn't too tired to conjure.

I do care about this man. How could I not?

He carries me around the desk to the window seat, laying me down gently so I face the sea.

"Thank you," I whisper, trying to say so much with just one phrase, because I realize that all that stands between me and everything I feared in the grotto is him.

"You're welcome," he replies, gently smoothing the hair back from my face and pulling it back. It feels nice. Then he leans down and kisses my temple. I smile, reaching up to touch his cheek. The hairs of his beard prickle my hand.

"I did it," I say quietly.

"I know. And you did wonderfully," he answers.

"The lantern shattered."

"It's alright. We have plenty. Now rest."

His warmth and presence drift away, and I hear his footfalls as he goes back to the table. The papers crinkle. The chair creaks.

And a long, deep breath works through me as I gaze over the water. Gold sparkles dance on the blue waves.

I've earned this view now.

And finally, I can drift off to sleep.

CHAPTER 15

"Well, it's not a lot of notice," Atiene's voice breaks into my sleep.

"Yes, but you know how grouchy he can be after travel," Ilano replies. "Just give him what he wants, and he'll be more pliable."

My eyes pop open.

Give *who* what he wants? The king? Is Ilano telling Atiene to hand me over?

"You're the one who'll have to deal with him after I'm gone. It's your decision. Put him in both rooms if that's what he wants."

Oh...Tension melts from my shoulders. It's not about me.

Night has fallen outside, and I can't see beyond the window now. Only reflections from within.

I was out for a long while...

Stretching, I rise and turn around. Ilano sits in the chair with his feet up on the table now. The chair balances on the back legs while his hands relax over his stomach.

At my movement, both men turn.

"Ah! Sister," Ilano says, his eyes cutting to his brother to see his reaction. "We were just discussing dinner. You'll join us?"

"Is that allowed?" I ask, deciding not to encourage him in his choice of appellation by acknowledging it.

"Brother! Have you not courted her properly? For shame. One must wonder where your manners have gone. First, you kidnap her and her family, transport them in those horrible moving prisons, hide your identity from her, and pretend to beat her family." He clicks his tongue in a disapproving way.

Atiene says nothing to his brother's teasing, but as he rubs his face, a small, tolerant smile plays over his features.

"You embarrass him," I point out, standing now, and moving to the wall near the table.

"It would be no fun if he weren't embarrassed. And if he didn't *want* to be teased, he wouldn't have given you his coat." His eyebrow flicks up. And as his eyes land on Atiene, he laughs. "Why, Whistle, I do believe his cheeks are...flaming."

Atiene shakes his head, and his eyes land on the papers in front of them. He prods them together, waiting for his brother to get it all out.

Picking up on the game, I lean against the wall and reply. "They do look a bit...singed."

"Seared really," Ilano returns, as Atiene leans his elbow on the chair's arm and props his chin into his hand, eyes locked on Ilano's with amusement.

"I do feel a bit...warm," he says.

"Positively sizzling. Roasted like a pig on a spit," Ilano replies, pulling his legs down off the table and repositioning himself in the chair, so his hands are steepled as his elbows relax atop the armrests.

"Perhaps a little scorched?" I put in.

"Yes, too heated indeed. Perhaps a fever?" Ilano responds.

"Absolutely burning," Atiene affirms.

"Shall I fetch some water to quench the blaze?" Ilano asks.

"Yes, I can almost hear the crackle and pop."

"Red as embers, brother. One might worry over your health."

"Simply glowing," I add.

"That must be due to the spark," Ilano surmises, leaning towards me as if sharing a secret.

"Oh yes, sparks generally cause flares," I return.

"Indeed, the conflagration must be watched, or it'll get out of control." He winks at Atiene.

"Agreed, can't risk what comes after kindling if it catches," I answer.

"How do you stand the smolder, brother?"

"Just hope that all this won't go up in ashes and smoke," Atiene says, sweeping a gesture to the papers, his brother, and me.

"No worries, brother. I won't...torch our family name. And I'm sure your love won't...flicker out."

I drop my head, blushing. Atiene and I haven't discussed anything like that. It's far too soon. Especially in the middle of everything else. To speak the way Ilano does is somewhat inappropriate for a delicate thing. He knows. That's why he does it.

"Yes!" Ilano claims victory. "There *is* a threshold at which your dragon becomes sheepish. I've got you both."

"Perhaps you, too, might be sheepish under the circumstances," I suggest.

"No. Never," he asserts, wrinkling his nose as if such a thought is appalling. "When I fall in love, it'll be completely. Like drowning with no desire to reach the surface. There's no room for embarrassment in love. Embarrassment comes from shame. I'd never be ashamed to be in love."

He sends a look at Atiene, who blinks slowly in reply, his face lost in thought. I can't decipher it. Then Ilano turns that look on me, too, brows raised as if waiting for me to disagree. Locked in silence for a moment, we each wait for the other to do or say something.

The older brother rises, pushing his chair back, and walks towards me, extending his hand.

"Dinner should be ready soon. If you're inclined to do so, you should join us."

I smile and take his hand, and he tucks it in the crook of his arm. Safely. Securely.

"Worry not, Sister. We'll make a gentleman of him yet," Ilano says, springing from the chair and gesturing for his brother to lead the way. "Oh, and I have a surprise."

Atiene exhales as if he's used to this sort of thing.

"What is it?" he asks.

"This way," Ilano says, taking the lead. His lanky figure strides out ahead of us. Through the corridor to the servants' quarters. Unable to help myself, I look for my family or a light indicating that they're here, but all is dark.

Into the stables we go and emerge onto the courtyard. Braziers light the scene. A long, dark table stands covered in a red runner, gold place settings, candelabras between platters of bundles of grapes, and several seats waiting for guests. On a makeshift stage covered in red velvet stand several instruments and the remnants of my family tuning the instruments.

Alessi has changed into the golden and cream dress combination, but she has indeed added her own flair. With what she's trimmed off the bottoms, she's created bows that cascade down the bodice, tightened the sleeves to the elbows, and added a higher collar with stiff pleats that shoot upward off her neck and toward her hair that falls in curls as usual. She's kept her pink fabric flowers but added some gold ones. It's her, but in a more sophisticated sense.

She doesn't use the crutch anymore.

Della is dressed up, too, but her dress hasn't been altered. It's a little too big for her short stature. It puddles around her feet, so she has to keep lifting the skirt when she walks. And the stiff material stands off her bony shoulders when she turns her head. Her white-gray hair has been twisted and pinned up instead of left long, but she's retained her single earring.

Big Henri and Little Benji wear new clothes and hats.

They're more in costume now than they've ever been.

Surrilo is there. I wish I had been there for the reunion. He hobbles as if his leg pains him and reaches for a crutch, which I can see now propped up against a stand for the instruments. He pops the crutch under his shoulder as if he's been using one his whole life and moves around Della to get to one of the larger stringed instruments. He plucks a few strings, noting the depth of the sound. Leaning his head closer, he plucks the strings again and then points something out to Big Henri that I can't hear.

"No thanks necessary," Ilano says to both Atienc and me. And his brow is crooked up as if he's proud of himself. Then he claps his hands to get everyone's attention. "Welcome all to the feast this evening. It's been great meeting you all, and I'm excited to partake again of your talents. But first, let's eat."

Most of them filter to the table, but Surrilo lingers over the stage, plucking a string here, tapping a drum there. Servants appear to accommodate. Their faces are stone. And that says more to me than if they showed emotion. This must look so strange to those who are particular about class hierarchy and the maintenance thereof. Nobles don't entertain people like us. It's supposed to be the other way around.

Atiene leads me to a place beside the head of the table. He pulls out the chair for me, which is nice. But surprisingly, as I sit, he doesn't claim the seat the noble would command. He chooses the spot along the long side of the table. Not where a noble should be. Instead, Della is directed toward that position of honor. Her brow draws down as she blinks a few times, her eyes darting between the two noblemen, but neither indicates that she shouldn't take it, so she does. Her hands land on the table, resting over the utensils as she studies Atiene as if trying to understand why he'd give up his rightful place to her.

Big Henri sits on her left, across from me. Little Benji gets sandwiched between Big Henri and Surrilo. Surrilo shows the child what to do with his napkin.

Ilano takes the other 'head' or the tail of the table...And Alessi sits between Ilano and his brother. I wonder if she orchestrated that. If so, that's skill. If not, that's luck. I'm inclined to believe she had something to do with it, though. Peeking around Atiene at her, I see her leaning on her elbow towards the younger nobleman as if he's fascinating. Her shoulder dances in a gesture as she curls her hair around her finger. His focus is on her, and interest lines his brow. Part of me desperately wants to hear that conversation. I don't even care to participate. I just want to see how it goes.

Atiene takes my hand on the table and squeezes it to get my attention. When I look at him, he gestures to the candelabras and the flames reaching a little higher than they ought, as if trying to caress the stars. Wax drips down the sides, melting faster than it ought to.

Oh, curse.

Is this what life is now? Controlling my emotions at *every* moment? Am I no longer allowed to just *enjoy* where I'm at? Perhaps if fire is far away, and I've no intention of sparking...That's a higher cost than I was prepared for. It'd better be worth it.

But I close my eyes, chest tight, and breathe out slowly, counting as I do. And I feel the release. As I open my eyes, the fire settles.

"Mother Della," Ilano says from the opposite side of the table, "If you don't mind, would you lead this evening?"

The old woman's lined features lift in a smile, and she slips back into her matriarchal role, raising her hands to direct the servants to bring food. They serve her first. She tests each thing before it's served, gesturing when things ought to be taken away from the table or passed along.

As she sends one servant away, Ilano shoots a look at Atiene with delight in his brow. His mouth hides behind his clasped hands. Elbows resting on the table, he savors the reactions of my family who taste vegetables, fruits, and fish. Each person is given a tiny loaf of bread just for themselves with butter. Our goblets are filled with some kind of juice that tastes like a mix of several fruits.

"What is this?" I ask Atiene, and Della's earring tinkles as she turns to listen.

"Grape, pear, and a splash of citrus. Ilano's favorite."

"It's delicious."

All of it is delicious. Though I'm not entirely sure why Ilano did it. To amuse himself? To tease Atiene? To make a point? Or is his motive more benevolent than I suspect? Is he just genuinely doing a nice thing, and I'm picking it apart because I'm me?

It feels more...settled than my family dinners usually are. We'd just sit around the cookfire, hang out of the back of the wagons, or even just grab something easy like bread and cheese before rehearsing. It's formal to sit at a table that's laid like this with servants moving between us and all around us. Structured. Stiff.

Caught between wanting to eat more and wanting to throw up, I finally put my fork down. It seems most of my family feel similarly. Except for Big Henri. Surrilo passes his plate down to the giant, so he can finish it off.

"Some music?" Surrilo says, and I see his fingers twitch as if already playing. Ilano nods and gestures him away. The entertainer shoots up from his chair and heads back over to the stand.

Alessi heads over too, eager to show her abilities. Her hand trails along Ilano's chair as she passes behind. Little Benji wiggles off his chair and moves to join the two.

"Tonight, you just dance," Surrilo says, keeping the boy from the instruments.

"Atiene, will you not join them?" Ilano asks with his brows raised. "Mother Della, I'm sure you'd be surprised at how well he can play. Perhaps you might persuade him."

The old woman raises her brows at Atiene now, but she remains silent. Her eyes turn inward as if considering whether or not she should push him.

He takes care of that for her, saying, "I will play if Whistle will dance."

"With fire?" I ask ruefully since his guards and servants are still around.

"If you want."

I pause, my eyes raking his face for clues as to whether he means it. His eyes gaze earnestly, and his face is relaxed.

Slowly, a smile spreads across my face, and I say, "We'll have to blow out the candles, but keep the braziers lit."

We rise, but I still have his coat on, so I hurriedly shake it off my arms and drape it over the chair, while he snuffs the candles on the table. He takes my hand, and we join the others.

Atiene grabs a gittern, plucking a few strings to test the sound. Then his fingers work expertly as the sound spills out. Surrilo's eyes flick from the instrument to the man, mouth slightly ajar as he assesses the skill. Then he picks up a flute while Alessi takes a timbrel.

Both pick up the tone of his playing and then join. Alessi, with a staccato sort of beat, interrupted by the tap of her hand. Surrilo with a melody that seems to wrap itself around Atiene's tune.

And Atiene looks at me now as if to say, 'I did my part. Now it's your turn,' but I'm enjoying the moment. I want this memory to appear forever in my mind exactly as I see, feel, and hear it now.

But eventually, I do reach for fire in the closest brazier, bringing it to me like a scarf, whipping it around my shoulders, and then flinging it off the other side. Snapping it back, I catch the other side of it and spiral it around me before shooting it into the sky and letting it burst like stars and fall like bits of ash, fizzling out before it lands on anyone or anything. I like that one.

Calling flames from the brazier again, I twist and twirl with them, stretching, wrapping the fire around my arms, and letting bits of it die as if it melts into me. Then I let it flare around me.

Proud of myself for controlling it well, I get bolder, sending the flickers out just a little farther and farther. Catching some of the blaze in my hand, I hold it up to my face and 'breathe' it out like a dragon. Not close to anyone or anything. Just safe in the gravel. But it's exhilarating to see what I can do, how big it can get. Twin swirls anchored in the rocks, large and reaching upward with me.

My insides bubble with the realization that this creation is mine. It responds to my will. To my emotion. The connection is raw, instantaneous, and complete. I suppress a shiver, twirling in the light of my fire.

I sense the end of the song coming, so I clap my hands to dissipate the flames. The light disappears all at once, leaving the courtyard significantly darker and silent.

After a beat of quiet. Alessi begins to sing, and Surrilo switches his flute for a fiddle. Big Henri comes to gather the drums to pat out a beat. A little tired, I pull out the whistle, melting back toward the stand to accompany them and give Alessi her moment. Atiene's fingers fly over the strings, adding a pretty backdrop for Alessi's soprano.

I keep the whistle's tune two lower notes away from Alessi's voice to create a soft sort of harmony. And at times, leaving off to create a sort of echo for her. Recognizing what I'm doing, she smiles, shooting me a quick look.

And we all get lost in the music, letting it exist outside of us. But halfway through, the gittern quiets, leaving a hole. I turn to Atiene to see why he's stopped, and he sets the gittern back on its stand. Then he holds his hand out to me as if asking me to dance.

Popping the whistle back into the holder, I take his hand, and we move onto the gravel to get some space. He shows me the proper way to place my hand on his arm, and then he places his hand on my waist.

Then he teaches me what certain pressures mean. Come closer. Move back. Twirl. At first, it's hard to make my feet follow this new constraint, moving when they should be and not moving when they shouldn't, but eventually a pattern emerges. I could get it with more practice.

I hear Della say, "Tomorrow may bring ruin, so tonight we live."

"Well, spoke, Mother Della. Words to live by," Ilano commends. "Shall we join them?"

He rises and helps the old lady out of her chair. She points to the instruments, saying something I can't hear while she hobbles along with Ilano supporting her. She takes up the timbrel that Alessi had and shakes the thing, so it tinkles to the beat.

Alessi smiles at Ilano as she continues to sing.

The song changes, picking up tempo. Not one that has words to sing. One for dancing, so Alessi moves away from the stage. Her boots tap the ground in rapid steps, heels then toes, kicking out in her boots as she holds her skirts. Swishing her dress this way and that, she moves and twirls. Her hands reach over her head to the sky as her face turns upward.

And it echoes everything we're feeling right now.

But all too soon, tomorrow presses onto my mind, seeping into my thoughts and then into the falling of my smile and the weariness in my movements. Of course, I want to enjoy all of this while I can, but I can't push off the inevitable simply by dancing.

As the others tire, the revel dies. And soon Surrilo alone soaks in as many of the instruments as he can while the servants clear away the dishes. Big Henri lets Della lean on him while they shuffle towards the servants' quarters. Little Benji rubs his eyes and follows. Alessi stares at the sky as if she can capture it and take it with her. Or join it.

I feel more like she does. Going to sleep only brings tomorrow closer. However, trying to hold off the dawn feels like cowardice. And besides that, the waiting in daylight will be infinitely worse.

I squeeze Atiene's hand lightly and then let go to check on my sister. I know Alessi hears me coming, but she doesn't turn.

"I never thought it might end this way," she whispers so the others don't hear. "I keep thinking we may not be a whole family after tomorrow."

"You're afraid, too, huh?"

"Of course, I'm afraid," she says as if it's a stupid question.

I don't reply. I don't think she needs one.

She inhales deeply and closes her eyes as she blows out her breath. Then she clears her throat and discreetly wipes away a tear while the men aren't looking.

"It may not be the end, but a new beginning?" I suggest. If the plan works, then certainly.

"Beginnings are almost as insufferable as endings."

Surrilo finally puts down the gittern. His face almost looks pained to leave the instrument behind, but he squares his shoulders and removes himself from temptation.

"We'll get through this? That's what we do?" Alessi says, watching him walk back to the servant's quarters with his crutch. "If Surrilo has the strength to leave all those behind, I can leave this island...This sky, these stars...this is my home. What if they're different after this?"

It starts as sarcasm and ends in truth. I push my lips together in sympathy and nod. She drops her head until it rests against mine for a moment, and we stare at the stars a moment longer.

She exhales dramatically.

"I'll relinquish you to your admirer now." Then she turns and gets Ilano's attention. "A woman needs an escort. Would you be a dear and assist me?"

He grins and then holds out his arm for her. She takes it with both hands, letting her skirts swish just a little more emphatically as she walks with him.

"This was beautiful," I tell Atiene as he steps to my side.

"Ilano knows, but I'm sure he'd love to hear it from you."

"If things go poorly tomorrow, will you take care of them?" I ask. Atiene's gaze meets mine.

"It's not going to go poorly," he answers.

"On the streets, we knew everything could go poorly. And it did. More than once. Remember that raid you planned on the butcher's shop?"

He smiles because while it was a fiasco, we did sit around the fire underneath the bridge telling stories about it for a few weeks after.

"This isn't like that," he answers.

"No. I know." That's what scares me.

He pulls me into a hug and kisses my forehead. "It'll be okay." His voice sounds deeper, like it comes from his chest, but the warmth of his statement doesn't quite reach my heart. *If* it happens to work out, then I'll relax. It's not pessimistic. It's realistic.

He senses that I haven't accepted it because he says, "You wanna know what I'm thinking about?"

"What?"

"How it will be when your family is together singing, playing, and dancing on the deck of a ship. Happy. Maybe a little seasick. But heading towards something better for them."

I smile at the thought and wrap my arms around his neck, wishing I had his optimism. I'll believe it when I see it.

He pulls back and walks me to the room.

Ilano leans against the wall while Alessi half hides behind the door as if she were in the process of closing it but got stalled. A game. And he knows it. But he's amused by it, so he allows her to reel him just a bit and keep him just far enough away.

The game ends when Ilano sees Atiene, though. He pushes off the wall and bids Alessi goodnight. Atiene kisses my hand, and we part ways.

Alessi closes the door without looking back.

“Do you think there’ll be fine gentlemen on the mainland?” she asks, brushing scraps of cloth from her bed and lying down with a hand behind her head.

“Most certainly,” I answer as she fiddles with a curl.

She flicks her eyebrows at me.

“Take care of that, will you?” she says, gesturing to the candle. “I’m already in bed.”

I reach my hand out to the flame and pluck it out of the air, closing it in my fist.

Chapter 16

Sleep comes so fitfully, I'm annoyed when outside begins to gray. I flip onto my stomach and hide my face from the window, wishing I could put the sun away for a few more hours.

As long as I can get back to sleep-

"Whistle?" Surrilo's voice reaches through the door with a quick knock. I groan and pull the blanket over my face.

So much for getting back to sleep.

"Go away," Alessi calls. I snort a laugh.

"We gotta practice for tonight," he returns.

"Good to know some things never change," she answers. She shifts on her mattress, pushing herself up tiredly and rubbing her eyes.

I groan. Gotta be responsible.

"I'll be there in a minute," I reply. And I hear his crutch plunking on the floor as he goes down the corridor. I'm sure it's that loud on purpose. A call for pity. Pity for a thing that didn't happen...

Oh...*this* is why they don't trust me with acting.

I stick out my tongue and roll my eyes. But I do push myself up and off the mattress, changing into my costume today because it'll feel more natural while I'm practicing.

"Good luck," Alessi says, fluffing her hair. She lets out a yawn.

"Same," I answer.

I run my fingers through my hair quickly and go out into the corridor. No knights this morning.

Hmm...

Hurrying to the study, I pass the hall, but my attention is pulled by Surrilo playing with the instruments.

"Are we practicing here today?" I ask.

"Yep. Gotta get comfortable in the space. And it'll be easier to see and feel the movements here." And then he dives right in, pointing me to where I'll be and tapping his foot while he waits for me to get into position. Then he launches into what he'd like the final result to look like, where I ought to direct fire and when. Without actually conjuring or directing it now, so I can conserve my energy for tonight.

We recreate his masterpiece from the grotto with a few changes. He has me run through it again and again. More so than we'd do for an audience in a town square. But this is the *king* we're performing for, and that comes through his tone and the way he stands with his hip cocked, mouth pursed, eyes judging.

And I'm tired enough by the fifth rehearsal, but he stands stiffly, one hand across his chest while the other props up his chin.

"Let's see that last bit again," he says through a heavy exhale. I do it exactly as he directed. "No, something's not right. From the beginning."

Chin lifting in a long-suffering gesture, I blow out my cheeks as I reset. And then I do the whole thing again.

At the end, he's silent. He taps his forehead while he thinks. Then he paces and hums the music. Finding himself before the instruments, he takes the gittern and plucks a few notes out, letting them die without being tied to anything tangible.

He sets the thing aside abruptly and directs me into a different sort of ending with the flourish he wants. Once I have it down, he declares it good enough and shoos me away, so he can fiddle with the music to his heart's content.

He's really going to miss these instruments.

Alone now, I consider heading to the study. But there's so much of the castle that I haven't seen, and it would be a shame to not see it all before I leave. Moving to the foyer, I climb the stairs to the second level. The landing protrudes over the hall only a little, and I can see the chandelier almost eye-level. Peering over the edge, I see Surrilo nodding to a beat only he can hear. Then he transfers the beat to his foot. It taps while he draws out some notes on the fiddle. From here, the purr of the instrument is positively haunting.

It's a good view of the hall, but not what I came for, so I look around.

Corridors stretch away from me on either side, so I go left.

Not sure how it'll be taken if I'm discovered here, I stay silent. But then I wonder if it'll *look* like I'm sneaking if someone comes upon me, and I'm being silent...on purpose.

I don't find a solution to that quandary. I don't care enough to make one. I'm just going to be quiet anyway.

The walls are white with some of the plasterwork of the lower levels, but not in the shapes of grapes and vines. More of it is stiff, column-like, with gold accents around the tops and on the doors.

I tread carefully to one of the closed doors. Gripping the handle, the cold feels like a shock to my palm. I turn it, holding my breath as I push the door open.

A soft, inviting sort of feel opens immediately. Walls painted like the sky with the moldings left white. Sheer, white drapes fall over the window. The canopy bed is made of dark wood, and the soft-looking blanket is embroidered with a darker blue thread.

I can imagine Atiene here, throwing open the curtains to gaze at the sea. But this room doesn't look lived in.

I turn to go, closing the door silently behind me. Continuing down the corridor, eager to find more beautiful things, I hear voices coming from one of the rooms with an open door. Pausing because I don't want to be found, I listen.

"Yes, but it's only for one more day. Then the king will take them away," a voice says.

"I heard the Chelees made some sort of deal with the king," asks another voice.

My heart stops, and my breath seems far too loud now. I hear it echoing inside me as I fight to contain it, so I can hear.

"What? For the fire girl?" A blanket fwips from inside the room. "Who told you that?"

"It's all over the market in town. The king commanded his steward to prepare the hunt through the king's forests. To make it more sporting, he's giving her a head start. But everyone knows his hounds are unmatched. They'll have her like that." Someone snaps their fingers. "He's set, and you know he gets what he wants. He'll have her head on a pike just like the others. Everybody knows."

"*I* didn't."

"Now you do." Another blanket snaps out.

Heat and prickles rise on my cheeks and the back of my head.

"What does the Chelees get out of the deal?"

"Not sure, but we'll know soon enough, eh?"

"Either way, it'll be nice when they're gone. The bonfires and music are un*bearable*."

"After tonight, it'll only be a memory. How long do you think that fire girl will last during the hunt?"

"Sounds like you're looking for a wager."

"Perhaps. I think-"

A slight shuffle of carpet from behind makes me jump, and I whirl quickly, heart thrumping in my chest. Ilano's eyes slide from the open door to me. He holds up his hand in a 'be quiet' gesture. Then he motions with his head that I should follow him.

Swallowing against the dryness invading my throat, I follow. Not bothering to stay silent anymore. I don't care that the servants (I assume they're servants) hear me now.

Ilano strides out through the corridor, and I follow over the landing again and down the right wing of the castle. Unfortunately, I don't have the time to admire or explore it now. Ilano makes it to a spiral staircase, kicking his long legs out as he descends. He looks back to make sure I'm still behind him.

I am, sliding my hand over the polished wood banister, wondering if I should be going with him or not. I trust Atiene. I don't believe for a moment that he made a deal with the king. It's likely just idle talk that one was struck. Perhaps a story put around by the king to press Atiene or to circulate stories that enforce his perceived power. But Ilano asking me to be quiet and follow him instead of confronting the servants feels a bit like hiding. Like covering something. That's uncomfortable.

Ilano hits the bottom step, lengthening his stride as he reaches for a door that leads outside. Sunlight strikes the floor, and I see bushes and flowers beyond. He waits for me to go through. I do, questioning him with a glance. His face is stone as he gestures to the path that opens up before us. Cream-colored stones mark a track through the carefully kept garden, but several feet ahead, they fork, one heading left, one heading right. Having never been in the gardens before, I'm not sure which way to go. Pretty flowers dot the bushes on either side. So, it would seem as if one way is just as good as the other. But I know one side leads to the courtyard and the gate. The other leads to the cliff overlooking the sea.

"Tensions are high today," Ilano remarks as he walks beside me. "What you heard was just humans being human."

Coming to the fork, I take the path to the left.

"I'm not bothered by what they think of us. That's not what worried me," I reply.

"You can't think Atiene would have made a deal."

"No."

"Good. Because he didn't."

Stiffness leaves my shoulders, and I breathe, pausing by a purple flower sticking out of a bush. I tilt it toward my nose. It's subtle, but sweet.

"He was offered everything the king could think of. And *threatened* with everything the king could think of. He wouldn't budge. *Hasn't* budged."

"What was he offered?" I ask, pulling away from the flower now.

"First-tier title, castles, wealth, vineyards, farms, ships. The king is desperate."

"What was he threatened with?" My fingers play over the velvety petals.

"*Is* threatened with. Imprisonment, being stripped of his title, lands, ships, wealth, and beatings. Lifelong torture. Execution isn't on the table. The king won't hear of an 'early release' for Atiene."

I can't look Ilano in the eye, so I drop my gaze and my hand. Hearing it, knowing it...my stomach churns. But I can't do anything about it now. The king demanded. Atiene refused. It's already done. Even if I wanted to save him from all he's done. All he's risking...I couldn't.

Ilano continues, "The king will leave with what he wants, or he will destroy my brother."

"No, he won't." *Because I will burn him.*

An amused smile flits about his mouth. "Isn't that the comfort we all give ourselves? That we can change things in a world that so singularly does *not* care? Don't we wish we could make it care? That somehow, someway, there's something we can do to make a mark? So, we matter in all this chaos before the end?"

I don't know how that's relevant. In life, there's what is and what isn't. And I *will* burn.

But I wait for him to continue.

"Atiene was never comfortable in this life. It stifled him. He ran away because our father loved me more. Pure blood. More...aptitude for politics." He smiles. "Atiene never held that against *me*, though, and we were always as close as brothers could be despite it. Nevertheless, he escaped once, tasted freedom, and he's been looking for a way out ever since. Did his duty all this time to honor the memory of our ancestors. And I think because it afforded him some space to do things he might not otherwise have been able to do. Like search for you. The point is that he's perfectly happy leaving all this behind. The one regret he has is that I won't be coming with."

"You could," I suggest.

He shakes his head and plucks the purple flower that I smelled. "No. This is my life. I love my brother more than anything in this world, but in order to keep all of this intact...to do right by us all...certain things are coming tonight that will seem to you to be harsh. Call it selfish if you like, but don't burn me for it, please."

His eyebrows lift as he smells the flower too. And then he shoots me an amused, yet intent look. He's waiting. He wants an answer. I feel it in the air, playing over my arms and face. The power dynamic has shifted. His eyes have never been leveled at me like this before. His brow hasn't had that set about it.

I don't understand what he's really saying, but I doubt I'll get a clear answer if I ask.

So, I nod as if I understand. And he claps a hand on my shoulder.

"My thanks, Sister. I won't be able to take care of him after this. Too much will move too quickly. Make sure he doesn't miss me too much, will you?"

Despite the hazy nature of the conversation, I smile. "I'm not sure that's possible."

He breathes a sort of laugh. "You're right. My absence will destroy him. The poor man. And you know, you're not how he described you before. I'd always thought him fanciful for chasing a memory all this time. But seeing you now, flesh and blood...getting to know your family. That's the dynamic he's been missing all along."

Somehow this feels like saying 'goodbye.' I don't know how to respond. It feels more like it's about *him* than Atiene.

"Well, enjoy the garden. I have business to attend to," he says. Tucking the flower into his tunic, he shoots me one last meaningful look. Then his face turns rueful again.

His hand drops from my shoulder as he turns on his heel, boots clacking against the stones. He touches his head in a friendly sort of salute before he goes through the door. Cut off from him now, I'm not entirely sure what we discussed.

What just happened?

I stand still for a moment, thinking. Finding no answers, I continue on the path until it slithers along the cliffs overlooking the sea. I pause here, looking down off the edge at the blue water breaking in white on the rocks. Battering over and over as if it can make a difference. And I suppose it does...through time. But certainly not enough in my lifetime to take note of.

A breeze lifts my hair and toys with my costume. It's a little chilly. Or maybe that's just me.

I'm not behind glass, looking out now. There's nothing between me and the sea but a long drop, and the wind teases and tousles at me as if I could just jump. If I look long enough at the waves, I'm sure I'll lose my balance and fall. The thought rattles me enough that I take a step back.

What did he mean? Is this part of the plan? Why was he warning me? Or was he extracting a promise from me? Or both?

'Don't burn me.'

Why would he need to say that?

My brow crunches as I try to reason it out, but I know that I'll just have to wait.

CHAPTER 17

My fingers dance and jitter as I walk back down the corridor to the servants' quarters. I shake them out to release the unnerving urge to shudder. My breath comes too fast, so I take command of it. Allowing it to fill my lungs to capacity and slowly letting it trail from my mouth. It helps a little.

It does nothing to combat the real issue.

The sun descends in the west, too slow and too fast all at once. Every tick of movement calls out to every nerve in my body to arrest its movement. And yet part of me wishes to hasten it so I can get this over with.

As I push open the door to my room, Alessi drops her red cloth project into her lap.

"There you are. Hurry up, you've got to try this on," she says, standing and holding the thing out to me.

"I'm not in the mood to try on clothes," I answer.

"I did all this work, so you'd have something striking for tonight, per request of Surrilo and your Chelees. So...give it a try."

Confused about why they'd have requested a new outfit for me, I take the dress and hold it up. The loose sleeves she's been working on hang on either side of the red underdress we were given. The bodice has black laces crisscrossing down the front. The skirt is loose enough to move in, but not puffed or wide.

It's a peasant-ish outfit. But somehow *dressed up* because of the sleek material and the additions she's made, like the different belt.

"I like it, it's just...ancient-looking," I remark, avoiding the phrase 'old-fashioned,' because I don't want a lecture.

She rolls her eyes as if I clearly don't understand. "It's *supposed* to look ancient. Like the dragons of old." She plucks up the sleeve, admiring her work.

"Ah!" Story.

"And...there are accessories," she says with a grin. She claps her hands and moves to the table, holding up a long necklace with rubies hanging off. And a headpiece of silver-gold with a ruby in the middle.

My hands find my stomach, touching my old costume. I get why they want the change, but is it...necessary? Why do I have to wear the new thing? I'm perfectly comfortable in my old costume. It's...cozy? Home? A piece of who I've been?

"You don't like it," she accuses.

"It's not the clothes or the things."

"Do you know how many times I poked my fingers with needles and pins making this dress? You don't get to back out now. Just put it on. You'll feel like a new person."

"That's what I'm afraid of," I answer, but I drop the dress over the back of the chair, and she turns to give me privacy to change. I remove the old, orange costume like shedding a skin, and the person I wish

I could stay. The girl who danced and played her whistle as Surrilo's partner on the makeshift stage in front of simple audiences. Moving from city to city with my family.

I hold up the red dress, facing it: the person they want me to be. Then I turn it around and slip it over my head. Putting my hands through the sleeves, I feel the smooth material sliding over my arms. It falls onto my shoulders and settles over the rest of me. And I do feel different in this outfit. Like stepping back in time and into armor.

That's not at all how I thought it would feel. It's...strange...and also comfortable. I can't find the right word.

"What do you think?" I ask, letting her know she can turn now.

Her eyes light up as her hands clasp with delight.

"My work is stunning. See what I've turned you into." I turn to the mirror, but she stops me. "Wait, no...accessories first. Gotta get the full effect."

She hands me the long necklace as she takes the headpiece and pulls it over my hair. The little cold ruby bounces against my forehead as she pins and tucks the rest of it into my hair, so it won't move when I dance.

I slip the necklace over my head, and it settles over the top of the dress, dripping as if the rubies melt.

"Aww! It matches your scowl perfectly," she says, wiping away a fake tear. "Okay, now you can see."

She snatches the mirror from the table, turning it so I can see myself.

There I am, though I'm not sure it's me in the finery. Bits of silver-gold strings drizzle over my dark hair. The golden headpiece pulls away from the ruby as if merely holding the thing like a burning droplet.

The dress hugs my frame in the middle, but the rest is loose so I can still move the way I need to.

I look fierce. And beautiful in a mythical way. This one's not a costume. Not really. This is what the ancient beings wore. Those whose blood flows in my veins. Those who fought for their lives, bled, and were killed merely because they had magic. Because they could command elements. I feel connected to them now. Their struggles are mine.

Power. *That's* the word. That's how this feels.

My blood tingles in my veins, and I feel the fire waking in my chest.

I've never wanted to be a dragon as badly as I do right now.

"See?" she says, vindicated.

"You did all this?" I ask, stunned and grateful.

"I'd never pass up an opportunity to show off my skills. And if I ever do, you know something's seriously wrong with me." She tilts the mirror on the table and steps behind me to fuss over the shoulders a bit more, and then she hugs me from behind with her arms draped over my shoulders, peeking into the mirror.

"Let's hear you roar," she teases.

I roll my eyes. She laughs.

"It's gonna be okay," she says. "Now, go find Surrilo and show off my creation."

Forcing out a breath, I peek out the window to see how far the night has progressed. Golden glow sinks into darkness. I can't see the sun, but I assume it's surrendered to the ocean by now. Quickly, I grab my whistle, because I won't be caught dead without it. And of course, some of my lock picks. I pop on my boots again, because I don't want to have to come back for them.

Alessi gestures impatiently to hurry me along. And I go, looking back to see her bend to pick up scraps of cloth off the floor. She catches my look and gives me a wink. And I pass through the liminal space into the corridor.

Ignoring strange looks from the servants, I lift my skirt and stride out toward the hall. Breaking into the space feels like falling through a layer of ice into a pond where cold water shocks my lungs.

How did they get this up so fast? It looks completely different.

The couches have been moved back to allow a hole in the center hemmed in by two tables. They're laden with golden plates, bowls, goblets, and utensils. A red runner trails down the center, accenting the piles of fruits and vegetables in pretty formations. Flowers scatter across the table as well.

The instruments have been set in front of the large window, the drapes of which are still open wide. Despite the sun's disappearance and the dying light over the sea, the large room is well-lit with the chandelier and candles along the walls. The fire in the hearth blazes. All these flames respond to my emotions as soon as I enter, fluttering a little higher. Atiene notices and turns.

He's wearing a dark blue and black striped velvet vest over a white tunic with loose arms. His hair has been combed back but has fallen a little unruly around his face and over his ears. Black trousers and black boots. I assume he'll put on one of those fancy jackets later.

His eyes take in the dress and the accessories, and then his gaze meets mine with a smile. He scoots a chair out of his way as he meets me on the threshold of the corridor and the hall.

He takes my hand and kisses it. "I'd ask how you're feeling, but…" he gestures to the fires.

"Ah." I breathe, trying to calm myself and them. Slowly they recede. A little. Only a little. Not enough, which pricks like panic in my chest. I swallow and try again to breathe the flames down by calming those inside.

Atiene can see the struggle, so he places his hands on the sides of my head and touches his forehead against mine, smiling at the ruby between us, pressing into both our foreheads. My hands find his arms, and my eyes close.

"It'll be okay," he whispers. "You can relax. I've got you."

"You've got *everything*," I answer, remembering what Ilano told me earlier. "What can I do for you?"

He pulls away. My eyes open, finding him.

"Just be you."

Knowing he means that douses the fear, quenching anxiety with a soothing balm. It feels the way the pool in the grotto does. The soft, luminous glow of blue light on the rocks. The silence of the place. The encasing of oneself. And the mesmerizing shafts of sunlight playing through the waves. Like an invitation to plunge in.

The fire dies down to a safer level.

He takes my hand.

"Come. See what we've done."

He leads me through the foyer that's decorated with plants and flowers that spill out of vases and twine down the staircases. The greenery adds life to this stone place.

Out the front door and over the balcony, the courtyard is lit with several braziers. The walkway is lined with them, and so is the outer edge of the garden, where streamers hang from bushes and trees. In the center, a fountain gurgles, water cascading into a large basin. Lanterns string from the castle to the gate, lit like fireflies. And down the lane past the gate, lights bob, hanging from the trees to light the way.

It's entrancing in the near dark of dusk. I want to dance underneath those lights. Maybe the way Atiene taught me last night. I do need the practice.

He squeezes my hand. "The king's ship arrived in the port two hours ago. He'll be here any moment."

The magic fades from this beautiful scene. I drop my gaze. My fingernail plays over the cracks in the stone banister.

The splash of water is accompanied by the strings of crickets in the forest. And from afar off, a rattle like a carriage drifts towards us. I look down the lane, but I can't see it.

"You should find Surrilo and prepare," Atiene says quietly.

"Okay," I respond, releasing his hand. Before I go, I stand on my tiptoes and kiss his cheek. "Whatever happens, I…and this…and you…" My throat seizes, and my mind trips over what I can't say. What exactly do I want to say? I'm not even sure. So, I just look at him, hoping he understands.

He smiles and touches my cheek gently. "Go."

Turning, I head back into the castle. Seeing the castle as the king will see it. The pretty things meant to impress. But more specifically, a direct line to the window in the hall. No. Not the window. Because there's nothing to see there now but the reflection of fire. That space between the tables is the stage.

It's me. The first thing he'll see is me. Framed perfectly.

Surrilo strides into the hall as if he's in charge. Glancing around at the tables, the instruments, the lights, and everything, he moves a chair here and a couch there.

"Ready?" he asks.

"Just like old times."

"And new times," he says, wiggling his brows. "This isn't our last performance."

He goes to the stand, taking up the instruments as Alessi appears in her golden and cream dress. Della leans heavily on Big Henri's arm and hobbles with a new cane and settles herself beside the instruments.

Little Benji, hair combed, joins them. Surrilo hands him a tinkling instrument.

At least we're together. No matter what.

A horse's whinny sounds through the foyer and into the hall as the clop of hooves bounces off the stone.

He's here.

It's time. But I can't shove down the terror because I'll need it. Just have to manage it.

Surrilo meets my gaze. "Remember what we talked about."

I nod, moving to the center of the room underneath the chandelier. Reaching for the fire in the room, I swallow the light with the flick of my wrist. Darkness falls in the hall, and we wait in silence.

Through the open door, I hear garbled voices. I strain to make out their speech, but I can't decipher.

Two lanterns remain in the foyer near the bottom of the stairs. There are no lights atop the balcony, so the extent of it reaches just outside the hall itself. Surrilo's flair for the dramatic.

Through the open door, I see figures moving. I can pick out Atiene and Ilano, who leans against the banister as he pulls off his glove, laughing at something the king says.

"Of course, your majesty. Of course," he says. "Welcome. We've taken the liberty of providing a little entertainment with dinner."

He pushes off the banister to lead the way.

"Your house is dark. You ought to beat your servants," another voice says, "Have the lanterns lit at once."

"Highness, this is part of the show," Ilano says as if sharing a secret. "The entertainers have prepared something special for you. I can assure you it's positively magical."

"Then you go first," the king commands, moving into the view of the door now.

He's shorter than Atiene with a dark wig of curls falling down his front. He sports a golden coat with many buttons down. Over his arms is draped a long, decadent-looking brown fur. His face is soft, but the hanging of his jowls pronounces his age along with the droop of his eyes and crook of his nose.

"Of course," Atiene says, leading the way. He comes down the foyer and stands just inside the hall underneath the balcony. Between the king and me, so I can't see the man anymore. I hear Ilano's easy stride across the stone floor, and then the king sends his guards in too, standing along the walls and moving into the space around the tables. I hear the clatter of chairs and the scrape of their weapons as they maneuver.

We're surrounded...nearly.

"Where's the optimal viewing position?" the king asks as he walks slowly through the home, so that he's backlit by the candles in the foyer. Just a shadow now. A specter for us to perform to.

Ilano pulls up a couch for him to sit on and snaps at a servant to fetch refreshment, as the king settles onto the soft cushions.

I open my mouth and let out the breath I've been holding. Swallowing at the sudden dryness in my throat, wishing for something to drink as my throat clicks.

Atiene moves aside now, taking a chair from the table and sitting to the side of the king. Ilano stands behind the noble, arms crossed.

"Well then. Begin," the king demands.

I roll my shoulders back, stretching my neck high.

Just like being on stage.

Releasing the pent-up emotions, I let a tiny flame loose in my hand. Just a little one. Just enough to see that it's there. The orange light plays on my sleeves and the bodice of my dress. And then, waving my hand in front of the blaze, it disappears as if blown out. Then I produce another flame.

But I don't make this one disappear.

I act as if I'll quench it, instead, moving it to my other hand, building it into three little flames that bob in the air by themselves, feeding off my energy. Giving them life, I let them swirl at the ends of my fingers, flitting and whooshing as they move through the air, melding into one as they settle with my hand, still glowing.

Then, bringing my other hand in front of my chest, I light it too.

Then the music starts. The fiddle lets out a long, energizing sort of note. And other instruments join in their turn. Alessi on the gittern. Big Henri on the drums. The thump echoes the beating in my ribs. The gittern and fiddle duel with their melodies, each trying to claim the honor of the ear.

Twisting my arms, the flames dance around each other, sometimes merging as if old friends and then dividing as enemies. I separate them like streamers falling on either side of me. Then I fling them both to the side, allowing them to fade just a little before calling them both back, so they splash into each other, sending sparks and flares that make my audience hide their eyes.

As the blaze mingles, I pull one side up and the other down, twisting my arms so the tides chase one another. I toss them both like scarves, allowing them to connect and spread into a disc-like structure overhead. Little drops like rain, spill out of it, falling around me like sparks that bounce on the floor.

Twirling with it, I draw some of it back down towards me, making it curl around my arm like a serpent, and then around my torso, and off my other arm. It reaches out like a snake's head, but I don't let it get too far. I snap to make it fold back on itself.

Swirling my arms together, I weave the fire in and out of itself, passing through me and around, making it bounce with the thump of the drums along my arms and over my shoulders. Clearly, building it around myself like a shield.

The music swells, and the king leans forward in his seat.

I throw my hands to the sides. Above my head, wreathed in fire, is the face of a dragon, snarling and hissing. As I let the fire snap and pop, its body builds out behind me until its wings spread across the hall.

Then I turn the dragon loose. Rising in the air, it shoots towards the chandelier, but before it gets too out of hand, I swirl my hand as if erasing the majority of the beast. Allowing the candles to be lit, but nothing else to burn.

The light spreads through the space now, and as our eyes adjust, I blow fire like a kiss to the remaining candles in the room, so that the whole hall is lit like before.

Relieved that the push and pull of emotion inside is working, I pull more to me now to finish off the dance with a flourish as the music dies. And I sink into a bow as the fire I hold filters around me and dies out.

"Marvelous," the king says. "The hunt will be spectacular. After the rumors, I wasn't sure she'd be up to it. But it seems she's more capable than was reported."

"She's quite adept, Majesty," Ilano assures, with his eyes cutting to me as if trying to communicate something.

"More, then," the king demands. "And bring the feast. I'll eat here."

Atiene gestures to the servants to bring a small table and food for the king.

"For your guards too, Highness?" he suggests, pointing to the tables.

"No, they'll remain on alert for this one." He gestures to me.

"If I may," Ilano says, leaning toward the king like he's an old friend. "She won't try anything while we have her family captive. In fact, that's how we've kept her subdued this whole time."

"I heard it was because Atiene romanced her," the king says with an eyebrow raised.

"That too. She'll do anything to protect those she loves." His eyes land on me for a beat too long.

"Then Atiene and her family will come along with me tomorrow," the king says as the servants place a large ham, a drumstick, bread, and an array of fruits and vegetables on the new table in front of the king.

What does he mean?

He looks from the food to me. "I said more."

I bow my head in reply, but my jaw ticks as I look back at Surrilo, who puts the fiddle under his chin and strikes up a tune.

"She doesn't listen well," the king remarks. "No matter. I'll have that beaten out of her."

"Her obstinance might make the hunt more enjoyable," Ilano suggests.

Alessi replaces the gittern and steps forward to sing while I bring fire to me.

Swishing my hands together, I bring the blaze into a medley of swirling circles and transitioning squiggles that build on each other. Then I cause the rain again, making sure the sparks and embers don't catch on anything. Some of them blink out, but others I let fly with, building them into sudden blazes that spring randomly in the air. Forcing them out before they spread, only a few scorch marks are left behind on the table runners. I'm not sorry.

Spinning now, I drop my hands to pull down the inferno, so it rages around me, spreading flares like the wind casts it about.

"Now then, Ilano. Have you told your brother the news?" the king asks.

"No, Highness. I haven't said a thing. I thought you'd like the pleasure."

"Watching his face will be enough. You tell him."

Ilano clears his throat. "Dear brother, please understand this is just business. But I've told the king of your plans to escape. As a consequence of your insolence, he's taking you prisoner. Not just for Whistle, but because you sought to defy him. Henceforth, your lands and all you possess are mine. As they should have been all along."

The king grins as he chews. His jowls bounce gleefully as he works the food. He watches Atiene's face with triumph.

My arms drop, and the fire dies. Is this what Ilano meant? 'Don't burn me.'

The cowardly swine.

My jaw clenches hard. He couldn't let us go? He had to serve us up like this? On golden platters?

Atiene's jaw works, but he doesn't say anything as he looks from Ilano to the king.

"What plans?" he asks. But even I can tell he's lying.

"Oh, come now, brother. It's over. He knows about the secret staircase behind the bookshelf in your study, the grotto, and the boat waiting on the beach."

"Ilano..." Atiene breathes, and pain etches his brow and pulls at his mouth.

"I'm sorry, brother," he says, not sounding sorry at all. "You know Father loved me best. He'd be appalled at how you've run our family affairs. And this..." he points to me. "Look me in the eye and tell me he'd not be ashamed of you."

The insult slices my chest *for* him. Calling me low is one thing. Striking at Atiene for it is unfair.

"Guards," the king says, pointing to Atiene. "Restrain him. Search the grotto. Ilano, show them."

"You touch him, and I'll burn you till all that's left is ash and smoke," I warn, flames warping wildly around my hands and reaching up my arms as the guard swarm Atiene.

An impulse lies between them and incineration. Flames lick the air, spreading over my shoulders as my body trembles with anger.

Try me. It would be a pleasure to remove you from this world for all the terror you've caused.

"*There's* your dragon," Ilano says to the king.

"Whistle, no," Atiene says quietly. And his eyes move from me to the chandelier and back. Forcing myself to breathe, I look up, seeing the candles burning high. Wax drips onto the tables and floors.

He's right. If this gets out of control, we're *all* in danger. To keep from burning this place down, I have to calm down.

My jaw ticks, and my breath is short and shallow, but I release the fire from my hands. And it sputters into nothingness around me. As the heat dissipates, the clamping down of the king's influence feels like chains weighing me down.

An amused look overtakes the king's face as he gestures for his knights to finish his commands. They grab Atiene's arms and force him to kneel, but he doesn't fight, and he warns me with his eyes not to fight either.

"I said perform, Sorceress," the king commands, his voice rising imperiously through the hall, and his dark eyes flash with derision.

"I will not," I return, barely able to speak through the tightness in my throat and the barely contained rage in my quaking body. My lip curls. "Release him."

"See what I mean about her?" Ilano says coolly, as he rises to show the guards to the study.

"Do you have no respect for your king?" the man asks, rising slowly, pinning me with a curling lip. His ringed finger points at me. "You will do as you're told. I dare you to test me."

This can't be part of the plan. They didn't mean for it to go this far...right?

Should I burn?

Atiene's face says 'no.' And I do trust him. So, despite what comes next, I must forbear.

So, like betrayal in my ears, I hear the door to the study open. The bookcase clicks. And Ilano says something about the staircase. Atiene's head hangs, but I can tell he's listening too. His eyes close when he hears the tromp of the knights down the stairs.

Is this really happening? Is Ilano really doing this? For power? For the title? For favor with the king? Or were the servants right? Except it was *Ilano* that made a deal with the king, not Atiene? Had he already begun to call himself the Chelees?

The king keeps his gaze on me. Waiting. And finally, he says, "For every second she doesn't perform. I want a stripe across Atiene's back."

The guards unfurl a whip.

My jaw clenches, but I conjure fire, which comes as naturally now as anything ever has, feeding off the seething in my chest, and for a brief moment, I imagine that this flame hits the king square in the chest.

But Atiene...

Swirling my arms, I spin, despite the silence, and the music falteringly follows. I feel the tension in the strings now as if they're my nerves and the bow rubs them raw. Turning, I see the faces of my family, shocked but playing through. None of them meets my gaze now.

Alessi's features are stone, but her eyes flick to the king as she backs up toward the stage and picks up the gittern to play. She focuses on the instrument as her fingers move over the strings. Surrilo sends a sad look my way, but it doesn't quite reach my face as he draws the bow across the strings. His eyes dart to the study as Ilano steps out.

"They have it from here, Highness," he says, stepping back to the king's side to enjoy the show.

I follow him with my gaze, eyes shooting daggers as he plants his hands on the couch behind the king and leans heavily over.

Scoundrel. No...No, that's not good enough. I'm not sure *any* word perfectly encompasses this.

He's not at all intimidated by my wrath. Keeping pointed eye contact, he simply reaches into his tunic and draws out the purple flower, which is a little wilted after having spent the majority of the day there. He spreads the petals the way I played with them earlier. Then he sniffs it, gently, and maintains eye contact as if there's meaning in it.

Yes, I gave my word. I acknowledge that. No, I won't burn him.

The window shatters, and I duck as a horrible wind blows through like a battering ram. Glass bounces on the floor while metal panes hang precariously, bent from the blast. The candles flutter along with the drapes. Not quite sure what I'm seeing, I catch sight of a streak of gray as it bulls through the knights and then circles around. Alessi and Little Benji vanish suddenly as the gray streak blows past them.

"No." I step to the window. What-Where did they go? What *was* that? How can they just be gone?

"Whistle, get back," Atiene calls out. And as he does, the gust is back, knocking over the things on the table. Grapes and apples bounce along the table and onto the floor. Red liquid unfurls as it flees the upturned goblets. The strange wind shoves the knights as Ilano moves to shield the king.

"It's another sorcerer," the king calls out, "Guards!"

Big Henri yells and rushes the guards, who draw spears to slash at the gale-like force. Della and Surrilo disappear next.

In the chaos, I'm not sure what to do.

"Restrain that giant. And bring all the knights back," the king demands.

"Of course, Highness," Ilano says, darting to the study now.

"You there. Get Atiene and the sorceress into the wagon," the king says, pointing to his guards. He stands now that the wind is gone and moves towards the door with his men on all sides.

Big Henri snaps a spear, but one of them stabs his leg. He roars as the gust whooshes through the room again, and he's suddenly gone. Stunned, I let the guards drag me off the floor. My eyes land on Atiene as he twists around to make sure I'm okay.

Shock rattles my breath in my chest.

What just happened?

The tromp of clanking metal echoes now as knights spill from the study, Ilano in the lead. He directs them to their sovereign, and they melt around us and into the courtyard. Ilano stops in the foyer, but his eyes land on me, and he smiles, flower still in hand as he lifts it like he'd lift a goblet for a toast.

Then he winks.

CHAPTER 18

The king hustles down the stairs and into his carriage. As soon as the door closes, the whip cracks over the backs of the horses, and they leap into motion, bearing him around the garden with the wheels spitting gravel as the thing tips. It levels out as it settles on the lane towards town.

A wagon with bars pulls forward for Atiene and me. We're shoved inside, and the door closes before I can even turn around. The chain rattles, and the lock clanks.

I hear one say, "Let's go."

Atiene moves to gather me in his arms. My head leans on his chest as I try to put together the pieces. I blink rapidly as my mind churns.

We have to get out of here. Lock picks, knife in my boot...What does Atiene have that will reach the chain? I can-

"Are you okay?" he asks.

"Are *you*?" I return, because...I don't know if I am or not. That will depend entirely on where my family is and what the king intends to do with Atiene. And because he just watched his brother steal everything from him and condemn him to the king's whims.

We don't know what comes next.

"Yeah," he answers as the wagon lurches. We're both on the floor, and through the bars overhead, I see the lanterns moving past in bursts. There'll be no dancing under them now.

At least my family is...taken care of? Who was that other sorcerer? Are they on our side? I'm inclined to think so, but after tonight...

I choose relief for the time being. I'll settle that once I get us out of here.

What of Atiene? Ilano ruined any chance I had of negotiating with the king for his release. I could have agreed to do whatever the king asked if he'd have let everyone else go. That was my 'bottom of the barrel' clincher tactic. Now he knows he doesn't *have* to let Atiene go to get me to comply. He simply has to threaten me, and I'll do it. All the way to my grave. And *then* what will happen to Atiene? The king won't take his insubordination lightly. Atiene will suffer.

And now that the king knows there's another sorcerer out there, he'll be searching for that one too.

I'm not alone, though...in these strange abilities.

"Who's the wind-conjurer?" I whisper.

"Later," he answers as the wagon stops suddenly, and the chain rattles again.

My heart tumbles over itself like falling down a flight of stairs.

No...not now? Not these woods? The king wouldn't hunt me right here, right now?

The door swings open, and I flinch hard, expecting to see knights, but a hooded figure reaches out a hand to us. Atiene clasps the stranger's hand, and he jumps out of the wagon. Turning back, he grabs me and hauls me out, too. The hooded figure closes the door, wrapping the chain through the metal loops and clamping the lock again. He smacks the back of the wagon twice like a signal.

"This way," a familiar voice says.

Gribble...

He leads us into the woods as the wagon rattles away down the road. We move quickly through the trees and the brush. Atiene's hand fastens onto mine to keep me close. My other hand grasps my dress to keep it from tangling around my legs or getting underfoot.

It seems we're traveling up. Not toward town or the port. Up. Toward the castle? Are we going to go into the grotto? Take the boat?

This could work...we could get free.

No. Wrong time to think that. We're not out of it yet.

Dodging the trees, Gribble leads us to a clearing to the edge of a cliff overlooking the sea. The water is nearly black, gently lapping the rocky shore below. The moon has risen now, and tiny lights dance over the surface. A strange shadow lies over the ocean, blocking part of my view of the sparkles. A shadow that looks sort of like a merchant ship. Sounds of people carry up to us, perhaps the crew, but there are no lights on the ghostly thing. It's too dark to focus on, but I can tell it's there.

My breath comes faster, but I don't let hope run away with me.

Okay...we got this far. And there's our way out. But there's a cliff between us and freedom.

Gribble hoots like an owl, and two figures melt from the shadows, both wearing hooded cloaks, so I can't see their faces.

"Ready?" another familiar voice asks.

"Riccard?" I breathe, looking to the other. Theliane scoops her hood back and grins at me.

"The ropes are solid, the harnesses set, and Big Henri and Surrilo are at the bottom now," she answers.

"We're going down the cliff face?"

"Harnesses are attached to the line. Unfortunately, Haweth is spent from grabbing the others, so he can't just get us down," Riccard says to Atiene.

"Well, he hasn't practiced in a while. We knew carrying everyone might be an issue," Atiene answers.

"Haweth...?" I ask.

"Later," he says, moving to the lines. I see now that there are two ropes wrapped around two very large rocks, and as the lines are messed with, I hear the metallic squeak of a pulley.

Riccard helps Atiene slip his legs through the proper holes of the harness. Theliane shows me how to fit my legs through with the dress. Then she and Gribble help me down over the side, so my legs are dangling over the ground.

My cheeks flush, seeing how far down it is between my foot and the ground below. My heart leaps into my throat. And I can't seem to breathe. I cling to the rope, mastering my breath because now is not the time to conjure fire. That would be *very* bad.

"Give two sharp tugs," Theliane says, as she expertly slides into the other harness. "That's how they know we're ready."

I grab the line below me and pull twice, and the line abruptly shifts, bringing me down. Gazing over the ocean as I descend to meet it, the movement makes me dizzy, and I have to look away. I understand the need for speed, but it's faster than I want.

Looking up, I see Theliane, very relaxed in her harness. Her arms spread wide as she pretends she's flying. She even twists this way and that as if she were performing her routine on a stage for the audience. I'm sure she doesn't need the harness. Simply uses it as a precaution.

It's so strange and exhilarating that she and Riccard were safe the whole time. That they knew of the plan. Were in on it. And did this.

Across from us are Gribble and Atiene. I guess two is all that they can do at a time...

Atiene hangs onto the rope, surveying the ship, the ocean, and the cliffs. Then he catches my gaze. He reaches out a hand, and I take it, but his line is moving faster than mine, so he has to let go after a while. And I watch him sink further and further away from me.

Below us, Surrilo works on mine and Theliane's line while Big Henri works Atiene and Gribble's. As soon as Atiene's feet touch down, he scrambles out of the harness, and Gribble is let down all the way. Big Henri immediately sends the harnesses back up for Riccard.

My feet finally touch down, boots settling into the rocky shore. Solid ground feels good. Better get my fill now. I won't get this feeling for some time.

Atiene helps me out of the harness, pats Surrilo on the back, and directs me to one of the boats bobbing with the waves. Theliane waits for her partner while Gribble, Atiene, and I hop into one of the boats. Surrilo ties off the cliffside rope and pulley system before he joins us.

As soon as the four of us are settled in the boat, Atiene gives two sharp tugs on the rope on the bow of our boat, and the thing thrusts out to sea as if shoved by some invisible being on the shore.

Faces peer over the sides of the ship at us, some familiar, others not. Alessi jumps up and down, clapping her hands. Della leans on the rail, and Ollio stands next to her. I breathe a little easier seeing that they're okay.

Is this real? Are they here? Is this really happening? This was the plan? We're almost there? I don't dare hope...Not yet. Not till it's the *only* real possibility, and we're far from the king's reach.

As the rowboat bumps into the ship, Gribble grabs the lines and secures the boat. Then we're directed to the rope ladder. I climb up first. And Atiene after me. Della grabs me in a hug and, despite her tiny size, pulls me into the ship.

"When you threatened the king, I'd never been prouder of you," she says, hugging me. Then she goes to Atiene and shakes his hand, patting their clasped hands as she says, "Bless you."

Alessi pulls me into a hug. Then whispers in my ear, "You made an amazing dragon."

"Your *clothes* made an amazing dragon. *I* did nothing."

"Don't worry. There will be opportunities to burn your enemies later."

"I don't have enemies on the mainland."

"Oh, you'll make some. No problem."

Then a sailor hands me a blanket. I wrap it around my shoulders, just...watching while Atiene moves to speak with Haweth and others.

Several sailors haul in the rowboat as Gribble and Surrilo crawl up the ladder. Alessi runs to hug them both. One arm around each of their necks. Then she takes their hands, bouncing on her toes with delight.

"Can you believe it? It worked," she says.

"Of course it did," Surrilo answers. "My plans always work. Our best performance yet, but I do have some notes."

"*I* was perfect," Alessi says. "Keep your notes."

The other boat with Riccard, Theliane, and Big Henri swishes water aside as it pulls up alongside the ship now. They climb the ladder too, receiving the same greeting from Alessi. She squeals with her hands on her cheeks, seeing Theliane, and they hug.

"You have to tell me everything that's happened to you," Alessi says.

"Tell me of the castle first," Theliane says as they clasp hands and move out of the way of the sailors.

Big Henri goes off to tend to the wound in his leg. Della follows, pulling her shawl from her shoulders and placing it around him as he sits.

Once we're all aboard and settled, Haweth moves around the ship calling orders to the sailors to weigh anchor and drop canvas.

I count my family.

Della, Big Henri, Little Benji, Alessi, Haweth, Surrilo, Riccard, Theliane, Gribble, Ollio...They're all here. (Letta, Lalina, and Braun, of course, are somewhere on the sea ahead of us.)

And Atiene. He's one of us now. That makes fourteen.

The ship turns slowly and the bow dips and rises, separating waves, heading...I think heading north? This is happening. It's so hard to grip right now. My mind isn't sure, but we're running with canvases snapping in the wind overhead, a slight breeze playing over the deck of the ship, and the pitch and yaw under our feet.

Elation bursts in my chest.

Even if the king finds out what happened, we'll slip away before he can get mobilized. And he has no power once we hit certain waters. I don't know where those boundaries are. I just know they exist.

Atiene moves to my side now that we're safely on the way. He does glance back once at the hulking mass of land falling away behind us. And so do I.

Goodbye, Home. Goodbye, Ilano, you rogue. Goodbye, view of the sea, every place we've ever performed, and all the memories made here.

"Shall we?" he asks, taking my hand and leading me to the front of the ship. He leans on the railing, looking ahead and leaning into the breeze.

"It's later," I say to him.

He smiles and dips his head. Then he shifts.

"Yes, this does qualify as 'later,'" he laughs. "Well, here it is: we didn't tell you because while your eyes were on us, the king's eyes were on *you*. In order for him to think we'd failed, we needed to convince *you* that we had. We had to keep you unsure, so the king's spies wouldn't know something was off. And when the king came, you were the distraction. A spectacle. A sensation. Your fiery temper kept him occupied. While he kept you in line, the others worked to get us all free."

"I guess I can forgive you for keeping me in the dark."

"If you were in the dark, all you had to do was spark," he teases, casting a sideways glance at me.

I shake my head. "Go on."

"Ilano picked up the king in town personally, 'dripping honey in his ears' as he likes to say, so his transition to Chelees could be smooth and fully sanctioned by the king. Though I'd already signed everything over to him, *now* he'll have the king's favor and be able to retain the lands without struggle. Ilano never betrayed us. He played his part perfectly."

"That's what the flower meant," I answer. A reminder of my promise earlier in the garden. A 'pact' so to speak, so I wouldn't kill him. And a half-admission. A half-confession. And yes, saying 'goodbye.' Asking me to look after Atiene...

'To keep all this intact,' he'd said. To carry on their family name and do right by their ancestors, because that matters to both of them.

"And Haweth can conjure wind," I prompt, because I did put *that* together at least.

"That's why he left the mainland all those years ago. Sought freedom here on the islands. And to hide."

"But now he's going back..."

"There's word of 'magic-users' on the mainland who stood up to the kings. We mean to find them. Their cause is ours."

That's too big for me right now, so I put a pin in that. One thing at a time.

"So...Ilano and the grotto?"

"He gave up information to the king to gain his trust. Then he took half the knights down to give Haweth time and room to grab your family. They were occupied, which left only a few in the hall to deter. Then, being under attack, the king hurried out of there, dragging us with him to the wagon that Ilano had set up with knights we trusted. Gribble was waiting in the woods to stop the wagon and let us out."

"But the king will be angry when he finds we're no longer in the wagon."

"Yes. Ilano will smooth over what he can. It's not as if *he* let us free. If it pleases the king, he's even prepared to send ships after us. But we'll be too far ahead."

"So, *he'll* be alright. And Riccard and Theliane were safe this whole time."

"Who better to set up the escape from the cliffs? Your family is a treasure of talent. They made this possible. Surrilo's knowledge of your family and penchant for flair. Haweth's skill at sea and as a wind-conjurer. Riccard and Theliane with the ropes and lines. Alessi with acting, sewing, and driving my guards and servants mad."

I laugh.

"Anyway, Ilano took care of transportation for Riccard and Theliane. That's why he didn't travel with the rest of us to Merincillo. It looked like they'd simply gotten away. Surrilo was 'beaten' by knights, then secretly let out of the castle to meet the others. He, Ilano, and Haweth sorted everything out. When Surrilo and Ilano came back to

Merincillo, Haweth kept the ship out of the port and off the coast so the king wouldn't know I'd bought a new one."

"How did you get Surrilo in and out of the castle without being seen?"

"We had another pulley system set up underneath his window. That morning he was in the grotto, I managed the rope for him, so he could get up and into the window."

I take a minute while all of it coalesces in my mind. Settling. Connecting.

Goodness, there were a lot of things going on. Things I wish I'd seen.

"Anything else I should know?"

"Most of what your family had in the wagons was brought with us and loaded into the ship."

I stare in shock. So, we *didn't* lose everything we had? Alessi can have her dresses, stockings, and trunks. Surrilo can have his instruments back.

I can't believe Atiene thought of that. Back *then*, no less. How-

"This ship is laden with delicacies that can only be found on the islands. We mean to trade with the mainlanders for some money to live on. I'll establish myself with the three kingdoms, opening relationships. Ilano should send more ships after we're settled. I'll act as his representative there. Should be a fruitful enterprise."

He smiles at my stunned silence. I try to wipe the sentiment off my face and fix my raised brows.

"I like that you don't scowl at me anymore," he teases.

Don't tell Surrilo, I say inside. *Outside*, I say, "You thought of *everything*."

"It was all of us. Group effort," he answers, but he still looks pleased at my reaction. I must be fun to surprise.

"So...we're free." A grin spreads over my face.

His grin matches mine. "Yes. We're free."

Laughing, I reach up to hug him.

"Wait," he says as his hands land on my shoulders, holding me back. His head swivels from side to side. What is he looking for?

"What?" I ask, suddenly worried.

What did we miss? Is the king coming? He couldn't have gotten his ship ready to sail that quickly, right?

"Just making sure there's no fire around," Atiene answers, teasingly. "We're on a floating mass of wood in the middle of the sea. We can't have you burning the ship down."

I roll my eyes. "I can just conjure it, you know."

"Then you'd better be careful," he answers as he steps closer, moving the hair from my cheek and leaning down. As soon as I realize what he's doing, flame erupts in my chest. I have to shove it down to keep it in check before his lips even touch mine. It's gentle, soft. New. A little hesitant and uncertain, but grows more confident. And his beard pokes my face, but other than that, this is nice. I could get used to this.

When Atiene pulls away, I bite my lip to keep the fire at bay. But I feel it in my cheeks. Several of my family members whoop or 'aw' at the sight, but I'm not embarrassed. Ilano was right. That has no place here.

"Hey," Della calls out. "You never asked my permission to court her."

"My apologies," he replies. "May I have your permission, Della?"

"I guess."

Laughs accompany her statement, as Alessi squeals.

Atiene steps behind me, hugging me from behind. I lean into him as his chin rests on my head. Breathing out a sigh, I gaze out to where the stars touch the water.

"Our future is out there somewhere," he says.

"It's exciting, isn't it?" I reply.

"It is."

This is it. The beginning. When anything can happen. This is the best part because there's so much ahead, and the possibilities are endless. The mind can't yet conceive of what it will see, but it can imagine. And imagination is powerful.

The End

Sneak Peek!

(Hint: Whistle pops up in book 3 of the Onyx series, so...there's that)

"Stop that boy! Stop him!" echoes down the narrow, stone corridor with the accompanied crushing 'clunk, clunk' of the knights' armor. I turn, seeing a young man leaping over crates, dodging townsfolk and merchant shacks, a proud grin splitting his face as he turns to laugh at the less agile, less flexible guards.

"You're a skunk's tail!" he shouts back at them, still barreling down the street, and with a jolt in my chest, I realize he hasn't noticed that he's going to collide with my stand.

"Watch out!" I scream at him, but it's too late.

Time moves achingly slow as he turns his head, and his eyes widen. His raucous smile melts from his face, pulling his mouth into an 'o.' He tries to stop, arms flailing, feet skittering, but it's too late.

I dive out of the way, rolling into the street, as he plows into the shelves with a crunch. They don't stand a chance; wood whines and splits, crashing to the ground with a cacophony of cracking and shattering ceramic bowls and pots. The young man reaches out, trying to grab anything solid. But instead, he catches the wool blanket that *used* to be my shade, yanking the shelves on the other side down on top of him with a crash. The image of pink and green herbs spilling through the air from an upturned basket presses on my mind like a memory I'll have forever.

He moans as the dust settles, and the scent of strong, earthy herbs wafts.

Rubbing my forehead, I assess the damage. My mind hiccups as I stare at the pieces of wood and broken things. What am I going to do about this? I can't sell this stuff now. And it will take forever to clean up and put everything back together.

The oaf pokes his head out from under the wool blanket, staring around wildly, his mirth subdued.

"We've got him!" one gravelly voice shouts, as the young man wriggles himself out from under the shelves, squishing herbs, nuts, and fruits under his hands as he pushes himself to his feet.

He darts through the crowd with a faint, "Sorry," whipping behind him.

I glare daggers into his backside. Thrashing metal armor rings in my ears, clashing off the walls as the guards part around me, still chasing their quarry.

I sigh, pursing my lips, narrowing my eyes, breathing deeply, and pinching the bridge of my nose to keep the rage at bay.

This is the last thing I need right now. My family can't afford this. We're poorer than the dirt we stand on. Barely able to scrape by with the earnings we get from the shop.

So, this is less than ideal.

The bare-bones shop is in pieces. Normally, it stands upright, rickety shelves holding aloft a bare blanket to keep the sun off my head, strong scents and spices invading my nose until I can no longer smell anything. It's usually meager at best. Now it's less than that. I bemoan internally as I stoop to pull the shelves off the goods. The splintered supports creak as I push them against the wall.

I get a few curious looks in passing as I clean. Not because people want to *buy* from me, but because people love drama. It breaks up the mundane.

Snatching the largest basket, I scoop handfuls of debris into it, tossing shattered ceramic, crushed fruits, and smashed herbs inside. I don't know how long it will take to replace it all. Mother has a few bowls I can borrow for now. I can trade for a couple of baskets. The stand, though, I'm not sure how it'll piece back together.

I don't have the time or energy for this.

We can't afford an apprenticeship for Cassian, my younger brother, and Mellen, my younger sister, is too small for hard labor (nor would I want her to have to put herself to some trade). Mother's energy is expended by taking care of them both, but she does a little mending on the side. Small favors for neighbors, for which we sometimes get a scrap of bread in return. In short, we don't have options.

I grab the dusty blanket and stuff it in the basket too, before making my way down the street to the lower town, into the quarter known as Muck Water to the locals. The name started as a joke about the terrible sewage system, but kinda stuck (Muck Water is actually the "nice" name for it). There's also Mouse Next near the northeast end of the lower village, which was a slur against an ancient people who mostly settled in that section and whose descendants still live there. And Bad Wine Row near the taverns that line the street, where traffic comes through the city gate. It's notorious for obvious reasons and leads up to the main street where the merchants gather to sell their wares. And the guilds are strict on where and when the taverns are allowed to solicit traffic to their own establishments. And to be clear, they don't run up this far. There are a few on the upper side of town, but not as persistent as the ones on Bad Wine Row. And with better wares, so I hear.

And as my stand sits at the crossroads between the main road and the one that leads into the lower town, you'd think the traffic would help with sales, but everyone knows the best wares are in the richer parts of town, so some people just hurry by.

Sometimes I wish I could live off the land, simpler, freer, harder perhaps, but less dependent on the shaky goodwill of others. I long for a trade more reliable, money more sustainable, and freer flowing. I just don't know how to make it out of this hole. I feel stuck. No matter what I do, I can't wrench myself from this dismal living. Can't save my family from going hungry.

I dump the contents of the basket into the scrap heap where skinny mongrels and beggars (and sometimes poor peasants like my family) try to make a meal. Two flea-bitten dogs snarl over the mushy fruit I've just tossed in, lips curling back, heads down, ears flat. I'd feel sorry for them and might try to help them, but I might just as soon lose a chunk of myself if I get near enough, not to mention the sickness or bugs they probably carry. So, I just hold my nose against the atrocious smell of rotting things and waste, and head back down the street, eager to put distance between me and the stench.

With nothing left to do, I head home. The stone houses give way to hut-lined streets where the one-story houses touch each other. Sad, sun and rain-worn homes with streaks in the wood, some tilting precariously, sit propped up with beams of wood. Old thatching, dirt floors, rickety doors that creak and flap in stiff breezes. My small home tucks between a cramped barn and another small home with an older, raucous mead-bibber and his old maid of a daughter.

Sunlight stabs the dusty living space when I open the door, and Mother's head jerks up. She sits in the worn chair near the empty hearth, with mending in her lap.

"You're early," she says, taking in my sullen appearance as she stretches her neck. "What happened?"

"Some idiot crashed into the stand. It's broken, and everything's crushed."

She has mousy hair with strands of gray, high cheekbones, a slightly rounded nose, and a thin face. There's a freckle above her left eyebrow and another along her jawline. Her hair is usually pulled back into a knot with a ratty rag to cover her head. I've always thought of her as pretty, but through the years, her age and stress have pulled her features, making sad lines in her brow and around her mouth.

She sighs, and her face tightens as she fights the concern away for my sake. It's too late. Her fears are my fears.

"I'll gather more herbs," I say, rubbing my temples. "But the stand will need to be rebuilt."

She smiles tightly as if to belay my worries but can't quite bring herself to believe we *shouldn't* worry.

"I can ask Gerdor to look at it," she offers softly, looking down at her work, purposefully avoiding my gaze. She knows I hate to ask anything of anyone, and especially of him.

The hut feels strangely empty suddenly. No sound, but for the creaking chair when mother shifts. No children messing about, helping mother with cleaning, mending, or playing. That's not normal.

"Where are Mellen and Cassian?"

"Mellen is down the way with Aidela learning to make pots and weave baskets. It's not an apprenticeship, though," she adds the last part quickly. "Aidela offered to teach Mellen a few things as long as we do mending for her. Her eyes are getting worse, and she has to strain to see these days. She said she could use the help."

I nod, breathing away my stubborn pride. "And Cassian?"

"Apprenticed to Gerdor," she answers, cheeks coloring, even as she keeps her gaze on mine because she knows what's coming.

"We can't afford that," I burst out. "Mother, his sleeping arrangements. His food and tools."

"Gerdor told me not to worry about the money. Cassian can come home every night. Gerdor said he has some old tools for Cassian. I can send him with some food," she answers, her face turning down as she draws the needle through stiff cloth. She means *her* food if it comes to that. I doubt it will, though. Gerdor will most likely feed Cassian. I know because I've seen Cassian munching on this or that as he sits atop the fence, kicking his feet and watching Gerdor at work. Sometimes small presents of food make their way home in his pockets. He always shares with Mother and Mellen, but that's not the point.

"We can't keep asking Gerdor for things. You can't keep relying on him like this," I admonish.

"And what would you have me do?" she questions, voice rising. "We have no alternatives."

"It makes us beggars," I counter, tears pricking my eyes at the implication. "All we have left is the roof over our heads, the little porridge or bread the mending brings in, and what we can scrounge from the forest."

"I am doing the best I can," her pitch rises, but she catches herself, regret etching her features a moment. "Gerdor can help us. I know you don't like him, but it's not his fault that your father left us in such dire circumstances. He wants to help, and we are fools to refuse. We *need* help."

Silence coats our outbursts. We do nothing to counter it, letting it hang while we lose ourselves in our thoughts. She continues stitching.

I know that Gerdor has feelings for my mother. I know she has a degree of affection for him that she tries to hide from her children. Well, mostly me, because she's afraid I won't approve. She's also afraid to love anyone. The social conventions surrounding her standing in society as regards relationships don't ease her fears.

My father disappeared when I was young. Rumors abound, and everyone in the lower town is always eager to share the story with anyone who asks. Seems everyone knows what 'really' happened. Everyone but his family.

Some people say he ran away with a younger woman. Or that he's a fugitive of justice. Or a magic-weaver assessing the castle's weaknesses. Or he was murdered.

Since his death can't be proven and the circumstances that would prevent his return cannot be corroborated, it appears to society as if we were rejected by him. We're 'damaged goods.' People don't like dealing with damaged goods. Unfair as it is, rumors are enough to hinder any progress we might make in the world. My mother is, in essence, a widow with mouths to feed, but worse than a widow, she's a woman seen as unworthy of a man (and it should be noted that this is a curse borne largely by the poorer classes rather than the rich...People with means don't have to deal with some of our limitations because they have money. Wrongs can be made right with money).

So, it is unlikely that she'll ever marry again, even if a man did want to take on children that weren't his. Which few men do. Making a living is hard enough. And for those children not to be his own...not to bear his name and continue his lineage...It's not exactly ideal for him. Thus, not a very tempting option.

Gerdor puts himself in a precarious situation helping us like this. Rumors will spread. His kindness might be interpreted in another way.

I should be grateful that some of our closer neighbors offer us these charities like Aidela. She's old enough to know that society's rules are dumb. And cranky enough to flout them if she can. Gotta love old people.

But even still, my mother doesn't deserve this life. She's tried hard to keep a brave face for us, but I've seen her at night with the firelight tracing tears down her face. She deserves more, and I shouldn't begrudge the help she's received from Gerdor. Nor should I fault her for accepting it. Life is hard enough.

I breathe slowly, taking the leather purse from my waist and handing it to her.

"If this won't cover the work on the stand, ask him if we can pay him over time, or maybe I can work it off somehow."

She takes the leather purse. Her thin, rough hands quiver. This is all the money we have.

I should have scavenged for food in the scrap heap before coming home.

It's fine. I'll bring home extra food for us when I scavenge from the forest. Mushrooms, onions, and fruit. Whatever I can get. Mother's Forest Soup will have to do for tonight. A probably tomorrow too.

"I'm going to pick more herbs," I say, slinging my hammock-like leather pouch over my shoulder and hooking the basket on my arm. Mother nods, trailing the thick leather string on the pouch through her fingers. Her cheeks seem more hollow than usual. Has she eaten in the last few days? I can't remember.

I step through the tiny door into the sunlight, the brightness brings my headache to a small throbbing pain in my temple, and I guard my eyes against the sun till they adjust. Kicking at stray stones in the road, I make for the southern gate.

It's not that I don't like Gerdor. For his quiet gruffness, he seems a kind soul if a little simple and slow with his words, but a true artist with his work. I only resent his kindness because I miss my father. Gerdor is a reminder of what I've lost. Like a hole that needs to be filled. I can't let it be filled because that means the one who left the hole isn't coming back. But if I keep it open for him...he'll be welcome when he does.

If, whispers through my soul but I refuse to hear it.

My father ran the shop when I was younger. I'd sit and watch him selling herbs, discussing the qualities of each, and terms of sale. Watching him was how I learned how to haggle, what certain wares were worth in terms of money, and fair trades (I prefer to deal only in money, but sometimes I take food or wares if my family needs them). After a hard day's work, he'd take me into the forest to gather herbs and fruits. I remember the feel of his rough hand holding mine as we walked, so I wouldn't run off and get lost. He'd point out the best spots to gather, which wares were ripe enough to take, and quantities based on the regulars who always expected him to have certain items. He always had the best to be found. We did well when he was here. With time, we might have even thrived. Moved up to the richer parts of town with our shop.

But anyway, one day when I was young, I'd stayed home to learn to make bread with my mother, at her insistence, but I soon broke free. Eating sticky dough from my fingers, I wandered off to find my papa at the stand, but when I arrived, he was gone. The wares were left out and unattended as if he'd been there moments before and had just disappeared. Thinking perhaps that he was just playing a joke, I just smiled and sat on his stool, waiting for him to pop back up. I watched every passerby, eagerly kicking my legs and giggling occasionally at how funny it was going to be when he returned. But as the crowds died down, he didn't show.

Dusk settled its blue-gray mist over the town, and all the other merchants closed up to head home. In a deserted square with the night coming on, I was sure my father would come soon, but he never did. I may very well have stayed the whole night waiting if my mother hadn't come searching. She found me calling out for my father, telling him he could come out now.

My mother spent the next few days asking the other merchants if they'd seen him. Not one of them had any information about his whereabouts. Abandoned with mouths to feed and no trade skills, my mother returned home defeated. I saw the panic etched into her brow, and silent tears of my own began. All that night, they didn't stop coming, and the next morning, without discussing it with my mother, I rose to take my papa's place at the stand.

It was my job. Or at least I knew enough of the trade to make it work, though I did have to learn to be sharper with customers who thought they could slip an unfair trade by a child. It was rough going, especially with customers who would push and bully to get their way. It taught me to be wary, to call for the guards when thieves attempted to steal things or things got too heated, to value the things I still had, and to take care of my mother whenever I could.

The memories fade as reality descends. Images in my mind dissipate into the corners and dark crevices of the stone walls around me as I walk, and my heart hardens against the incessant question before it surfaces. Always the same question whenever I think of him: Where did he go? I know there's no use wondering anymore. Wondering doesn't bring him back.

"I'm innocent. I've done nothing wrong. Please," a small voice cries, echoing off the walls as I turn down the street toward the main gate. Clumps of people have gathered to watch. I stop on the fringes out of curiosity.

"You know the penalty for using magic," one of the guards dragging her says. Her bony hands are in shackles that look way too big on her small frame.

"It wasn't a lot of magic. Please, the children were starving." Her eyes are wild with fright, her thin, white hair sticking out, and her back and shoulders are rounded.

"Isn't that Ol' Woman Ferdy? From Ilfrain?" someone asks.

"The one with the goats?"

"No, the one with the lame cow."

"If she has magic, why didn't she fix the cow?" someone jokes, and a few laugh. But I don't.

"Magic is magic," one of the guards says, pinning the laughing people with a warning gaze. The crowd falls silent and stiff.

"It was just enough to feed the children. That's all. They would have died," she says, pulling back in the weakest and most pathetic way, it almost hurts to watch. Her thin arms are like sticks bent at odd angles from the men's fists, and her knees are bent as she plants her feet. But it does no good. She's dragged along anyway. And I can't watch anymore, so I turn and go about my business. I try not to think about things like the old woman. Thoughts turn into whispers. Whispers are dangerous. As dangerous as rumors.

The guards barely glance my way as I approach the gate. I barely glance at them.

Outside the city walls and across the drawbridge, I veer from the worn road to the deeper parts of the woods where hardly anyone else goes. Wild raspberries, grapes, apples, crab apples, and pears grow aplenty in the forest, though not all at once. I suspect this place may once have been a farm before the wild took it back over.

Blackberries, mushrooms, watercress, any edible leaves I can find, and wild onions make their way into my basket, and then I begin searching for medicinal herbs. I wish winter wouldn't come and kill all the green and rot the fruit with its icy touch. I could feed my family from the forest if the plants didn't die, but already the spring fruits rot, and the flowers get replaced by ones hardier and more acclimated to the warmer weather. Later in the year, there will be apples and gourds.

I gather as many of the strawberries as I can. The King's Stable Master has a taste for them, and he was a friend of my father. He takes enough pity to visit my stand on occasion. When the strawberries die, he buys wild carrots and apples for the horses. His patronage keeps us afloat. Another form of pity that I begrudgingly take.

Then there's the King's Physician and the King's Cook, who come occasionally when they can't find the exact herbs they need from the other merchants. I always keep their favorites on hand. One is an old man who doesn't like to walk far, though, so he tries to stay in the main square, which is closer to the castle. I only see him in emergencies. The cook sends his apprentice to shop, and the apprentice has eyes for the servant girl at Verdon's stand, so the boy spends his time wooing her and shopping at the stands closer to her.

Still, I try to have the best of everything each of them could want. And my family eats the leftovers, so they don't go to waste.

My mind turns to my two younger siblings.

Cassian and Mellen don't really know our father. They were very young when he disappeared. But Cassian looks like him, same shape of the face, nose, and brow. Mellen has Papa's gray eyes and a slight figure like a wisp. She's always been quite small for her age. For a while, Mother wasn't sure she'd make it. Mellen had to have special milk, and she was sick often, keeping Mother up at night. But the tiny bundle pulled through somehow. Mother swears we could have been twins with the shape of our faces and noses, though I have more freckles than Mellen.

We all have dark hair. Mellen has to make do with my hand-me-downs, and Cassian wears Papa's old clothes, which are too big, but Mother insists he'll grow into them. Mother and I have two dresses between us, which we've worn nearly threadbare. Her mending won't hold them together forever. We'll need new ones soon.

I'm seventeen. Cassian is thirteen, and Mellen is eleven. Mother's right to apprentice Cassian. It's beyond time. It's years later than most boys. And Mellen needs to learn skills she can't learn from our mother. I know that. My issue lies with the money.

It's always the money.

Hours drag, passing me by, and darkness falls as I wander slowly, sometimes on hands and knees, to find the plants I need. Finally, I decide that there's enough to fill the stand and feed us for tonight and tomorrow. Mostly, I just can't fit anything more in the basket, the pack, or my pockets, so I stuff one more apple in my mouth, cringing at how the sourness bites back. I shoulder my pack and head for the city gate.

As I near the road, I hear muffled screams and yells from the forest, probably travelers on the road. A sharp, cutting howl rips through the air. I freeze breathlessly to listen, heart thrumping in my throat. It doesn't sound like baying wolves or the high-pitched cry of a hunting bird. It sounds larger. Much larger. I hasten my step toward the city gates, eager to put distance between the blood-curdling squeal and myself, but it slices through the thin veil of night like a blade. Shaking, I desperately hope it doesn't hear or smell me as I break into a run, hoping I'm far enough ahead to get to the gates before it catches wind of me.

I break through the tree line and see the torches on the city walls like fireflies against the night. So far away still. So much space between safety and me.

The ear-splitting scream is closer now, raking through the descending night like a wolf declaring territory.

"What was that?" one of the guards asks.

"Close the gates!" orders the Captain, and a flurry of men along the walls position themselves for defenses just in case.

"Wait!" I call out. A deadly choice if the animal hears me. It might even see me running and give chase, but if the guards don't hold the gate for me, I'll be trapped outside the walls with the creature.

"Hold! There's a girl," one of the men calls. I pump my legs harder, wind whipping my skirt, basket jostling in my arms, pack shifting across my back. I hope the contents survive. I can't afford another day out of work.

The screech pierces my ears. Louder. Closer. Malignant and hungry.

"Drop the basket, Girl!" one of the guards shouts. It weighs me. Even though I know it's slowing me down, I can't leave it. I *can't*.

Breathing harder, face heating with fear and exertion, I run harder, but the earth begins to sway under my feet as a sudden burst of pain in my head flashes white across my vision. I try to shake it away. The frenzied guards blur into spots of color. The breath catches in my throat as I fight through the panic.

"Someone fetch her," a voice floats through my ears. My legs grow heavy, and my heart thuds in my ears. I try to pull fuller, deeper breaths, but my lungs convulse, and I stagger, dropping the basket, and watching the contents scatter in a beautiful cacophony of color that soothes the vision and calms the mind.

I don't feel afraid, though I know I should. I just feel tired as the world grows farther and farther away, grayer, and my dulling senses watch it all happen with tired curiosity. I fall, but the jarring pain loosens my grip on reality rather than drawing me tighter. Instead, I float in a sea of gray, wondering at the beautiful dark blue sky with silver stars peeking out.

Many Thanks!

Acknowledgements

This poor book has been through...a lot of rewrites....over like 15ish years? (I had some growing up to do before it came together. Did I actually grow up? ...No...still it came together somehow.)

So here's the thing...I'm INCREDIBLY grateful for those who stuck with me through it.

Mariam for getting me out of the house (because I was an absolute cave troll during this last rewrite). And for letting me gush about the characters and the story.

Marissa for for being a FANTASTIC writing buddy.

My friend Jeramee for also letting me gush about the stories and gossip about the characters. So...many...spoilers! But she said she's fine with that so...I don't feel so bad about it now.

Seriously...gushing is part of the process. It NEEDS to happen. So I'm grateful to those who let me pour out my heart and soul for HOURS about these people and places that don't exist. Thank you for letting me waste some of your life. Hopefully, it was fun for you, too.

My mom for reading the first, terrible drafts, but not making me feel bad about how dreadful they were. Thanks, Mom!

About the Author

D.B. Forest writes high fantasy and tiny psychological thrillers that are... Ish? Like they exist and contain words which counts.

Currently self-publishing the Onyx Series, a 5-book fantasy series that started as a quick throwaway story and ended up taking over my life for a year and a half. I used to be meh about it... Now I love it. Yay! Character development for ME.

Also author of "Scythes of Onyx" and "Tales of the Immortals," short stories set in the same universe as the Onyx Series. The universe keeps expanding because characters just keep doing things. In fact, I'm writing another 5-book series snuggled right smack dab in the middle of the short stories and the novels. It's HARD, but I love 'em so...

I have an ellipses problem I'm not ready to address, a tendency to use italics, and a habit of starting sentences with conjunctions (you'll see). I'm not even trying to be professional at this point. Just having fun with this whole bookish adventure of writing and self-publishing. I am indeed human (and not fantastic at grammar. Exhibit A), so there will be typos. We could make a game of it though. Highest count wins! Prize: Emotional damage borrowed from fictional people. Woohoo!

I am not responsible for what my characters do, but I do accept angry letters on their behalf considering I'm probably just as surprised as you by how the stories go. I tried to tell them. They just do whatever.

When not wondering why my fictional people won't listen to perfectly reasonable advice, I can be found hanging out with my dog who believes I should do that full time. He might be right. We'll see how this goes.

Want free pics and stuff for the Onyx series? Scan to grab those.

Also by D.B. Forest

Books in the same universe

Onyx Shadows

Onyx Mist

Onyx Dust

Onyx Whispers

Onyx Essence

A Dance with Fire

Scythes of Onyx

Tales of the Immortals: A Ballad of Love

Tales of the Immortals: A Song of Death

Dystopian Action/Adventure

Let's Call it a Game

Smoke in Our Veins

More to come! Are you as excited as I am? I'm like, "Let's GO!"

Sign up for new releases here

Dive into the World

Because this story is just one part of a universe.

You're more than welcome to follow along this journey or more accurately this explosion of randomness. I can't promise it will always be entertaining...but there will be terrible jokes and chaos.

Interested in keeping up with the releases? And also getting pics from the books? And see the character chaos and me weeping over the complications of corralling characters who act like a house-full of toddlers who definitely don't take direction while I follow them around begging them not to destroy the furniture and eat their veggies?

And if you want to follow on Instagram where I post a lot of this randomness, check me out at @dbforestauthor

Also, just feel free to say 'hi.' I don't bite. That's unsanitary.

Please leave a review

Your voice matters.

Plain and simple. A casual browser may or may not buy this book because of what you tell them in your review. That's why reviews are so important to authors.

So...I'd be INCREDIBLY grateful if you left a review to let people know what YOU thought of this book.

But also...if you don't want to, no pressure.

Thanks a million!

-D.B. Forest

www.ingramcontent.com/pod-product-compliance
Lightning Source LLC
LaVergne TN
LVHW090559110826
845146LV00001B/187

9798999822390